MANGOES AND QUINCE

In Nonna's Kitchen
Celebrating Italy
The Italian Baker
The Hill Towns of Italy

MANGOES AND QUINCE

A Novel

CAROL FIELD

BLOOMSBURY

Published by Bloomsbury, New York and London.
Distributed to the trade by St. Martin's Press.

Library of Congress Cataloguing-in-Publication Data

Field, Carol.
Mangoes and quince: a novel / Carol Field.-- 1st US ed.
p. cm.
ISBN 1-58234-114-1
1. Amsterdam (Netherlands) – Fiction. 2. Runaway hus-
bands –
Fiction. 3. Women cooks – Fiction. 4. Cookery – Fiction.
I. Title.

PS3556.I3668 M36 2001
813'.54–dc21

First Edition
10 9 8 7 6 5 4 3 2 1

Typeset by Palimpsest Book Production Limited,
Polmont, Stirlingshire
Printed in the United States of America by
R. R. Donnelley & Sons Company, Harrisonburg, Virginia

For Jean McCann

ACKNOWLEDGMENTS

In an ideal world every writer would have a supporter as enthusiastic and insightful as Cyra McFadden. I truly can't imagine what this book would have been without her sensitive reading and suggestions.

I want to thank Eleanor Coppola for providing me with mangoes at a critical moment in my life and for cheering me on from the very beginning.

I thank my wonderful agents, Bonnie Nadell and Fred Hill, for believing in the novel and helping me every step along the way, and to Irene Moore who kept everything flowing smoothly, my extraordinary editors, Karen Rinaldi and Panio Gianopoulos, and James Walsh, an exemplary copy editor.

This novel owes an immense debt of gratitude to the following readers: Whitney Chadwick, Morley Clark, Jane Downs, Mathea Falco, Mary Felstiner, Ann Goldsmith, Carolyn Hall, Barbara Jay, Else Jensen, Diana Ketcham, Annegrete Ogden, Diana O'Hehir, Alison Owings, Mary Priest, and Ruth Snow.

Thanks to Rosmarie Stanford for the beautiful image on the cover, to Gillian Riley for her generous help, and to Sandy Mullin and members of the Bloomsbury office for testing the recipes.

When Linda Connor gave me the catalogue of an exceptional photography show, *Towards Independence: A Century of Indonesia Photographed* by Jane Reed, neither she nor I would have guessed what a profound impact it would have in inspiring much of this book. Finally, I owe a great debt of gratitude to Charles Corn for his two extraordinary books on Indonesia, *Distant Islands: Travels Across Indonesia* and *The Scents of Eden: A Narrative of the Spice Trade.*

CHAPTER ONE

CIGARETTE BURNS SCAR THE old mahogany dresser on which a mirror swings slowly on rusting hinges. The knobs have long since disappeared, leaving the drawers lying open at odd angles in the still morning air. Inside the top one a monkey, sinewy and slender with silvery brown fur, stretches languidly on its stomach as it toys with a white marble, pushing it between two paws, playing an indolent game of catch with himself. Suddenly he leaps out and lands on the dusty green chenille bedspread, his prehensile fingers and toes combing through the tufts, feeling them, smelling them. He begins to dig in the fabric frantically as if to unearth a treasure, a secret. His nose nuzzles the worn cloth. In a frenzy he tries to penetrate the soft bedspread, sinking finely pointed teeth into the fabric, ripping and shredding through to sheets pulled taut over a mattress that sags in the shape of its earlier inhabitants. His nose quivers, then fills with a complex layering of soft powders, rosy scents, and the smell of man. Electrified by a deep subdural knowledge, he seems to shrink to a fragile earlier state, plunged into memory.

The spray of tangerine juice, a pale perfume of roses dried and crushed and left in a cracked bowl, the thick scent of lovemaking trapped in the folds of sheet, the powdery residue of shades frayed from being pulled up and down too many times: these are the smells that pull the monkey back to a time when the room was full of pleasure and sensual delight.

The monkey belongs to Diana. With her ginger-colored curls and soft faded clothes, she looked even younger than her seventeen years. For a few weeks that spring, she was often alone with the monkey, who clung to her and rode on her back like an animated knapsack. Diana gave him the run of the place. He scampered up and down stairs and into the several rooms that opened onto a central hall. He knew the worn floors, polished to a faded gleam by the feet of so many visitors, the rugs that were frayed at the edges, and the old mismatched furniture that made each room distinct within the possibilities of such a place.

Once, before calamity came, the room had been part of a great house built in the eighteenth century by a family of immense wealth. Leaders of business, government, and society had gathered in its impressive rooms, but by the time Diana came to live there, the family house had already begun the steep descent from its years of greatness.

Diana's father had fled from its confines many years in the past and, when he returned home from a sea voyage to Australia not long after the end of the Second World War, with Miranda, his unannounced fifteen-year-old bride, his mother was so cold and disdainful that Miranda immediately persuaded her new husband to take her traveling. 'She's a child, Anton, an ill-bred, unmannered and grasping child' was his mother's uncompromising verdict. 'Let's leave, Anton, please. We can go anywhere, I don't care where. Just don't make me stay here.' Miranda grabbed his hand and took his thumb into her mouth, sucking at the juices. His eyes locked on hers. She tipped up her chin so he could stroke her palate, so his fingers could stroke the soft flesh at the sides of her mouth.

When they returned to the house ten years later accompanied by Diana, their one child, Miranda had changed. With her darkly tanned skin, her hair plaited in a single long braid, and her ripe body wrapped in an indigo sheath, she had become a singularly outspoken and commanding woman.

She strode into the house and strewed the canvas bags and trunks in the rooms she chose for them. 'We've come home,' she informed Ria, her husband's mother, who watched silently as she snapped open the hasps and locks of their trunks and pulled out objects of beauty and strangeness. 'We have something for you,' she said, plunging her hands into a trunk full of hair ornaments, rugs in dazzling colors, a clump of tightly braided jute ropes connected to one another with elaborate hooks, and journals bound in soft leather covers. The old lady stared as Miranda extracted a brilliant green scarf sprinkled with tiny yellow blossoms, a gigantic black and crimson shawl shot through with golden thread, and boxes of stained bamboo and bark that stacked into a tall tower. They hardly fit in with the porcelain plates Ria had so carefully collected or with the soft pastels and silvery grey shawls she wore, but she thanked Miranda as she tied the scarf at her neck, sniffing suspiciously at the foreign odor it emitted.

Anton, Diana's father, a purveyor of implements for ships, left home frequently on sea voyages, and in those days, the three women – grandmother, mother, and daughter – lived in suspension, waiting for his return. Every evening Diana sat in the kitchen as Miranda chopped vegetables and stirred a pot of spicy stew or soup. It was then that she acquired her first monkey and it was then that she first heard the tales of the earlier times in her parents' marriage.

They had lived a watery life, drifting from island to island, settling for months at a time before Anton's curiosity and wanderlust forced them to move on. Diana's first bed was a tiny hammock strung between two low green plants. As her ginger-colored hair grew thick as a bird's nest, her father carved little moon-shaped combs for her. He showed her how they fit into the soft flesh of her palms and taught her to draw them through her hair until it rippled like a mermaid's. As the light of day faded, he taught her to hold a comb up to the distant surface of the pale moon and draw it back and forth until the opalescent circle shone strong in the sky, spilling out into pinpoints of light that were the stars and constellations. He taught her about the Milky Way, Cassiopeia, and the big bear who fished in the streams of the sky. He taught her to cup her hands and dip them into warm waters, pulling out silvery fish whose flashing tails tickled and caused her to drop them back into the sea. The family lived easily on the abundant fruit that grew on the trees, on vegetation that grew in the rich earth, on the fish of the sea and the eggs of the immense colonies of sea birds that floated on the waters every evening at dusk.

Each time the three of them moved, they packed up their growing possessions – the cloth made by native women in colors like flowers unfolding at dawn, necklaces of spiky coral, cutlery made of bone with glowing stones set in the handles, basins and mortars and pestles scooped out of local rock. Everywhere they went Diana's father collected ceremonial fetishes, fertility symbols with swollen bellies or huge stiff members, old men with the heads and wings of birds spread to protect young women with blank expressions in their eyes. He carried away with him crocodiles that appeared to be swallowing the moon in the shape of a maiden, and masks of multicolored serpents encircling a man and woman joined together.

Their moves became more frequent as Diana's father sought for a solution to a deeply felt, nameless need. Satisfaction seemed to slip through his fingers as the waters through which they traveled rushed through the fingers he trailed in the sea. When she was six, the family left the soft air of small islands for the windy expanses of an inland town.

Cautiously exploring her new environment, Diana encountered a colony of monkeys. They lived in the huge enclosed garden of a local merchant and their chatter and activity instantly attracted her. At any opportunity she escaped from the confines of the house and ran to the gates of the garden to watch the monkeys as they leapt from branch to branch, talking and grooming one another with an easy intimacy. The guardian of the gates of the garden, a squat bald man with butterscotch-colored skin, eyed the child with suspicion.

After several days of studying her intently, he crept from the shade of a large leafy tree, clamped a thick hand on Diana's bony shoulder, and commanded her not to move. She went rigid with fear. When she opened her mouth to scream, vocal cords tensed thin as taut wire, she could make no sound at all. The clutch of terror wrapped her in a numbness as isolating as a thick blanket of fog. She broke into terrified sobs and began to shake, so unnerving the man who had planned to send her away forever that he reached into his back pocket, brought out a large and very dirty piece of cloth, and shoved it at her.

Then he whistled through the gap in his front teeth and Diana watched as the mother monkey swung hand over hand with a baby clutching her chest, landing on the branch of the tree nearest the gate. His voice, so different from the original growl she had heard, was a sort of chatter in a choppy sing-song rhythm. The monkey responded ecstatically, swinging its head from side to side and leaping up and down so enthusiastically that the branch swung dangerously close to the earth. The man's hand now reached into another pocket and brought forth a handful of vermilion seeds, which he thrust through the iron grillwork of the gate. Instantly the monkey swooped down and grabbed them before returning to the branch to feed herself and her baby. When the man found another handful of the brilliant seeds, he gave them to Diana so that when the monkey returned it was from Diana's hand that she ate.

On her third visit the man unlocked the gates of the garden and allowed Diana entrance. There was a whole colony of monkeys with spiky grey-brown fur that darkened to smoky black on their feet, palms, and faces. Their screeching and chattering filled the air, causing the leaves to stir as if their voices were the wind and the leaves waves on the water. Soon she became as familiar to them as the guardian and they allowed her to feed them slices of papaya and mango, glowing orange loquats, sweet green plums, and red-fleshed fruits whose rich, custardy interiors were studded with watermelon-like seeds.

Miranda might have noticed her daughter's absence earlier had her life not become much more complicated in their latest move. Anton had entered into dealings with several local traders, which entailed his setting off on sea journeys of some length. He always returned with more money than he had before, although it seemed to evaporate swiftly and require yet another trip, and then another. In his absences, Miranda began cooking for some of the local women, who were enchanted by her ability to cadge new flavor from local ingredients and to present them in enticing dishes. Reveling in their praise, she soon was so busy shopping and chopping and cooking that she wasn't aware of the length or frequency of Diana's absences. It was only when the girl came home with a tiny monkey on her shoulder that she realized her daughter had a life about which she knew nothing.

'Where did you get that animal?' Miranda asked, backing away from the small, furry bundle in her daughter's arms. The women of the village all knew, of course. They saw her disappear every morning; they even called her Monkey Girl. They speculated on the questionable business that took her father away, for they had learned that he strapped a finely honed knife to his calf whenever he went out. They had heard about his luck at cards and his bouts of drinking the cheapest local potions at the only bar in town. Diana's mother began to suspect that he was trading in contraband, but she was afraid to ask and when she hinted at her worries, he grew cold and turned away, neither answering her questions nor confirming her doubts.

Not long after an awkward conversation with her, he left on a brief voyage, and when he returned a deep circular cut surrounded the fleshy part of his left breast and broad marks striped his back. He refused to answer Miranda's questions about his injuries and merely gave her a furious look. She realized that she had grown afraid. The time had come to leave the places of their wanderings and return to the home to which he had originally brought her.

Overhearing pieces of their arguments, Diana fled to the monkeys. She had given names to the ones that were special to her. She played games with them, fed them, and sang songs made up especially for them. Often the mother monkey rode on her shoulders, arms wrapped loosely around her forehead, and they voyaged together beneath trees with thick trunks and roots that extended into the earth in rich complicated patterns. The babies snuggled under her neck and chattered with her, and she rocked them back and forth, stroking their soft fur.

Diana fought furiously against leaving. She screamed at her mother. She pleaded to stay with Majine, the keeper of the gardens. She raged and sobbed until her tears turned into deep body-shaking hiccups that left her unable to speak or even catch her breath. She all but spat upon her father. She begged to be allowed to take one monkey with her. Diana's mother tried reasoning with her, explaining that the monkey could not survive without all its family members and the garden that contained them. Diana refused to listen and stormed in and out of the house as her mother continued calmly to pack. Soon after, they loaded their belongings on to the boat and sailed away from the only existence Diana had ever known.

CHAPTER TWO

NOTHING ABOUT THEIR NEW life was familiar. Not the big house with its upholstered chairs in high-ceilinged rooms, not the massive dining room where they ate their dinners, not the many mullioned windows that began high on the wall like a clerestory, allowing light to flow in but permitting no view out, and certainly not the tall, bony grandmother whose hooded sapphire blue eyes followed Diana relentlessly. The carefully landscaped garden with its beds of tulips and floppy-stemmed ranunculas was entirely unlike the lush tangle of fragrant vines and flowers that had overrun their island homes. Diana hated the cool grey air and the tight grid of the city with its endlessly long curving streets, hated the chilly people who wrapped themselves in layers of warm clothing and wore thick-soled shoes. Even the dense mists and the smells that rose off the sea were entirely different from the soft steamy breezes of her island life. 'I hate this house,' she said to her father, kicking the leg of the high-backed chair she was forced to sit in when they ate their meals. 'Why couldn't we have stayed where we were?' Consumed by a sense of loss, Diana walked through the rooms in a state of bitter confusion, barely able to fathom the immense change in her life.

The city of Amsterdam was shaped like a huge half moon. A river ran through it, cutting it in half. Canals divided the neighborhoods that were threaded with much tinier canals.

Tall brick and grey stone buildings lined the boulevards, where leafy elm trees softened and punctuated the flat expanse of streets. If she closed her eyes, Diana imagined that she could see almost all the way from the front of the house to the port where big freighters and liners docked at the piers.

When she accompanied her mother on shopping expeditions, Diana usually walked dejectedly, dragging her feet and falling further and further behind until, on one of their exploratory trips, she saw a pet store. Immediately she ran inside where she reveled in the familiar, ripe animal smells. She scooped up slices of plum and seeds from baskets perched on a counter and approached a cage with a small smoky grey monkey inside. 'Here, monkey, monkey,' she called as she coaxed it toward her outstretched hand. She puckered her mouth and made little clicking sounds with her tongue. The monkey advanced tentatively, swiveling its head from side to side to check for danger, and then scampered to the front of the cage and ate everything she offered. Diana replenished her handful and returned to the cage several times until the shop owner asked her please to stop. At this the girl wheeled on her mother, who had discovered her in the store, and asked the inevitable: 'Please let me keep this monkey. There is nothing in my life here that I care about and nothing that cares about me. Please – I promise I will be happy when it lives with me. Please.' When Miranda hesitated, Diana promised to take care of it and to keep it out of her grandmother's presence. And so she named the monkey Majine after the keeper of the monkeys on the island and he came to live with them.

Her father still left on voyages across the sea. As time passed, he seemed to be gone for longer and longer periods, but no matter where he went, he continued to collect his sculptures. He stored the pieces, which came to number over a hundred, in two rooms to which he alone had the key. When he was home, he spent hours gazing at them, but he never spoke of them.

He didn't reappear after a trip that was supposed to take

no more than a month. Days went by and then weeks passed without a word from him. Bills piled up and creditors began to threaten Miranda. She put them off by paying a bit to each one but soon the small amounts no longer appeased them and she feared that they would turn off the electricity and refuse to bring the wood that stoked the large fireplaces in the dead of winter.

With no relief in sight, Miranda was forced to take people into the house as paying guests. 'You'll have to move to the back of the first floor,' she told Ria. 'Move downstairs? From the rooms that have always been mine? So some tramp, some sailor, some . . .' Miranda slid into the space left by her sputtering: 'That's right. So someone willing to pay to live here will have a place to sleep.' She moved furniture from room to room, placed beds and chairs where none had been before, and stuffed Anton's clothes and possessions into trunks and boxes as she effectively erased him from their existence. Only the two locked rooms remained beyond her reach.

Anger at her wayward husband gave her the energy to transform their lives. She and Diana each moved into a small room in the front of the house while the grandmother commandeered two rooms in the back. The older woman could barely contain her fury as she was forced to accept the first of many men who came to board in her once elegant house. She watched through narrowed eyes as Miranda opened trunks to decorate the rooms for strangers: out came a rug woven by islanders, dresser scarves crocheted by the sure hands of old women, brushes with the bristles of wild pigs, scarves to drape around bare light bulbs to lessen their harsh glare and create a soft, shadowy atmosphere. She dug out old records so music was always playing on the phonograph and in this way shrewdly created an aura of such warmth that her rooms were always full.

Miranda wrapped herself, as well, in gauzy fabrics printed with whorls of color in concentric circles and put on the dozen bracelets and long dangling earrings acquired in those years of travel. She strode confidently through the place and whenever Diana went with her, the monkey came as well. Diana let him ride on her shoulders, his fingers holding tight to her burst of ginger-colored curls. 'Chee chee, chee chee,' he chattered happily as he bounced in the rhythm of her steps. He was both friend and confidant to the girl, whose smoky blue grey eyes sent out signals of uncertainty and fearful compliance.

Miranda became an enchantress of sorts in her own small kingdom. With her newly appreciated talents for cooking she made soups with golden squashes and stews flavored with apricots and almonds. She haunted unusual grocery shops to find green papayas from which she made a piquant, spicy chutney. From her capable hands came the dough for flatbreads that she slapped on a hot griddle, then cut open and spread with a garlicky paste. She was often up late in the night cooking, so that aromas danced through the house at odd hours. At dinnertime a crowd always gathered around the massive mahogany table that all but filled the dining room. Miranda softened its unequivocal statement of power with a brilliantly patterned tablecloth, bouquets of wild flowers, and a lazy susan that revolved slowly in its center. She piled bowls full of food and let people serve themselves, and though she permitted no distilled spirits, she poured wine into goblets made from molten glass in which bubbles and ridges still remained.

Sailors, yachtsmen, wanderers, and businessmen with an adventurous nature found themselves in her rooms and at her table. There were only men. Some came for a few days, some for a week, some kept a room to which they returned intermittently, and a few stayed for more than a year. Behind her back Miranda was sometimes known as Circe, for her beauty and culinary wiles did indeed bring men to her and keep them ensnared by the appetites she stirred but never fully satisfied. She moved among them in her diaphanous robes and she laughed and drank and flirted with them. She kept her distance, although it often crackled with electricity, and it may be that the erotic tension created by her presence was the attraction that brought more and more men to the house.

In those days mother and daughter were often taken into the confidence of their guests. Most of the men gravitated to her mother, but some, missing their own daughters or remembering their childhoods, took an interest in Diana. One played cards with her and helped with her homework. Another took her walking through the streets of the city and taught her to look with new eyes at the tall houses with their roofs defined by ziggurats and by gables pointed like circumflexes. Yet another took her to a theatrical performance, giving her a first taste of the appeal of stories told in the dark, men and women caught by the enchantments and terrors of the world.

Once, in the long light days of summer, Fritz, a naval architect, who had lived with them on and off for many months, took her fishing in the river that flowed from the distant foothills and emptied into tributaries that reached the waters of the nearby port. He showed her how to tie flies and how to cast, as they waited for a bite, told her stories of his childhood in Copenhagen and in turn learned about the importance of the monkey in her life. When Diana felt a tug on the line, she panicked, nearly dropping the pole, until he took charge, his hands over hers, and showed her how to let the fish fight, playing with it, letting the line go slack, then tightening it up at the right moment and pulling the struggling fish through the calm waters, reeling it in. Together they drew from the water a silvery fish with a sprinkling of orange scales, plunged it into a bucket, and at the end of the day brought it home for her mother to cook.

'Thank you,' Miranda said crisply, swooping up the fish in a single motion and moving swiftly to the kitchen. She seemed to be speeding through life, her motions ratcheted up a notch or two, with less time for Diana as she became busier and more distracted by the numerous chores connected with running a house full of guests. Noticing Miranda's simultaneous presence and absence, Diana's grandmother made herself wander the halls in an effort to protect the girl from the men. She studied their faces and sent out signals with her eyes that were meant to keep them at a distance. She tried to make Diana wear dresses with full skirts that disguised her body, but in the heat of summer the girl insisted on wearing light cottons and dresses made of gauzy fabric, even shorts, when her grandmother wasn't looking.

One hot day, a tall sandy haired man from Kinderdijk, a small town in the north, asked Diana to come to his room. He wanted to show her a picture of his daughter whom he hadn't seen for many months. She went to get her monkey, but when she saw him sleeping so deeply on the soft pillow in his wicker basket, Diana left him and followed the man, listening as he told her that he kept the picture in a little silver frame next to the bed and talked to it every night before he went to sleep. He saw a resemblance between the two girls, although when Diana looked at the picture, she couldn't find any similarity between the younger girl with her plump cheerful face and straight brown hair and Diana's own long face framed with ginger-colored curls.

The man was wearing a batik shirt so long it reached to his knees and caramel colored leather sandals that exposed feet with thick-ridged toenails. He wanted to show Diana all the presents he had purchased for his daughter on his travels in Indonesia, and when she appeared interested he reached into the room's shallow closet and brought out a box with clothes unlike any she had seen before. He spread out a skirt with tiers of white blossoms woven in red cotton and another with a pattern of parrots in golden and pumpkin colors. From crumpled tissue paper he drew out several soft blouses in muted pastel patterns and one made of dazzling red and purple silk sewn with shiny metal threads.

'And here are rod puppets. I will show her how to make them come alive with stories, just as they do in Indonesia.' The puppets were made of paper cut into lacy patterns as delicate as the doilies Diana's grandmother kept on her plush velvet armchairs. One was a dainty young girl with almond-shaped eyes who was gazing down at her elegant, narrow feet. She was painted all in white, whereas a gargantuan man with big eyes, fat lips, and an unmistakable sneer was colored a fiery red. 'This one,' he said, gesturing at a puppet with a golden face, 'is Shiva, creator and destroyer of worlds, and this one is the monkey king, who rescues the beautiful girl after she is abducted by the ogre.' He showed her how they were mounted on rods and described how a puppeteer can make them tread gracefully or stomp furiously or mince in silly steps. 'He knows all the episodes in their lives and he speaks their words in many different voices – some soft and sweet, others deep and threatening and angry.' As the man described them, she saw the puppets like figures in a dream world and imagined them casting shadows on a taut white cloth lit from behind with incandescent gaslight.

In his pleasure at her company, the man reached out to rumple Diana's hair and then gently to touch her knees. His hand stroked the kneecaps, and then he smiled, wanting her to know how happy he was to have her with him.

'There are so many different stories within the plays that it could take years to perform them all. Here – would you like to try using a puppet? You can be the girl,' he said, and he put the rod in her hand, showing her how to move it slowly back and forth, like a fan, as if she were walking in a beautiful garden. 'I will be there, watching when you aren't aware, and then I will slowly approach when I think you won't notice.' He pantomimed clumping, throwing the puppet's weight from side to side in an exaggerated way. 'But you do notice,' he said, taking the rod in her hand and showing her how to jump back in surprise, 'so then I will snatch you from the safety of your royal enclosure and take you into the jungle where I rule.' Diana took the rod and made her maiden struggle fiercely. He let her move gingerly before he overpowered her and took her into the darkness of the forest. Seeing Diana's distress, the man stopped to explain. 'It's a famous story in Indonesia, and everyone knows that the monkey king will appear when the ogre is fast asleep, unbind the maiden, and take her in his arms, swinging with her through the trees and back to freedom.'

'Oh, good, a monkey,' Diana said, clapping her hands in excitement. 'Is he the hero?' 'Yes, yes,' the man said, giving Diana a small squeeze and a hug. 'Now put down the puppet and come sit on my lap. I'll tell you two or three of the stories and perhaps you can help me find the right one for my daughter when I first give her the puppets.'

Diana knew that, at eleven, she was too big to sit on someone's lap, but she was afraid to say so. She didn't want to hurt his feelings. She climbed tentatively onto the edge of his knees, perching as far forward as she could, but he pulled her back, putting his arms around her shoulders. 'Call me Daddy,' he said softly. 'Daddy,' she said tentatively, in a voice full of yearning that stirred the man. 'Daddy.' 'Say it again.' 'Daddy,' she whispered. 'Yes,' he crooned, stroking her hair. Something stirred. 'Look,' he said, gently lifting her off his lap, unbuttoning his long shirt and putty-colored trousers and drawing out a pale white thing with a single eye. As she watched, it grew thicker and longer and darker, a hooded serpent swerving drunkenly upward. 'Here,' he offered. He took her hand and placed it around the thing that was swelling and careening toward her. It was stiff, solid, muscular. 'You can stroke it. Yes, like that. Now hold it tight. Don't be afraid.' In her frozen amazement she watched him close his eyes and smile, saw him arch his back, heard him grunt, and then she felt a thick viscous liquid pool in the palm of her hand.

She opened it, letting the thing drop without warning, and stared uncomprehending. Looking at her through his drooping eyelids, the man warned Diana that they now had a secret. One that was just between the two of them. 'You mustn't tell anyone. Not your mother or grandmother or anyone. Something terrible will happen to you if you say anything. Worse than anything you can imagine. And I will know. You can count on that.' Nodding, she lurched backward, upsetting the table in her rush to get away. 'Don't forget,' he shouted after her. 'Don't ever say a word or you will be sorry.'

Diana ran to her room, taking deep breaths that turned into sobs as she opened the door. She rushed at Majine, scooping him up and holding him tight. 'I'll never go anywhere without you again. Never ever ever. That awful man. Oh Majine, how could I have left you behind? He told me a story about a monkey who saved a girl and you would have saved me, I know you would have, you wouldn't have let him do that awful thing, but you weren't there. Oh Majine, you weren't there.'

Pitching herself into the shower, she stood under its scalding spray for long minutes, scrubbing her skin and washing her hands again and again. Climbing out, wrapping herself in an old threadbare towel, she felt betrayed by her body. She couldn't even look at it. Her skin ached. She wished she could rub it off and become clean again. For the next few days Diana had no appetite and sat uncomfortably at the dinner table, evading the dark looks the man shot her. Even after he packed and left, she was distracted by the surge of complex feelings that spiked through her, although in time the feelings submerged, sinking in the darkness of her interior, leaving a residue of fear and anxiety like the exhausted froth left on the sand by a retreating wave. She did not speak of what happened, but she grew wary of the men in their passage through the hallways and shrank against the walls when she had to walk where they did.

Every day Diana wished that her father would return and

send all the men away. She watched Miranda become more and more wrapped up with the boarders and her own life and wished she could break through the invisible barrier that separated them.

Diana and her mother spent most of their time together doing the chores that kept the house running. At their most relaxed, they cooked, Diana toasting walnuts, whisking eggs, sifting flour into the big blue-banded bowl while Miranda took the ingredients and transformed them into puddings and cakes. Sometimes Miranda sang island chants as they waxed the floors and sometimes they drank tea and ate leftovers, but more and more Miranda seemed distracted, ready to be elsewhere. Majine was almost always with them. Every once in a while he would leap into Miranda's lap, so unnerving her that she automatically swatted him away. Diana would immediately slide to the floor to comfort Majine as he whimpered. 'Are you all right? Here,' she'd say, hoisting him gently onto her lap, moving first one arm and then the other, one leg and then the next, making sure that nothing had been harmed. Concern etched her face until she proved to herself that he was all right. 'Mamma, don't. He doesn't mean anything by it. He just wants to be with you.'

Diana couldn't turn to her grandmother. The older woman was outspoken in her loathing of Miranda for the profligate atmosphere she had created. She resented the intrusion of men in her house and was merely tolerating the situation until Anton returned. While she waited in her isolation at the back of the house, she continued to polish the family silver and display pieces of it on her bureau. She knitted sweaters. She became tighter, fiercer, more imperious, like a dowager empress whose kingdom had been reduced to insignificance.

Her only solace was the garden, where she planted flowers and tended trees, organizing a little corner of the earth with tenderness. The garden, a sizable portion of land behind the house, was laid out in a careful formal pattern, with the yew trees that marked its borders enclosing several separate cutting gardens. She was particularly proud of the parrot tulips, whose brilliant reds and oranges were striped with soft washes of yellow and pale pink. She nurtured other tulips as well, some with ruffled edges, some with marbled petals, and some in unusual colors, like a purple so deep it was almost chocolate.

Diana often sought out her grandmother when she was in the garden. 'Nanna,' she would call as she unlocked the gate that formally separated the house from the garden. 'Nanna, are you there?' Then she would spot the big canvas hat that kept the platinum light of the sun out of her grandmother's eyes and set off for the tulip beds. Sometimes she came with a purpose, as when the nursery man arrived with new plants and needed to be let in, but often she just liked to sit on the earth and talk with her grandmother.

The older woman felt a direct infusion of energy when working in the garden. Tidy, careful, and perfectionistic in the rest of her life, she relaxed into an easy intimacy with the earth as she knelt in the dirt and weeded, pruned, and planted new flowers.

As she thought about it, she wondered if perhaps the brilliance of her garden was her way of compensating for the lack of mountains or trees that contain the geography of other cities. Yes, canals circumnavigate and wind throughout the city, but it was her garden, hidden behind the stone and brick house with its stepped gables, that gave her the deepest pleasure and contentment. It was, she sometimes thought, her signature upon the earth.

She had been only slightly older than Diana when she married and left behind her life as Ria Van der Lin, moving from her country village to the grand city house of her husband's family. She had spent her childhood enveloped in the colors and fragrances of the flowers her father raised and sent to market – paperwhites and narcissus, flamed tulips and extravagant cabbage roses, daffodils and ruffled carnations. Every day she had put on her wooden clogs and walked up and down the rows of flowers in the greenhouses, rows and rows of them, breathing in their aromas and feeling entirely at home in her world. One day Thomas de Jong arrived to arrange for masses of tulips for the party he was giving for his parents' wedding anniversary. She was the one who greeted him. Over the next months he returned to see her every week, and when they married and she was transported to the city threaded with its watercourses, the garden behind the house became her refuge.

It had originally been planned as a formal space with parterres, clipped hedges, and colored pebbles, but it had fallen into a kind of genteel neglect. Ria was overwhelmed by the scale of the house and was properly intimidated by her mother-in-law, but the garden – yes, that was something she could understand. There were no flowers in it at all when she arrived, so she asked if she could please plant the languishing areas with color. Thomas, who was used to seeing flowers only when they were arranged in pewter bowls, silver vases, or globular glass bottles, thought it a fine idea and convinced his mother to let Ria try her hand.

It was the beginning of a long and happy relationship with both the garden and the nursery from which she bought plants. She made low green walls to separate the cutting gardens and set about finding the flowers that gave it the color and life that continued to draw her. The nursery man, Mr. Mieskeeper, and his family became her first independent friends when she moved into her new life, and they had remained her mainstays for three generations.

The old man Mieskeeper began bringing his son, Andreas, to help with the work when the boy was only ten. He wanted to show him how trees and flowers, when planted with foresight, created pattern and color, how the spill of light alternating with shade and shadow could transform an ordinary plot of land into a world of solace and serenity.

Ria's own son, Anton, was Andreas's age but had no interest in the garden. To him a tree was to be climbed, a branch to be snapped. His idea of pleasure was loading a slingshot with pebbles from the squares in his mother's garden to use against birds, neighbors' cats, and boys at school. His teachers had warned him never to bring the weapon to school again after he had narrowly missed hitting a classmate's eye, but he continued to hide it in the inside pocket of his jacket. Slow, sleepy-eyed, slightly pudgy Anton and muscular Andreas attended the same school. Anton took pleasure in deriding the boy in front of their classmates for working after school in his family's garden. It was a large and important garden, as Anton pointed out to whoever would listen, and their house was full of valuable possessions. He sometimes showed off ancient silver coins he had filched from the trays that held the collection made by his great-grandfather, a merchant banker who had accumulated the tapestries, oak chests, tables, and chairs carved of exotic woods, fanciful birdcages, harpsichords, and ebony-framed mirrors that filled the rooms of the family house. Most of them were still in place during Anton's childhood, before a wave of financial reverses overtook their lives.

Ria was infuriated by Anton's arrogance. 'What gives you the idea that you are so superior? Have you forgotten that your own grandfather grows flowers for people like the Mieskeepers? That I used to help raise plants in the greenhouses and watch them be sent all over Europe? Andreas, at least, is doing honorable work, unlike some boys I know, who seem to think they're above it all.' It was only one of her many lectures meant to improve Anton's character. In response he closed his eyes and smiled smugly, throwing his head back and forth, as if to shake off an irritating insect circling about his ears.

Ria became even more concerned when she realized that

Anton was using the fascination of the family's great house to lure and impress girls. They captivated him, stimulated him, and intensified his secrecy and bravado. For all his roughness and arrogance, the boy was transformed when he was in the presence of girls. He spoke in a voice as soft as the silken filaments that float out of a cocoon.

On the day that he invited Laura Klees, a particularly beautiful girl in his class, to the house, he knew that only the servants would be at home, so he felt safe promising to show her the collection of old silver coins, the hand-blown glasses, and the porcelain plates with griffins encircling the incised golden rims. The girl entered the great hall timorously. She was dazzled by her first sight of the ancient leather trunk holding dozens of vases of paperwhites. 'It's so big. I've never been anywhere like this,' she said in a whisper, as she followed Anton into the main room with its paintings and carefully constructed shelves with trays full of old coins. He allowed her to handle the coins, to feel the raised ridges of the portraits of the great monarchs and merchant leaders whose faces graced the currency of the country.

'Let's go upstairs. There are lots more things up there.' 'Is that all right?' she asked nervously. 'Where's your mother?' 'Don't worry.' His voice was soft and reassuring. To overcome her trepidation, he held her hand as he led her up the winding staircase into the dressing room, where his mother hung her velvet gowns. 'Here, feel this. Soft, isn't it?' he spoke in his low, magical voice. Laura ran her palm over the surface. 'Try it on,' he encouraged her. 'It's all right, there's no one here. Just put it on over your dress. It's OK. I promise.' She slid the long gown over her head and felt it fall in place on her shoulders. She smiled at her reflection in the dressing room mirror and let her hands feel the sensuous material as it lay across her stomach. 'Doesn't it feel good? You look beautiful in it,' he said, and he slid his hands up and down one arm. 'Oh, that feels so good.'

He went to his mother's dressing table, took the fluted crystal top off a flacon of perfume, and dabbed tiny circles of it on the pulse at the base of Laura's neck and the insides of her wrists. 'Let me smell it,' Anton said, pressing his nose against the soft notch at the base of her throat. Teased by its smell, he lifted her long blond hair with his hand and rubbed little circles of the fragrance behind her ears. 'Do you really think this is all right?' she asked nervously. 'Of course,' Anton replied. 'I do it all the time. My mother's happy that I like to be here.'

When Ria appeared without warning, she found the two of them touching tongues, the tip of his slowly inching its way into the moist pinkness of Laura's mouth. She was shocked. 'Anton, who is this? What is going on?' Laura burst into tears. She began to shake so hard she could barely pull the dressing gown over her head. Ria called one of the servants, who ushered the terrified girl to the door. 'Anton, how could you? Whatever made you think you could bring this girl here when I was out, and then . . .' Unable to continue, she left it to Thomas to punish his son.

That night when his father confronted him, Anton refused to back down. 'What did you think you were doing there, with that girl? In your mother's dressing room? Explain yourself.' No response. 'You'd better apologize now, if you know what is good for you.' Still nothing. 'I'm giving you one more chance.' Anton stared at his father, looking him straight in the eye, and said nothing. 'Answer or I'll give you a thrashing you won't forget.' Infuriated by the silence, Thomas took off his belt, told Anton to put out his hands, and breathing deeply and slowly, brought the strip of leather down over the boy's knuckles. The boy braced himself each time he heard the leather slapping at the air and exhaled hard each time it stroked across his hands. Once, twice, three times. At first he was surprised at the pain, but he held out, so unnerving his father that the man shouted at him. 'Talk to me. Now. Apologize now or you'll be sorry.' Nothing. 'Doesn't hurt then, I guess?' his father inquired, eyebrows raised in a quizzical circumflex. Goaded by the silence, he curled the end of the belt around his fingers with the buckle dangling downward so the lash would sting all the more. Anton's eyes teared but no words came from his mouth. By the time his father had finished, he had kept his promise to himself and said nothing. A wave of pleasure surged over him, moving into the cold places between his ribs, behind his eyes.

CHAPTER THREE

URING WHAT SHE CALLED 'the years of Miranda's men,' Ria spent more and more time in the garden. She worried about Diana and often invited the girl to join her there, where they sat quietly together, Diana pulling up weeds or sliding bulbs into the holes her grandmother dug. 'Don't pay attention to the men in the house,' Ria said to the girl again and again, as if repetition would keep her safe, 'and don't let them pay attention to you.'

'I keep Majine with me all the time, Nanna. He will protect me.'

'Maybe so,' the older woman said, guardedly. All those coarse men and a monkey in the house that had once been the scene of opulent parties filled with great bankers, merchants, and captains of industry, she thought to herself. It was bad enough that her husband had failed to keep strict watch over the bookkeeper, who grew rich at their expense, and worse still that Thomas had died unexpectedly, leaving a severely diminished estate. His sudden death had been such a shock that she still had difficulty comprehending her position. All those years of bearing her mother-in-law's slights and then reduced to straits not of her own making, Ria felt unable even to protect her own granddaughter.

'Do you mean the monkey might attack if a man . . .' Ria stopped, uncertain how to continue.

'Don't worry, Nanna. I'm sure he would. And if you let him come out here with us so he could get to know you, I'm certain he'd protect you too.'

Ria's response was always the same. 'No, dear, I don't think so. Such a little beast.'

She encouraged the girl to come to her sitting room without him, to curl up in the big wicker rocker and read books from her bookshelves for as long as she wanted. She took Diana shopping and bought her clothes. Velvet skirts, soft blouses, and hand-knitted sweaters were a palimpsest of another life, a world beyond the crude sensuality that Miranda exuded, according to the older woman, who insisted that she keep her new wardrobe where her mother couldn't see it. 'These clothes are for you,' she told Diana, opening the door to her closet where they hung behind her tweed suits, 'but only for the times when we are together. Your mother doesn't need to see them or even know about them.'

One day when she came home from school, Diana went to her grandmother's room for the book she'd been reading. She knocked and almost immediately opened the door, surprising her nanna, who was rummaging in one of two big bags that lay at her feet. 'Come in, dear. Your timing is perfect. I need your help. In fact, what I really need is both your hands. I bought some yarn to make you a sweater, but I have to wind it into balls before I can get started.' She reached down and pulled out a skein of deep blue-grey yarn. 'It's beautiful,' Diana said, walking over to feel it and look more closely. 'Yes, I think so too. Now if you'll just sit right here' – she pointed at the floor in front of her – 'and hold your hands out in front of you.' She slid the first skein of wool over Diana's outstretched fists and slowly started to roll it into a ball. One after another, she made balls from the big loops of yarn and as she did she told Diana about her life in the house when she was much younger.

'Everything was so strange, so different from what I was used to. The first time I tucked my napkin under my chin, everyone laughed. I didn't know which fork to use. I picked up my asparagus in my fingers and they looked at me as if I were a savage.'

'No wonder you missed your own family.'

'Yes, but it all changed when your father was born. A boy! I had produced the miracle child, an heir to carry on the family name. They hung over his crib at all hours, cooing and exclaiming how clever his every move was. Suddenly I was acceptable.

'I'll never forget his christening. There he was, angelic in the magnificent christening dress that every baby in this family has worn for generations. How he hated it all. He shrieked when the minister drizzled a little bit of water over him. Howled, absolutely howled. Of course, why wouldn't he? There he was, safely cradled in my warm arms and some man in black leans over mumbling a lot of hocus pocus and out of nowhere pours water over his little head. I tried to comfort him, but he was still wailing when we all went in to drink a toast to his health in champagne.'

Many afternoons during that cold rainy season Diana returned to her nanna's room to hear stories about her father when he was a little boy. 'As he grew older, the nurse took him off to the park for walks every day while I was in the garden. He'd come home with his cheeks all rosy and he'd run into my arms. "Mamma, mamma, birds, boats," he'd say, so excited. He saved what he called his treasures, things he'd collected on that day's walk, and put them away into his special box. Sometimes I'd slip into his room and watch him holding them and talking to them. "My special rope," he'd tell me with such a serious face, and he'd hold out a dirty old piece of fraying rope and touch it with a kind of reverence. I couldn't always make out what he'd gotten – twisted pieces of metal or old clips of some kind – but they were very important to him. They all went into that box, which he kept under his bed. He told stories that he wove around them and sometimes he clutched them so tightly that his knuckles turned white. He could be fierce in his attachments. He loved me ferociously then, you know, and the nurse. Oh, she was special.'

Each afternoon Diana listened, lulled by the rhythmic click of one knitting needle against the other. 'Taking a walk with Anton, even when he was three or four, was an adventure. He'd disappear suddenly. We didn't know if he'd climbed a tree, dashed into an open door, or simply slipped around the corner when no one was looking.'

'So he always loved adventure,' was Diana's response, 'even when he was little.'

'Always. Hold still, dear. I have to measure the length of your arm. What we didn't know for a long time was that the nurse had met a sailor who she . . . well, cared for, and she began taking Anton to the docks on their walks. We should have figured it out. His vocabulary was full of new words.' 'What kind of words?' Diana wanted to know. 'Oh, goodness, it was so long ago. Let me think. I remember "rigging" – he loved the word "rigging" – and "hold," I remember that. I thought he wanted me to pick him up and put him on my lap, but that wasn't what hold meant to him any more. It seems the sailors let him explore the ships. They told him stories. They even let him sip their beer. You can imagine we were horrified. He was supposed to be in the park climbing trees, not spending time with a bunch of unshaven men with dirty hands doing dirty work.' The old woman suddenly looked tired. 'I think that's enough. But look at how much progress I've made,' she said, and she held up the front and back panels of the sweater.

Diana was too embarrassed to bring anyone from school home with her. How could she explain that the bedrooms in her house were inhabited by men who came and went, men who could be gentle or coarse, men who might stare at her friends with unconcealed curiosity or even longing, who might try to speak to them or even invite them to their rooms? She had no one but her monkey with whom to share her feelings. Her body, caught up in onrushing adolescence, had begun to sprout breasts. Clumps of silky hair grew under her arms and wirier hair in the triangle beneath the navel that signified her once profound connection to her mother.

Had it not been for Majine, she thought later, she might have collapsed into a dark kingdom over which she could have ruled with the same commanding presence as her mother did in theirs. She knew not to mention her father, although she missed him intensely. In her imagination he had become an important explorer, making voyages that relied on the complex instrumentation he invented. She was sure that his wizardry was responsible for breakthroughs in understanding the depths of the oceans and the creatures that lived in it. Perhaps he had even invented implements responsible for the rescue of people who had had accidents on the water and been marooned, waiting and clinging to the wreckage. She worried that he was himself shipwrecked, and though he had compasses and knew all the constellations, he might still be waiting for help to repair the damage wrought by a storm or an iceberg. Diana felt certain that he missed her but could not write because he was always away at sea on watery passages that permitted no letters, no links except the ones they kept in their hearts.

In Diana's thirteenth year, three years after her father's desertion, Max Madoqua, an anthropologist from Rotterdam, arrived, sniffing around Anton's collection. He had heard rumors about the unusual content of the two locked rooms and hoped to persuade the abandoned wife to open the doors and allow him entrance. Of medium height, with a deeply wrinkled sunburned complexion and dark hair that sprouted from his shirt top, grew in tufts on the backs of his hands, and even exploded in a luxuriant rush from his ears, he was entirely unprepossessing save for two piercing blue eyes and features so plastic that they changed expression with the speed of clouds flying across the sky. He saw himself as a protector of the treasures of innocent and rapidly vanishing cultures and was fierce in his putative stewardship of them.

He went about trying to gain entrance to the collection with admirable directness, bringing documentation of his expertise and letters from scholars. Miranda looked at him with scarcely controlled disdain and explained that she had no keys to the collection and had no interest in finding any. She meant to be dismissive, but he stayed on, and one night, after a curry dinner served with tangles of coconut and one of her homemade apricot chutneys, he invited Miranda to join him in the living room.

He settled in an armchair, poured them each a glass of wine, and set about wooing her. First he admired her house, then her cooking, and then her inimitable style. 'You remind me of the glorious women of a Polynesian tribe who stand as straight as a stick. You move in an explosion of color. I can't tell you how much pleasure it gives me to watch you, to see your long fingers pick up a piece of bread, a bone, a bowl.' He paused, suddenly uncertain, worried that he'd overdone it. 'Oh God, you're going to think I always talk like this, but I assure you I don't. You have a rather heady effect on this placid anthropologist.'

'Umm,' she smiled, dipping her head very slightly in acknowledgment. 'Such nice compliments. I'm glad you like my cooking, my clothes, my . . .' She shrugged, briefly looking as if she were searching for the right word and then giving it up. 'But I do wonder exactly why you're still here. Do you really expect that I'll just open the doors to the rooms with their unknown treasures for you? It's not that I'm waiting for my husband to come home and you certainly shouldn't either.' No, she felt those rooms were some sort of obscure threat, a link to a marriage that began well and ended disastrously, and the objects in them were going to stay there, unseen, until Anton came to collect and sell them, and pay her what he owed.

Leaning close to her, thrusting his chest forward – his

colleagues and competitors would have recognized the anthro-pologist's wind-up at once – Max tried to explain that the objects she was reviling had meaning for scholars who needed to see and study and understand them. 'From what I've heard, these are no ordinary pieces. They were made for rituals in cultures that saw in them the fire of creation and the sacred force of life.' He half-closed his eyes, and speaking in a tone only slightly above a whisper, voiced the opinion that they would obscurely haunt this house until they were allowed into the world. Miranda smiled wryly. She might not have all the degrees this man had, but she could detect a line a long way off.

Almost immediately thereafter he turned his attentions to Diana. 'Call me Max. Let's get to be friends. I expect to be around for a while.' He lit a cigarette, tossed the match in a huge crystal ashtray, and picked a tiny speck of tobacco off the tip of his tongue, flicking it lazily toward the floor. 'I have a general sense of the house, but I'd really like you to show me around. I'd like to meet your grandmother. And hear about your father. What do you remember about him?' Diana hesitated. She held the monkey in her arms, smoothing his fur, stroking it all in the same direction. She had let him sniff at the anthropologist, nose around the short socks that barely covered the man's ankles, but now she didn't want him to leave the warmth of her lap or rob her of the sense of assurance and protection he gave her. There was something about the man that made her feel queasy in his presence. Maybe it was the way he related the sculptures to Diana when he explained that there were figures of young women like her with their new breasts. He talked a lot about bodies, about the waxing and waning moon with its pull on the tides and women's internal rhythms. As he talked, she noticed his tongue licking in and out of his lips, noticed that they left a large wet imprint on the end of his cigarette. Unsettled and confused, Diana worried about giving the man what he wanted. She didn't have the key to the locked rooms and she no longer remembered the sculptures.

Max opened a leather case and brought out pictures similar to what he expected to find in the forest of carved sculptures behind the locked doors. He showed Diana a spiky toothed crocodile devouring a young girl with breasts like newly budded flowers, a gigantic female painted in curves and zigzags of bright oranges and reds and blues that scrolled from the head over the breasts into an intricate mosaic of colors in her pubic region, and a man with a cape of brilliant feathers and immense genitalia in the embrace of several women with snakes writhing over their lush bodies. Some of these, he explained, were sacred symbols of ancestors, were the glorification of fertility, affirmation in the face of death. Some illustrated the cycle of growth and decay and the endless renewal of nature, and some, he let out a smirky laugh, were just plain tributes to the glories of mating.

With his fingers tracing one recumbent maiden's delicate body, he looked directly at her and spoke, using obscure words that swirled around her in a thickening fog. She was aware that his speech was splitting into phalanxes of nouns and verbs and rich clusters of adjectives that were moving ominously toward her. She wanted him to go away. Words of refusal were imprisoned in the darkness of her interior by her irresolution and in their place she felt as if canker sores were blooming on the walls of her mouth. Her tongue sought them out, sure she would find their inflamed centers, exploring, touching, unable to believe they weren't really there.

Anxiously she realized that in some of the sculptures she was seeing the same thick heavy flesh that grew out of the center of the body of the man from Kinderdijk. She wondered if what he had enjoined her to keep secret was something that men everywhere used with abandon and, presumably, impunity. Diana barely heard Max explain, 'I wanted you to see why your father's collection is of such importance. Every one of these sculptures is in a museum or private collection where people can see them and scholars can photograph and write about them. I'm here because I want to keep your father's sculptures safe for the future.

'And I want you to help me. This collection might make your father famous. Otherwise who would ever hear of him, a man who simply walked away from his life? Away from his own wife and child, from his mother and the home he grew up in. I daresay that publicizing the sculptures might even bring him back.'

Diana stared at Max. All this time, she had tried to keep believing that one day he would walk in the front door and tell them of the fabulous adventures that had kept him away for so long. If she might play some part in hastening his return, how could she refuse?

Without asking Miranda, she took the monkey with her to rummage in the closet at the back of the house. She talked to him softly. 'It's okay, Majine, she'll forgive us once she understands why we're doing this,' and coaxed him to take the lead as if this were his idea. He rooted around for a minute then leapt, landing with a thud on the biggest trunk in which her father's belongings were stored. Diana examined his discovery but found that the padlock was securely in place. As she looked around, Majine leapt into the casual clumps of possessions piled on the floor. He had just begun digging with his small, agile hands when Diana heard the sound of metal on metal. 'What did you find?' she asked. He swirled his discovery around on the floor and then began a game of catch, chuckling to himself as he tossed the bunch of keys into the air and dove to retrieve them. 'Majine, let me see,' she said, putting her hand out, but he clutched them to himself and turned away. 'Naughty boy,' she said, inching toward him. 'Let me have them.' As she stroked his stomach, he lost interest in the keys and she caught them when they fell from his hand. 'So many!' she said, and began inserting one after another until finally the padlock sprang cleanly open.

'Well, here we go.' She had a momentary pang of guilt and then, inhaling sharply, she lifted the top of the trunk. The smell of powdery mildew and sharp rot that assaulted her senses was overlaid with her father's masculine scent, hints of sea salt and the metallic bite of chains, clasps, and hand-hewn knives, all bringing him back in an unmediated rush. Sucking in her breath, she plunged nose first into the pile of his old shirts and inhaled deeply, drawing the smell of her childhood into her nostrils. She remembered how tenderly her father had cared for her, how clever he was at catching slippery fish with his bare hands and at lighting fires by the water's edge, where they cooked their meals. She remembered his narrow, good-natured face with its sleepy eyes and crooked smile, his deeply tanned muscular back and arms. She remembered waiting with him to hear the frogs croak their deep burps and climbing on his shoulders to pick fruit from the heavily laden branches of trees. She found the paddle he made to go with a canoe he had scooped out of the bark of a fallen tree, and the fishing pole he created in seconds by snapping off a bamboo branch. He had taught her to delight in the richness of nature. She had never been able to understand the almost imperceptible changes that came over him as mysterious moods washed away his sunniness, pleasure becoming shadowed first by fear and then by an edginess that drove him obsessively to the sea.

She was so hungry for his return that she could have plunged her teeth into the contents of the trunk, chewed and swallowed them down. Where was he, her much beloved father? If Max thought his sculptures might bring him home, all right, she would help him. Diana slid her hands very carefully through layer after layer, touching rusty metal and something in an advanced stage of decomposition. She gagged but refused to stop. She tried bouncing her fingertips lightly across the contents – Majine imitated her by jumping up and down – until she came upon an iguana skeleton and a box of matches that still exuded a strong smell of sulphur. At last her fingertips hit a long, narrow metal container. She extracted it with care and perched it in her lap, setting it across her thighs. The monkey reached up to touch it, but she didn't move. She took time to admire the design of wild boars chasing one another around the edges of the top and then, breathing slowly, slid the lid along the ridged grooves at the sides until it came off, exposing a tangled mass of keys. Some had multiple flanges and were big enough to have opened large entrance gates while others were smaller with oval holes at the top to hang over a nail or hook.

Diana was sure one of them must open the door to her father's locked rooms, but she knew that her mother would be furious at what she had done. She wondered if there were some way to hand over the keys without Miranda's knowing. She picked up Majine, plunked him into her lap, looked directly into his dark eyes, and asked for advice. 'Majine, can you think of some way for me to explain how the keys suddenly ended up in Max's hands? What if you had found them and then left them lying around and Max just picked them up? No, I don't suppose she'd believe that.'

On the morning that she handed him the keys, Diana felt queasy with guilt and excitement. The minute she heard Max's heavy footsteps, she opened the door of her room. He took a fast look around and then extended his hand, palm up. 'So, where are they?' Sensing her hesitation, he pressed harder. 'You want your father back or not?' 'More than anything,' she whispered, clutching the keys so tightly they etched a mark on her palm. 'How do you know he'll come home? What if he doesn't even know about your show?' 'A collection like his – there will be lots of publicity. And from what I know about your father, he'll lap up all the attention.' When she finally took the keys out of her pocket, Majine made a leap for them. 'No,' she cried, and swept him away with her free hand. 'Promise you won't tell my mother how you got them.' Max smiled at her naïveté. What did he care? He held the keys to his future in his hand.

Miranda noticed that Max was turning to Diana and worried that he might be trying to pry memories from her. On a Saturday morning, after she had served her buttermilk pancakes with homemade preserves to the men, she sat down with Diana at the breakfast table and told her how much she wanted Max to leave. 'I just don't like him. I keep feeling that he's sniffing his way around like a ratty little terrier, determined to get what he wants. He doesn't care who he uses or how he does it as long as he goes home with the prize.'

A day earlier Diana would have been thrilled and relieved that her mother had intuited her own conflicted feelings, but now that she was surreptitiously helping Max, the girl was afraid to say anything. She wanted to right the balance of her withheld confidences in some way, so she tentatively mentioned the man from Kinderdijk, saying that he'd made her sit on his lap, that his hands had found her knees and . . . She had stopped, unable to go on, the corners of her mouth pulling downward, tears welling in her eyes. Finally in a voice so low that Miranda could hardly hear it, she continued, '. . . and more.' She couldn't bring herself to say what had happened. Anyway, she thought, her mother really didn't want to know. She was enjoying her admirers and would not want to imagine that they presented a threat. Miranda was silent for a long time before speaking. 'Oh Diana, who knows what to make of these men? Here they are, sailing all over the world, doing business in places we've never heard of, constructing bridges or making discoveries that they bring back here to sell, and then they just melt when they see girls beginning to become women. They just take leave of their senses. No that's not quite right. They don't know what to do once their senses are stirred up. They are carnivorous, and when they are hungry, they want to feed upon young flesh. They should turn to older women who understand, but that doesn't always happen. I'm so sorry if he did something to upset you. Anyway, I'm glad for you that he's gone now.' It was the last time Diana spoke of the incident. She felt colonized by feelings she could not name. She had no way of knowing how to deal with the shame that came to suffuse her inner being, marking the territory as its own, moving her slightly off-center in her own life, as if she saw and felt everything in double vision.

Leaving Diana, Miranda walked distractedly through the dining room, stopping to peel parchment-colored drops of wax from candlesticks and remove drooping tulips from the bowl in the center of the table. She was on her way back to the kitchen to make mango chutney that would go with the ragout simmering slowly on the stove. She had poured mustard seeds into a small ceramic bowl, grated fresh ginger, and piled red-golden mangoes in a heap on the long wooden counter.

As she pushed open the door, she saw a flash of fur. 'Get out, get out right now, you horrible beast. Diana,' she yelled. 'Diana!' the second time even louder. Heart beating fast, the girl came running and found Majine sitting on the floor in the middle of a pile of mangoes. He was sampling them one by one, tearing at their leathery skins and taking bites from the juicy orange flesh, then pouncing on another and another, tasting each, then discarding it before moving on. His eyes were bright with pleasure. Each time Miranda lunged, he escaped easily, leaping onto the counter or the top of a cabinet or under a chair, cradling a mango in one hand. Staring boldly at her, he settled back on his haunches and sank his tiny sharp incisors into the sweet fruit. Miranda approached stealthily, her eyes staring into his. He looked back undisturbed, a glint of provocative amusement playing across his face as he opened his mouth wider to taste the soft fruit. Miranda leapt, but he jumped sideways so quickly that her fingertips barely grazed his fur. Thrown off balance, she slipped on the scattered mangoes that shifted under her feet like marbles. Skidding into a bank of kitchen drawers, she lost her balance and fell into the fruit, which splattered as she hit it. 'Beast,' she yelled. 'Diana, get him out of here. I don't ever want to see him in this kitchen again. Ever.'

'Oh Mamma, he was hungry. You forgot his bananas and sunflower seeds and he hates the dried peels that you put in his bowl. The gatekeeper used to cut mangoes into little cubes and feed them to all the monkeys. Poor Majine. Maybe they made him think of his mother and his life before we got him. Come on, baby,' she said scooping up the monkey and heading for her room.

'Don't walk away from me. Put that monkey in his basket and then come right back and clean up this kitchen. I needed those mangoes. I'm going to get on my bicycle and go to Dagstrom's to buy some more. I expect to find this place totally in order when I return.'

As Miranda cycled to the emporium, she remembered picking mangoes in armloads right off the trees and letting the juices run down her face. She didn't mind the big flat pit, just gnawed her way around it. The women on the little island where they had lived believed that a mango once enclosed the daughter of the sun. They used to tell the story that she was being chased by a wicked sorceress and to get away she jumped into a lake and turned into a golden lotus. The king came along and lost his heart to the lotus and the next thing you know the sorceress set it on fire and turned it to ashes. A tree grew from the ashes and flowered, or so they say, and the flowers became fruit, and the fruit was a mango. When it ripened, it fell upon the ground and split in half and out from it walked a beautiful woman who was the daughter of the sun. The king recognized her at once as the wife he had lost long before and he swept her into his arms.

A romantic story, Miranda thought, as she moved around

the store, scooping fruits and vegetables into brown paper bags and finally spreading her selections on the wood counter near the brass cash register with its fat white enamel buttons. She unconsciously ran her hands over the smooth surface of the wood, feeling the grain polished by hundreds of customers over the decades the Dagstrom family had been in business. This generation's Mr. Dagstrom carefully wrote the price of each item she'd chosen, using a pencil he'd sharpened with an old penknife, and then totaled them up before adding them to her monthly bill. He put them into the expansive string bag she'd brought with her and reminded her that a big storm was on its way. 'Wrap up well, Miranda. It's cold out there. There'll be good skating soon.'

Yes, she thought, and I'll be on the ice, in the silent expanse of cold, taking long gliding strokes with my skates, carving arcs into the frozen canals. I'll take Diana with me on the nighttime walk over the frozen streets with candles and torches lighting the way and then on the way home we can stop for hot chocolate and talk. Miranda knew she needed to make a bridge to her daughter, and she thought about it as she pedaled home. She found it hard to concentrate, dodging around the cars that were filling the city streets and squares. She hated the smell of their exhaust, the grey fumes and luminous slicks of fuel they left on the roads. She hated their horns and squealing tires, and she particularly hated their arrogance, pushing walkers, cyclists, and mothers with prams to the edge of the road.

CHAPTER FOUR

P RODDED BY MAX, DIANA began to ask Miranda about her father. Miranda rarely mentioned him any longer. At the beginning she had been furious at him, worried that he'd found another woman, hoped for revenge, and wished he'd come home, a cycle of emotions that she could go through in a matter of minutes. But slowly, as she became the support of three generations of women, and as she saw herself a desirable woman wooed by the men who swarmed through the house, she began to remember how happy she had been during the first few years of their marriage. Anton drank, yes, but for a long time the liquor made him calm, full of warmth and high spirits. She couldn't put her finger on when he began to drink more and more, becoming angry, secretive, and vindictive. If there were other women while he was away, she ignored the clues. She had always relied on him as provider, so when she insisted they return to this city and the house to which he had brought her as a bride, she assumed that he would make a life for them that was less fraught with danger.

Instead he was gone. Disappeared without a word of explanation or even a message to keep a fragile connection to his mother, his daughter, and her.

Miranda sometimes thought of trying to explain to Diana how devastated she was when she understood that Anton would never come back. 'I hated his constantly leaving,' she could imagine herself saying to her daughter, 'but I never thought that he would leave us forever. For a long time I blamed myself for not trying harder to understand why he was behaving so strangely.' But there was no way that she could tell a fifteen-year-old girl that she refused to let Anton bind her, that she stopped making love in the sea, even in the bathtub, after he held her head beneath the water to provoke her desperate flailing. Terror aroused him. He loved it when she fought him, thrashing and clawing at his flesh, leaving marks on his back and face.

Instead, at first, she told Diana stories about happier earlier days. 'When we first went to the island, he made up songs that he sang to me in his thrilling voice. He taught me to weave strands of sturdy grasses, to tie knots with them, to know the constellations and the patterns of the tides. We lived with the sun and moon as our clock and calendar.

'How he loved watching my belly swell as you grew inside me. He rubbed his hands across my stomach, stroking as if he could feel you swimming inside me, doing tiny kicks and flips and weightless turns.

'"My two women," he called us. He loved us, but he grew restless. He loved the liquid movement of the sea, the ocean and the waves. He was powerless to resist them. I think that his love for them finally claimed him.'

Miranda couldn't admit then that she was as much Anton's captive as Diana, although what were enchantments for the little girl were powerful blasts of need for Miranda, provoking dangerous couplings in a darkness in which she was held by ropes and tiny pointed anchors that bit into her flesh. He fed upon her, biting, eating, and sucking her juices until she was no longer enough. She had opened up and taken him in and together they rode waves that took them far beyond themselves. She had given him her being, but it turned out that he needed to be yoked to others and to lose himself in them. He needed to thrash and terrify and control them. Finally she could not follow where he had begun to lead.

Still raw with loss and need, Miranda could hardly bear Diana's mythologizing of her absent father. 'Your father deserted us!' she lashed out one morning. 'Left us with little money and no provision for the future. I did what I could. But don't expect me to be full of gorgeous memories of him. Why should I? Your hero capsized my life.'

She was constantly amazed that she had somehow compensated by sliding toward smells and tastes and juicy stews. 'And what do I have now? Fruits and fish and spices and whatever exotic ingredients I search out. I slice and sauté them, pile them into bowls and heap them on platters. It still amazes me. I don't quite know how I turned to cooking and let it take me over but, oh Diana, while I've been doing that, I can see that I've left you too much on your own.'

She hoped that Diana knew that she had never succumbed to the temptations offered by the men who loved the succulence of her food. Not yet. No, she was still hurt and furious with Anton. Men! Her body craved them. Instead she gave it apricots and venison, quince and apple tarts, scented basmati rice and figs stewed in red wine flavored with cloves and cinnamon. Men! They feast on women's flesh until they have eaten their fill, she thought to herself, and then pass on, leaving us to grapple with a world we only chose because we knew nothing else, and because we had fallen in the broth of sexual surrender and were forever changed.

Unknown to her, Max had managed to open the doors to the two rooms populated by the sculptures. And Miranda had to concede, when triumphantly he took her to see the results, that it was like coming upon a magnificent, if slightly deranged, private island on which every square inch of ground was claimed by an extraordinary person, animal, or totem. She stared at a bird as big as a man with a horned beak, sinuously carved plumage, and erect penis while beside it a clutch of multicolored serpents slithered across a couple plunged into the darkest recesses of each other's bodies. These works, the expression of Anton's obsession and unexpressed needs, struck Miranda dumb. She swore later that she was sure she'd been hit by lightning, that she had smelled burning flesh and, as if she were both bystander and wounded, looked to see if a line of flame had streaked up her arm to darken and encircle her eye sockets, before scorching the ends of her hair, frizzing them like crazed wires. While she had long suspected that the man to whom she had been married had buried a secret self within his flesh, only now had she seen it clearly exposed to light and time.

So she made a deal with Max. He could buy the sculptures, photograph and write about them all he wanted, but he first must leave her alone with them. Then they would be his. Max ran his fleshy tongue around his lips, literally licking them. He tried to compose his excitable features but failed utterly. He foresaw a brilliant career, envious colleagues, honors and riches raining down upon him. She bargained shrewdly, laughing at the figure he offered for the sculptures and countering with a much higher number. They dickered, but Miranda knew that she could name her price and, if she weren't greedy he would have to agree.

Miranda was so astonished by the collection of figures, adumbrations of her husband's internal landscape, that she hardly knew what she had done in asking for time alone with them. She tried looking at them as works of art, but it wasn't long before it dawned on her that they had undoubtedly inspired Anton to go in search of a kind of gratification that horrified her. 'Oh God,' she whispered to herself, as it occurred to her that his disappearance might be an unacknowledged gift. Her breath came short and shallow, as if the wind had been knocked out of her the way it had been when she was tumbled in the waves as a child, tossed and disoriented by the surge of the ocean.

Miranda was barely fifteen when she fell in love with Anton. He had arrived in Australia to do business and when his transactions with her father took longer than expected, the older man invited him home for dinner. Tall, tanned, with sleepy brown eyes and a barely suppressed grin, Anton, with his outsize feet and long legs, looked puppyish, a good deal younger than his thirty years. Miranda was immediately fascinated. She saw in him the possibility of life beyond her father's violent outbursts, beyond the arid provincial city where she was quarantined in a girls' school and kept as far from the baying ranks of boys as her mother could arrange. The four of them sat down at the small teak table and, while her mother served watery soup and overcooked lamb, Anton never let his eyes leave her. She leaned across the table, mouth slightly open, chin resting on palm, listening attentively to his voice, and she realized with a start that her body was growing softer, warmer, responding to the provocation of his frank fascination. He managed to answer her father's questions and ask some of his own, did complicated mathematical calculations and currency transactions in his head, plotted shipping and delivery schedules, all the while feeling like a man going down for the third time. 'My siren,' he whispered to her when both her parents had left the room. She opened her mouth to speak but he put his finger across it, cautioning silence. She wanted to take it between her lips, let it ride on the rise and fall of her tongue, but managed only to lick a stripe across it, tasting the finger's thick salty fleshiness. His eyes widened. He was close enough to feel the warmth of her body, sense the softness of her breasts; he could smell the fragrance she exuded, a cloud of honeysuckle and frangipani. She was breathing deep and slow, this innocent girl whose body had never known the touch of a man.

He prolonged his stay, first by days, then by weeks. He did more business with her father than he needed, but it was his only way to see Miranda. The two were never alone until the evening her grandmother was stricken. When a neighbor came to tell them the news, her mother gave a strangled cry, clutched her husband, and the two of them rushed to the small cottage where the old woman lived. She was lying in bed half paralyzed, one side of her body frozen, the affected eye staring listlessly from its sunken socket beneath a prickle of grey eyelashes. One side of her mouth drooped. Husband and wife lit candles, piled on blankets to keep her warm, and massaged her limbs until the doctor came.

By the time they returned home late that evening, Miranda had given herself to Anton. She who had only kissed the local boys with their dry lips was electrified by the shock of his tongue in her mouth. His fingertips were like matches, igniting her dry limbs, causing flames to lick at her breasts, her thighs. Later she could barely remember how he helped her shed her schoolgirl clothes and laid her all pink and rosy on the rumpled white sheets of her narrow childhood bed. She remembered how he slowly stroked her stomach with the heel of his hand, how he traced the fine path of hair from the scoop of her navel to her tender triangle blooming as thick as moss. She remembered how he gently parted her legs and helped her raise them around his back, and then it was all noises and pantings and ploughing and riding, galloping across landscapes she had never imagined.

Days later, afraid sparks would erupt if he were merely to graze her body, she could hardly speak when he whispered, 'I have to leave, darling Miranda, but I can't leave without you. I will die if you don't come with me.' Easily he convinced her to go away with him. Her parents were scandalized. Anton was twice her age, and worse, a foreigner. Except for the appointment with the justice of the peace that her father took care of, she made all the arrangements. She bought a simple suit and her first pair of high-heeled shoes at the town's only apparel shop and packed a suitcase with the few possessions she wanted to take with her. She smirked openly, unable to hide her feelings of superiority and relief as she made a quick round of visits saying goodbye to friends and teachers. For the ceremony she made her own bouquet of calla lilies that grew wild at the stream curling through the dusty backwash, and held it proudly during the wedding that took place at her grandmother's bedside that same week. Two days later they sailed across half the world's seas to reach his family home.

From the beginning she had delighted in their lovemaking and been profoundly changed by it. And so she traveled with him into unknown territory, far from her home, and then from his. She bore his child and watched him change slowly before her eyes, first wounding her by his remoteness and finally by his disappearance.

Now, as she looked at his sculptures, the unexplained experiences began to make some fragmentary sense. She remembered finding him with a beautiful, tiny, fine-boned island woman who was naked save for a piece of cloth tied like a thong, riding him like a beast, making deep guttural sounds as she rocked back and forth. Miranda recalled coming upon him a year later locked in a strange posture with a fisherman and a young girl, the three captured in an intimate tangle beneath a net that bound them more tightly the more they moved. She saw his hands grab the buttocks of the fisherman as the girl swam against him like a fish in the sea, her hands winding through first his hair, then the other man's, and the three slithered against one another in the rhythm of sea serpents cresting the waves. When Miranda spoke to him of what she had seen, he turned away. He barely acknowledged her for several days and she became so fearful of his coldness that she never mentioned the episode again.

She wondered whether to show the sculptures to Diana. Her impulse was to have Max crate them up and send them away as quickly as possible. It was one thing, Miranda decided, to have a collection named for her father in the recesses of some university museum and something else to see the dark sexual content associated with what he had amassed. She still felt obscurely uncomfortable about Diana's unexplained experience with the man from Kinderdijk. Surely the girl felt her sympathy without any words being exchanged. Miranda knew in some part of herself that she had been wrong, that she could have opened the stream of feeling between them instead of allowing it to silt up. At least now she was doing the right thing. It was a fait accompli: first Max would sign a paper promising not to bother her about the sculptures ever again and then he would hand over a large check and take the sculptures away. The two rooms, locked in darkness for so long, would at last be open to light and air and feeling would flow freely again between mother and daughter. Miranda might not be able to retract her dismissive remarks, but she had convinced herself that she could make it all right by sending the sculptures away.

She hadn't reckoned with Max. Since Diana had allowed him entrance to the sculptures, essentially handing him his golden future, the anthropologist thought that the least he could do was to give the girl a glimpse. Once he had concluded his negotiations with Miranda, he went to find Diana.

'I'm going to be leaving soon,' he told her, 'but I wanted to thank you for helping me with your father's sculptures. I'll be making an exhibition of them and writing a book about the collection, but before we pack them all up, I thought you might want to take a look.'

'Are they like the photographs you showed me before?'

'More or less.'

'I don't know. I don't think so.' Diana was curious but wished Max weren't around to watch her.

'Tell you what. I'll open the door to one room so you can get an idea what's there. You can look at the ones that are right near the door and decide then. How about that?'

'Maybe. OK,' she agreed reluctantly, 'but Majine comes with me.'

'It's up to you. But hold the monkey – don't let him go running all around in there. God knows what damage he could do.'

It took Max a few minutes of fiddling with the keys before he could throw open the doors. Bowing, one thick eyebrow raised quizzically, he left her with the inhabitants of the room.

What she saw was a visual cacophony, animals and monsters, men, women, and children, some standing, some crouched or sitting with legs akimbo, some with blank eyes, some with fat tongues, some wrapped in feather capes or bound and plaited in ropes, some intertwined, one with the other, most painted in brilliant colors and dizzying patterns. A larger than life size male standing as stiff as a pole with lips like a figure eight, tattoo marks on his body, and exaggerated, colorfully painted genitalia stood beside the door of a tall thin house incised with a crescent moon, palm leaf, and blazing sun. They formed a threatening community that pointedly kept her out. Diana nuzzled Majine's fur and squinted nearsightedly, as if she couldn't understand what she was seeing. She hesitated, not wanting to enter the room.

'But will they bring my father home?' Diana pressed Max for reassurance. He shrugged. 'I don't have any way of knowing for sure, but I'd say it was a good bet.' 'OK,' she said reluctantly, 'you can take them. I don't need to go in there.'

'Whatever you want.' Anxious to leave before the masses of clouds gathering darkly in the sky exploded, Max thanked Diana. 'You've really done something great for me,' he said. 'And for your father and his collection, of course.'

Diana shrugged. Then, without any warning, Max threw his arms around her and planted a wet tongue in her ear, blowing into it as into a conch shell. At the same time, he used his pudgy fingers to tap out some sort of syncopated rhythm on her stiffened back. Looking pleased with himself, he held her at arm's length to explain in his best professorial tone that he had just given her the same farewell that one of the most important tribes represented in her father's collection would have used.

Diana couldn't get away fast enough. Running down the hall followed by Majine, she doubled over with revulsion. 'I'm not coming out until that horrible man is gone. I hate him. I hate him. He's disgusting,' she said, shaking her head violently from side to side, trying to dislodge the spittle his coarse tongue had left behind. She shuddered, reached down to scoop up the monkey and rubbed his furry head against her cheek as he stretched his arms around her neck. 'I can't believe I decided to help him.' She stormed around the room, kicking her shoes out of the way, throwing books onto the floor.

A sudden roar of thunder was followed by crackling zigzags of lightning that lit up the entire sky and left a sulfuric smell in the air. In the space of the next few hours immense amounts of rain fell from pewter-colored clouds, flooding streets and pulling down trees in the city. Lights flickered on and off. An eerie silence gripped the house. Miranda wondered if she should lay a fire. Diana found a flashlight and read with Majine curled in her lap. In the quiet between strikes of lightning and roarings of thunder, she thought she heard a voice at the back door.

When she looked into the darkness she saw the outline of a man balancing a large crate in his hands, rain sluicing down his dark rubber coat and high rubber boots. 'Who is it?' she called out uncertainly, before she made out the familiar dark green truck with the name Mieskeeper stenciled on the side. It must be Mies, she thought to herself, who often brought plants and helped in the garden.

'Three generations,' her grandmother had told Diana not long ago. 'We've known each other since I was slightly older than you are now when I came here as a bride, knowing nothing, fixing on the garden as the thing I wanted to do.

Old Man Mieskeeper – that's what everyone called him even though he probably wasn't all that old – he was a big gruff man, at ease only with his bulbs and his plants, but he decided he'd help me learn, so he'd come by and drop off plants and tell me what to do with them.

'When his son Andreas grew up, I saw the promise in him and made sure he had an education. And then I insisted that the old man let him train with a fine landscape architect and apprentice at a garden in Italy before he came home to work at the nursery.'

Diana knew Andreas as the man who ran the nursery now. He had two sons: the older one turned out to be a mathematical genius and was now a professor at the university, but the younger one, who everyone called Mies, was slower, in need of nurture like the plants in his father's nursery. He spent his days in the greenhouse and in the fields of flowers, helping things grow and transporting them in the family van. He often came to help her grandmother, who was gentle and encouraging to him. Watching them together, Diana realized that touching the earth opened otherwise buried parts of her being. She sat with Mies for hours as they weeded together, digging holes to make homes for bulbs and transplanting bushes when they had grown beyond the space allotted to them.

Mies stood patiently, his big boots almost covering the thick jute mat at the back door. Balancing the box in his left hand, he reached out with his right and again pulled the long cord to ring the bell. Diana turned on a light as she opened the inner screen door. 'Oh Mies, Nanna must have forgotten that you were coming. All this rain . . .' A puzzled look came over her face. 'But Nanna never forgets. She was talking about you yesterday. Wait a minute and I'll find her. Do you want to come in?' She gestured in the direction of the room where he might wait in his muddy boots and dripping raincoat.

'No,' he shook his head.

'You're sure?'

'Mmm.'

Diana walked quickly down the hallway and knocked at the door. She knocked again. Still no answer. She was uncertain whether to actually enter the room, remembering her very private grandmother's strict instructions, but after calling out twice with no answer, she opened the door slowly and tiptoed in. The shades were still down, her grandmother still asleep under the goose down comforter. Diana moved quietly, calling 'Nanna, Nanna.' In the quiet of the room, she stood at the head of the bed, looked down at her grandmother sleeping peacefully, and placed her hand gently on the soft cheek of the old woman. It was as cold as ice on the river.

She tried to keep panic out of her voice as she called Miranda. From somewhere far away she heard an explosion of rain pouring from the skies in solid sheets, falling and falling as she stood there, one hand on the old woman's cold cheek. Minutes went by before her mother arrived, drying her hands on a kitchen towel. She walked into the darkness, turned on the bedside light, and understood immediately. Miranda tried to find a pulse, to feel a wisp of breath, and finding none, gently brushed back strands of the old woman's silvery hair.

Diana kept looking at her grandmother, unable to absorb the reality. She felt an immense need to stay and have one final conversation with her. Instead she studied the face she had loved for so long and bent over it, letting her lips brush the cold cheek as she mouthed a silent goodbye.

Then she remembered that Mies was still waiting. She walked down the hall in a trance, scooped up her monkey, and carefully placed his little arms around her neck. Only then did she walk shakily to the boy.

'Oh Mies, I . . . I'm so sorry . . . Oh, it's terrible. My nanna has died.'

The boy shifted awkwardly on his feet and put his box down. 'She was my friend,' he said. 'She loved the flowers too. The ground. We sat on the ground together. Sometimes she sang. She listened to me.' His voice broke. 'Who will listen to me now?' Tears falling from his eyes, he slipped the rain hood back over his head, pulled open the inner door, and turned to Diana. 'I'll tell my father. He'll be sad too.'

The rain continued to sluice from the skies. First came the doctor, striding up the stairs to the front door in his high rubber boots. Miranda took him to the room where the old woman lay. He felt for a pulse and finding none, held a finger under her nose, and with an imperceptible nod acknowledged what he already knew to be true. He whispered a few words and wrote in his notebook. While he was still there Andreas, patriarch and commander of his empire of bulbs and flowers, arrived. A tall redheaded man with mottled reddish white skin and a barrel chest, he spoke to the doctor, saw him out, and then turned to Miranda.

'I've brought hyacinths and candles. Let me surround her,' he said, more in the form of a statement than a request for permission. He arranged dozens and dozens of white hyacinths on every surface, their silky cones shining as if woven of fine luminous ribbons. He laid a row of them at the threshold of the room and encircled the old woman's bed with them. Between and around them candles flickered, embracing her in the luminous glow of flowers and light. When he had filled the room with flowers, Andreas stopped and looked at the woman who had made it possible for him to have the life he loved. He knelt beside her and placed his rough weathered cheek next to hers. He took her thin, fine boned face in his big callused hands, and at that moment Diana saw flowers burst into bloom before her, until she thought she saw her grandmother become a giant bouquet of her beloved hyacinths and tulips, and then she watched as the color slowly drained away from them until they were pale and soft and lost to time.

Sitting with her after the simple service for Ria, Andreas

felt sorry for Diana. Her grandmother had died, her father had disappeared, and her mother was so relieved at the old woman's passing that she was almost heedless of Diana's grief. Dazed, the girl wandered through the house clinging to the monkey. She could not bear to be in the old woman's room, but found comfort in the garden.

Diana had rarely been in the garden alone, but now she knelt on the cool earth, just as her grandmother had, and trailed her fingers in the dirt. She felt her grandmother's spirit all around her, in the tulips and the hedges, the border of river-washed stones and the yew trees anchoring the long rectangle of land. She felt both nourished and bereft, but it did not take long for her to realize that taking care of the garden would soon be beyond her.

She went to the nursery to see Andreas, and told him she worried everything in the garden would die.

'What was I thinking? How could I be so stupid?' Andreas berated himself. 'Of course you'd worry. Anyone would. I know what your grandmother had in mind and I can easily choose the plant materials. I'm sure Mies would be happy to come and work the way he used to when your grandmother was alive. Then we'll keep the garden just as she would have wished.'

'Won't it be hard for him to be there all by himself?' Diana wondered aloud.

'You're right. He would be sad being left there alone. Why don't I come by more often, and maybe you could sit with him some of the time.'

Yes, Diana thought, she could do that. 'It's where I am these days anyway. Majine comes with me – Nanna never allowed him anywhere near her, and now he's ecstatic, leaping onto the branches of the tree, swinging hand over hand, making his funny little noises of pleasure. A lot of the time I just walk up and down or sit on the ground. Last week I made a circle out of some of the river-washed stones she has. Had. I lapped them one over another, like wafers. I don't know why, but it felt right.'

Andreas came to visit two days later and saw the simple circle of stones that Diana had laid out to honor her grandmother. He admired their integrity. 'What if I were to make a second circle of stones?' he asked. 'And maybe Mies could add a third. Three concentric circles of deep grey pebbles, three circles that embrace her spirit and contain it in this garden.'

'I think she'd approve,' said Diana. 'The three of us come here more than anyone else.'

'Yes, a memorial in her garden. It's the right thing.'

Andreas took to saving stones in a burlap sack. He came by twice a week to see what progress Diana and Mies were making. One day seeing Diana in a cloud of grief, he called her over, sat her down, and asked if she'd ever heard the story of the trip he and her grandmother took to Italy. 'I don't think so,' Diana replied wearily, shaking her head.

'I started coming here when I was only ten. I came after school to work with my father in the garden when all the other boys were free to play ball or go to their music lessons or just do nothing. Anton – your father and I were in the same class – was always slipping off to the port, much to your grandparents' distress. He loved everything that had to do with ships. I could always tell he'd been to the port just from the metallic smell that came off his hands, the smell from the anchors and hasps that hold the ropes and secure them, the salty smell of the sea. You can probably guess how your grandmother felt about the men who were there, but Anton didn't care. Nothing could keep him away. As he hung around with the sailors, he learned how to tie all kinds of knots, how to read a compass, and how to use the stars as a guide. He was a much better student there than he was at school. He used to tell me how easy it was to haul a large net full of heavy cargo once he'd gotten the hang of how to take its weight over his shoulder. I remember him bragging that he'd brought a piano onboard all by himself, but your father had a way of exaggerating. Doesn't matter. He really did love all the instruments that made a boat go, the implements that showed how to set and stay on a course. He once proudly showed me an old telescope one of the sailors had given him. He kept it carefully locked inside an old wooden box.

'By the time he was fifteen, he was aching to ship out, but of course your grandparents wouldn't hear of it. He was supposed to join the family business, a fate he swore he'd do anything to avoid.' Andreas stopped. 'Have you heard all this before?'

'Some of it,' Diana said, 'but not in the same way. I know how much he loved the sea, but I hadn't thought about how he might have felt about being told that what he loved most was beneath him. No wonder he was a rebel.'

'I guess you could see it that way.' Andreas picked up one of the grey stones and felt its smooth surface before returning it to its place in the circle. 'Of course you're right that your family's prohibiting him from spending his afternoons at the port made him lie about where he had been.' He stopped, wondering how much he should elaborate. 'I remember how mercilessly he teased me at school because I came to work in your garden with my father. Anyway, I think he took some sort of strange pleasure in thwarting *his* father. Your grandfather was a gentle man, who wouldn't have hurt anyone or anything. He would have picked up each snail eating your grandmother's flowers and removed it from the garden cradled in canvas gloves. Not Anton.'

As she listened, Diana pulled up a few prickly weeds that intruded on the integrity of the circle of stones. 'I watched him squash snails and then throw their broken shells against the wall as hard as he could. He loved shooting birds out of trees. And in the coldest days of winter, he used to take a sled onto the frozen waters of the river, cut a hole in the ice, and harpoon fish with an old barbed spear. I remember his smile as he tossed them down on the ice and plunged a knife into them, taking real pleasure in watching them thrash. Maybe I'm exaggerating,' Andreas said hastily. 'I love to fish too, but I don't think I take the same kind of joy in the kill. Do you mind hearing these things?' he asked.

'Oh no. I love knowing anything about my father, even things you don't like saying. He taught me how to catch fish, you know, using just my bare hands in the warm waters of our island. He told me stories about the beginning of the world, how fishes swam in rhythm with the waves and how those waves were like the waves in my hair where he said the fishes yearned to swim so they could remember the beginnings of their lives. "My little mermaid," he called me. He told me that it was all connected – moon, tides, waves, and sea, the fruits that grew on the trees. He made us a hammock by tying knots together with rope and then strung it between two trees, and the holes he had made held us in the air. Sometimes we would swing in it together. He always said that the steamy heat of the islands made us flow with the currents of the air and the rhythms of the sea and that we were in paradise. "Remember that," he told me, "we're in paradise."'

'Paradise,' smiled Andreas. 'That's right. I started to tell you about going to Italy with your grandmother when I was eighteen. How old are you now?'

'Fifteen,' she answered, taking him aback. How young she seemed, how different than he had been at her age.

'Your nanna was insistent that I develop my talent. Somehow she managed to convince my family to let her take me to Italy where friends of her father had greenhouses. They took us to nurseries in the Tuscan countryside so big we had to climb into a little open car and be driven up and down the rows just to be able to see all the different varieties of trees. There were trees I'd never even heard of before – ilex and holm oak – and others I'd never seen – all those tall, dark green cypresses that marched across the landscape, and great old gnarled olive trees with silvery grey trunks and dusty green leaves. We must have seen thousands of ruffled carnations and even more hydrangeas and cyclamen. And the roses! They were creamy or copper colored, salmon, and apricot. I remember one that was such a delicate pink that the color seemed an illusion when you looked again.

'We stayed with a family who were friends of your great grandfather's. There were seven children in the family, all crammed into a bunch of smallish rooms. I was stuffed in with the one nearest my age, but I didn't care. They lived in an old stone farmhouse with an immense kitchen. The mother was always cooking something in the fireplace or the big wood-burning oven, where they burned branches trimmed from their fruit trees. She made everything – breads, soups, big stews, pasta sauces – in quantities large enough for a small village. She put up all kinds of preserves from the fruit. When the figs were ripe, they had a little droplet of honey oozing out at the stem. We cut them in half and sometimes would drape a slice of prosciutto over them like a sheet. I was there when the tomatoes were sweet and juicy. I ate so many the whole family was worried I'd get sick.

'In winter the family threw sheets of plastic and burlap bags over the lemon trees that were planted against the house, and by early spring they had not only survived the cold and frost but were already budding. Bougainvillea and vines with scarlet trumpets climbed everywhere, covering fences and hiding the big ugly gas tanks that country houses have. Flowers grew everywhere. Even people in tiny houses had geraniums in window boxes or spilling out of tin cans set on the ledge of a balcony. It was heaven. Plants and trees and being outside all day long, a house filled with the smells of food at night when friends appeared and everyone sat by the fire in the kitchen, the men smoking and telling stories, the women knitting and crocheting. So I always associate your nanna with those two months in a country that opened up my heart.'

Andreas paused and looked at Diana. Seeing that his story

had briefly erased the sadness in her eyes, he smiled. 'Your grandmother treated us – my father, and me, and then Mies – as if we were her second family, her other family. So Diana, never worry.' His voice told her how strongly he meant this. 'Anything you ever need, you can count on me. I'll always be there. Always,' he said.

CHAPTER FIVE

D IANA MISSED HER FATHER even more after her grandmother died. Not only had she lost her nanna, she had
lost her connection to her father as well, and the life he had
lived in their house.

She told Andreas about her father's collection when she
was showing him the two rooms. 'I remember these rooms,'
Andreas exclaimed, his features softening as he entered into
memories from almost a half century before. 'They were
your father's. One was where he was supposed to study,
but really he spent most of his time here making models of
ships. Beautiful schooners, three-masted sailing boats, elegant
liners, old pirate ships. The room reeked of glue.' Diana
nodded, sorry that the earlier boats had been supplanted by
such embarrassing substitutes.

'There were dozens of carved sculptures of men and women
together, of naked girls younger than I am, and some of them
were doing things that weren't . . . nice,' Diana said. 'Max, the
anthropologist, kept talking about their bodies. I could hardly
look.' She winced. 'The way he talked made me feel sick.' Yes,
she thought, his words were like swarms of insects. The soft
powdery dust on their wings filled the air when they flew and
she was sure that a black cloud of them was aimed straight at
her. She could feel what it would be like for the dust to settle,
sift through her, and choke her breath away. 'Max said the

sculptures were important and that the university would give a big show of them. So maybe they weren't so bad,' she said uncertainly.

She remembered that she had only given Max the keys to the locked rooms in hopes of bringing her father home and she still felt the surge of pleasure she had in first coming upon his belongings. It had been a long time since she'd plunged nose and hands into those overflowing trunks. She waited for Miranda to leave to do her shopping before going to root through the small heritage he had left behind. The metallic smell that Andreas had mentioned still floated off his clothes. She put one of his shirts over her own and twirled around the room, smoothing it over her body. She stuck her nose under her arm to smell him and flapped her arms as if she could fly to him. She put on a second shirt and twirled around, showing off to Majine, and then tried on a long flowing blue and white ikat garment that looked like a skirt.

She moved her fingers gingerly through layers of cloth in the big trunk until she found the brass box that had contained the keys to his collection. Pieces of spiky coral and smooth shiny shells lay on the bottom. She slid her hand carefully under the homemade knives, took one out, and saw a piece of sand-colored paper under it. The paper was stained and looked as if it had been in water for a long time before being spread out to dry. Diana moved next to the window to hold it to the light and saw that the first words were faded but still legible. *Miranda, if you find this and I am gone for more than a year, I am gone forever . . . water . . . danger . . . love . . . trance. Beyond the beyond. Debts. If anybody finds this . . . one more message . . .* and then she saw her name. *Diana*, yes it was really there, *Diana*. In his handwriting. At the bottom four words floated up off the page. *House. Palm. Half moon.*

Diana stared into the trunk, lay her cheek against the clothes folded on the top. After a while she folded up the paper and carefully placed it between the pages of a book that she hid in her bureau.

For the next several days the note was all she could think of. Maybe it referred to one of the houses they had lived in on the islands. Or a house he went to visit on one of his many trips. No palm trees grew in their city, so it couldn't be nearby.

House, palm, half moon. She strapped on skates and let her mind wander as she moved smoothly over the ice. Ice laps, she called them, her voyages out and back across the same patch, a meditative trip prompted by a mystery. House, palm, half moon. Out and back she skated, over and over in a mesmerizing pattern, her legs grown so accustomed to the path that her mind could wander freely.

'Majine, Majine,' she called excitedly as she took off her skates and flew into her room after a third session of contemplative skating. The monkey leapt into her arms, making little smacking noises of affection. 'I've got it. I know what "house," "palm," "half moon" are. One of his sculptures. I suddenly remembered.'

The next morning at breakfast Diana informed Miranda that she had to find Max. 'Good Lord, Diana,' said an amazed Miranda. 'I remember how thrilled you were when he packed up and left. I wouldn't have thought you'd ever want to see him again.'

'I don't. I'd give almost anything never to see him again. But he's the keeper of my father's collection and I have to decode the message I found in his trunk.'

'What *are* you talking about?'

'I was missing him.' She shrugged her shoulders involuntarily. 'So I looked into the trunk again. Way at the bottom I found a faded letter that mentioned one of his sculptures. One of the only ones without women and men . . . or girls . . . you know what I'm trying to say . . . but I think it means that he left a message for us inside the sculpture.'

Miranda looked at her daughter. So young for fifteen, she

thought to herself, remembering that at Diana's age she was already married to Anton. Full of passion and hope. Not like this withdrawn girl who spent all her time reading books and whose closest friend was a monkey. A girl who sometimes spoke in fantastic images. 'It's important enough that you'd actually see Max again? I remember how you physically shrank away whenever he approached you.'

'Would you come with me?'

Seconds before Diana blurted out the question, Miranda was thinking how little she wanted to encounter the repellent Max herself. 'Are you even sure he's there?'

'He teaches at the university, doesn't he?'

'Why don't you call and make sure you'd find him if you went.'

Finding Max's phone number and address was easy. Finding Max was more difficult. Anthropologists travel, and just during this semester, according to the secretary of his department, he'd been to Uppsala, Paris, and Montreal. Diana learned that he'd be away for another week.

Miranda continued to fret. She couldn't spare a full day to travel with Diana but couldn't bring herself to let the girl loose in Max's company. She was more relieved than she wanted to admit when Andreas heard of the problem and offered to accompany Diana.

They went by train, carrying a picnic Miranda had packed for them to eat. Andreas found seats with no one sitting opposite so he could stretch without cramping his long legs. He was a big man whose girth was exaggerated by a thick-wale brown corduroy jacket pulled over a heavy knit sweater. His sandy hair was thinning noticeably, and he had taken to wearing a slouchy felt hat to keep his head warm. As they ate the sandwiches Miranda had prepared, he promised to stay with Diana until it was time to leave.

Max had arrived at his office in the anthropology department that day prepared to go through all the mail that had accumulated in his absence. He was stunned to find the girl waiting for him with a man old enough to be her father. My God, he thought to himself, it's Anton, come to demand the return of his collection. Could he have convinced Miranda that Max had coerced her into selling what wasn't hers to sell? Did he want it back, and was he prepared to make trouble to get it? Max saw everything collapsing, his sure tenure evaporating. He was about to proofread the text of the catalogue for the show that was scheduled to open within the year. And now this girl had come to ruin it all? He eyed the man by Diana's side, wondering what it would take to pacify him, thwart him, even to buy him off.

Relief flooded his features as Diana introduced Andreas. 'He knew my father when they were growing up. He came with me. He was curious.' Andreas towered over the squat anthropologist, who reached up to shake hands.

'You want to see the collection now? When it was in your house, Diana, you let me take it away without giving it more than a glance. Has something come along to change your mind? Or have you simply grown up enough that the sculptures no longer look threatening? Look interesting? You want to see the copulating couples, the nubile maidens?' Not even Andreas's presence deterred the unflappable Max.

'*No!*' she shouted. She couldn't believe it. He was at it again, pressing at her with his disgusting innuendo.

'Then why?'

'There's one piece that I have to see. I think my father left a note in it.'

Max sighed heavily. Now that I have no more use for her, he thought to himself, now she shows up. 'Well, if he did, that's too bad. Nothing here belongs to you anymore. We paid your mother handsomely. Remember? The university owns everything, even little notes scribbled by your father.

'Remember that,' he snorted, and began walking briskly to the room where the sculptures were being prepared for the exhibition. He paused dramatically and then opened the door.

Andreas stared at the array of figures in every posture and position. He was both appalled and fascinated at the huge collection, and was grateful that Ria, a prude at best, had never seen it. He was especially glad now that he had decided to come with Diana and shuddered to imagine what the anthropologist might have said or done had she been alone.

Diana had already moved into her own world. She threaded her way through the dense forest of figures until she stood in the center. She looked around, hunting for the house, trying not to be sucked in by the more threatening pieces, trying to steer her vision away from all the erect penises, the suppliant women, the birds with their wings spread wide. Majine wasn't there to keep her company, so she did the next best thing she could and imagined that she was a lighthouse, a calm white tower on a point of land jutting into the sea. She imagined that it was dark and slowly she swiveled the strong beam of light everywhere, looking only for the house with the palm tree and half moon. After several long min-utes she said under her breath, 'There,' as she spotted it. She slithered between columns of sculpted wood until she reached it. She looked it over carefully, searching for drawers and hiding places, then closed her eyes and ran her hands over the surface. She stuck two fingers into each of the openings between fronds of the palm but found nothing. She walked around the house, looking carefully for slots or miniature drawers, then hit the palm of her hand against the surface in several places, thinking she might jostle loose a concealed panel.

A wary Max stood at the door, his eyes trained on her movements. 'What's she doing now?' he asked Andreas, who hadn't left his side. 'Is she hitting . . . wait a minute,' he shouted out. 'That's a delicate work.'

'It looks pretty sturdy to me,' Andreas countered, as he

watched Diana slide to the dusty floor in search of a way into the sculpture.

'Where'd she go? Where is she?' Max asked in a tone that was both belligerent and aggrieved. 'I wouldn't put it past her if she snuck something out of there,' he said, stepping forcefully into the room. Andreas grabbed his arm. 'Good Lord, man, what makes you so suspicious of a fifteen-year-old girl?' Momentarily thrown off, Max began to sputter, giving Diana time to continue her explorations. 'Yes,' she whispered to herself, as she found that under the door of the house was a tiny drawer with an ebony knob the size of a small stone. She grasped it between her thumb and index finger and pulled very gently. It stuck momentarily but she wiggled it loose, and when the drawer opened she could see a letter, facedown, its words rubbing against the pale wood. Diana turned it over and glimpsed a message written in sea blue ink. 'What are you doing now?' Max barked at Diana, who very gingerly removed the letter and slid it into the deep pocket of her skirt.

In the tense moment, she closed her eyes and drew in her breath. She missed Majine. She wondered if she'd feel better if he were sitting on her lap and she could ask him what he thought she should do. Before she could imagine his response, she heard the thrum of wings beating, saw an image of two birds, one an ibis, the other a heron with a golden beak. The ibis was tall and elegant with a curved bill the shape of a scythe. It looked Diana straight in the eye, then slowly flapped its elliptical wings, like a dowager fanning herself in the stifling heat of a tropical afternoon, and gracefully lifted off the earth, its long skinny legs silhouetted against the rapidly darkening sky. The other bird snapped its golden beak, opening and closing it like a pair of scissors. It threatened to cut up the message and let it whirl away into the sky in a thousand pieces. Snap, snap, edging closer to the precious letter. Snap, snap. Mine, said the bird, lunging forward and grabbing the corner. 'Not for you, no, not you, no never,' it hissed, opening and closing its golden jaws.

'Why not?' Diana wondered, holding tight to the paper. 'I know he left it for me.'

'For you. Ha. That's funny. Not for you. You don't want to read it.' 'Yes I do,' she thought to herself, although now she wasn't quite so sure. What if he had disappeared because something had gone very wrong? Or had left because he didn't love them anymore? Would she really want to know? Diana wavered. The ibis, as elegant as her nanna, had gone and now she was left with the argumentative heron. He stuck his golden beak in her face and snap, snapped again. Diana opened her eyes. Anxious as she was to know what the paper said, she kept it tucked in her pocket and decided to wait until she was in her own room by herself before she read it.

'What are you doing in there?' She heard Max's impatient voice. 'That's more than enough time. Come out now. I've got more important things to do than stand around watching you feel a bunch of sculptures.' 'OK,' she said quietly, and when she stepped into the well-lit hall, he shouted, 'Hold out your hands. Come on, come on.' Clearly he was anxious to leave. She waved them toward him, palms out and obviously empty. 'You didn't take anything, did you?' She shook her head. 'Good. I've got appointments to keep,' and he left them to find their way out of the building.

A cab took them to the station, and when they were safely settled in their seats, Andreas leaned over and asked what she'd discovered. He was almost a foot taller than Diana and he bent down protectively when he spoke to her.

'A piece of paper. He hid it very well. It took a lot of poking around to find it.'

'What does it say?'

Diana stared into his friendly face with its deeply etched smile lines. The pores of his skin were so large that the wen near his mouth, neatly tucked inside the deep creases, looked like an inverted dimple. A single fold of skin on each side of his mouth draped downward, reminding her vaguely of a soulful bloodhound. Could she tell him about the birds and the warning? She thought about how much she trusted Andreas, but it wasn't enough to speak about her inner world. 'I put it in my pocket so Max couldn't see.'

Andreas's eyes widened. She could see the flecks of gold in the dark brown irises and read perplexity on his face. 'You mean we've made this trip for a single piece of paper and you're not even going to read it?'

'Oh, I'm going to read it. Just not yet. Not until I'm home.' With Majine, she thought to herself.

'You mean the anticipation is almost as delicious as the actual discovery? That's how I used to feel about the special caramel candies my mother gave me for my birthday. I would eat one or two and then keep the rest for months, hoarding them. I would eat one at a time, letting the flavors dissolve slowly in my mouth. I could make one last a whole hour if I really tried. Is it like that?'

She shrugged, uncertain how to continue. 'What if there's something bad in the message?'

'Oh. Not like my birthday candies at all. Well, how would you feel if there were?'

'Sad. No, awful, then sad. I don't want anything bad to happen to him.'

'Of course not. But you know, your father relished trouble when he was younger – adventure and trouble and excitement. So you mustn't be surprised if that turns out to be the case. Will you make me a promise, Diana? Once you've read the message, will you tell me what it says? I could help you figure it out, if there's a puzzle.'

She shrugged, lowering her eyes, not wanting him to see her confusion. What if she were the cause of her father's leaving? Wouldn't her mother blame her and be even more distant than she was now?

When Diana got home, she went straight to her bedroom and closed the door. Majine leapt off the bed and jumped into her arms. She stroked his fur, rubbing it in the direction of its cowlick-like whorls, then tickled his stomach so she could hear his sounds of pleasure. She nuzzled his nose with hers. 'OK, Majine, now we have to get serious.' She patted the space next to her on the floor and Majine joined her. The two sat quietly while Diana removed the letter from her pocket, laid it flat, and smoothed out its folds.

The writing was tiny, tight, and knotted, as if the letters were made of string that had been balled up for a very long time. She read as best she could, skipping over the words that didn't make sense.

Miranda,

If I have been gone for more than a year, then I am gone forever. What began well has ended badly for us. I fell into a dangerous world. Each time I left I traveled farther from our simple lives. Then once after unloading a shipment, I was taken to a ceremony in which men stabbed their chests with knives and danced into a trance. My heart beat fast as I watched their wild eyes and thrashing limbs as they slid to the floor. Now like them, I have crossed over beyond the beyond. Shiva has come to rule my being, but like a door closing, he is also a door opening. More and more do I live on the edge of enchantment. I have a new life.

Forgive me, Miranda.

Forgive me, Diana. Perhaps we will meet again when the dance enters your being.

'Oh Majine, he's gone! He's really gone and he won't ever come back. He doesn't even say where he is. Who's Shiva? Why do these men stab themselves? What does he mean, that we might meet when the dance enters my being? How can we meet if I don't even know where he is?' Diana cried until her ribs ached and her eyes stung. She cried until she fell asleep, exhausted, still wearing the clothes she had worn all day. Late that night she was woken by a nightmare in which her father appeared dressed in the black-and-white-patterned sarong she had found in his trunk. A knife was tucked into the waistband. He began to yell out savage cries, then took his dagger and attacked himself violently, stabbing his chest in a fury. His arms and knees began to twitch. He thrashed and then slid to the earth, eyes wild and vacant. A blind man sang a haunting melody. A beautiful woman with many golden bracelets danced with a puppet wearing a lacy fan-shaped headdress. Someone picked up a brazier of burning coals and leaned over her father, casting a shadow like a death mask.

Diana woke in a state of terror, cold and sweaty. My father's in trouble, she thought to herself. Terrible trouble. I'm afraid he's going to die. I don't know what to do.

Next morning she went to the kitchen to talk to Miranda, but the spatter and sizzle of frying and the clanging of pots drowned her words. She had to wait for a lull in the frenzied preparations before telling her mother about the message. 'Let me see it,' said Miranda, wiping her hands on a dishcloth. She read slowly, once and then again. 'My God,' she whispered. 'I guessed something was wrong, but the daggers, the trance, the strange ceremonies' – she shook her head – 'I never knew.'

'Why not?' the girl asked. 'Didn't you talk to each other? Didn't you ask where he'd been?'

Miranda swallowed hard. 'Diana,' she said guardedly, eyeing her daughter through narrowed lids, 'you couldn't possibly understand. You may be fifteen, but you're still a girl. You've never been married. You've never even had a romance. And you've certainly never been isolated on an island with no one except a man who is becoming more and more secretive and a girl who cared more for monkeys than her own family.'

Diana blinked. 'I loved the monkeys and they loved me.

They rushed to see me every time I came. They didn't leave me alone or forget about me,' she said sullenly.

'Oh Diana, your father was so cold when he came back from his trips. So remote. I asked but he wouldn't talk to me. I knew something was wrong.' Miranda narrowed her eyes, as if looking into the past to see what she hadn't seen then. 'He was gone too much. Came back with wounds on his chest that he wouldn't talk about. I thought he was getting into fights because he drank. Or gambled. I knew he was unhappy but I couldn't help him. I couldn't have guessed.'

'I don't understand. You don't let the men who are in this house tell you what you can and can't talk about. Did you mean to let him leave us?'

Miranda pulled out the nearest chair and sat in it. 'It's so easy to ask the questions, isn't it? Well, what do you know of being married to a man in over his head? A man whose idea of an answer is a slap. A punch. That's right, he couldn't talk but he could use his hands to let me know what he thought of those questions. Now are you glad you asked?'

'That's mean of you to tell me that, Mamma.' Diana felt terrible, as if she were the one who had been hit. She grew quiet. She would talk this over later with Majine but she didn't want to think about it now. She changed the subject.

'Who's Shiva?'

'A Hindu god, I think.'

'Where do they do these dances?'

'Somewhere your father sailed, I guess. On one of the bigger islands. I suppose.'

'What does he mean – maybe we'll meet when the dance enters my being?'

'How should I know? I don't have the vaguest idea what he's talking about.' A long sigh escaped from her. 'Your father has become a different person from the one I knew. He was already changing before we left. I don't know what dancing means to him. He hasn't done anything to let us know about his once secret life, hasn't done anything to show that he cares about us at all.'

Diana shot her a dark glance. 'He left the note, didn't he? I'm going to the library. Maybe I'll be able to find him.'

'Find your father?'

'Shiva. Maybe the islands. I might learn enough that I could figure out where he is.'

'Don't get your hopes up, Diana. He's a long way away.'

In the library Diana looked up the words that she didn't understand in her father's note. She wrote down the definitions.

Shiva: One of the principal Hindu deities, worshiped as the destroyer and restorer of worlds. Shiva is often conceived as a member of the triad also including Brahma and Vishnu.

Brahma: The creator god. Variant of Brahman. The holy or sacred power that is the source and sustainer of the universe.

Vishnu: One of the principal Hindu deities, worshiped as the protector and preserver of worlds.

Creator, protector, destroyer. And her father had chosen the destroyer.

She studied the phrase 'beyond the beyond'. In one dictionary she read of beyond: that which is past or to a degree greater than knowledge or experience; the unknown.

She checked out several books and brought them home. For three nights Diana slept fitfully. No dreams came. On the fourth she saw a school of silvery fish clumped together in the moonlight, riding waves that rippled like Miranda's hair when she loosed it from its braid. A single chair with teak slats that curved like a half moon appeared at the edge of the sea. Solid and simple, it sat alone facing the silvery waves as they lapped at the shore. Above it the heavens arched in vaults of indigo, dusted with handfuls of comets and constellations as if a great cook had dipped into a heavenly salt jar and tossed the seasoning across the firmament.

Diana watched as a man with cloth wrapped around his waist and tucked between his legs, like a giant ikat diaper, began to dance slowly. Eyes closed, he whirled to an arrhythmic beat, moving as if a funnel of energy were spinning from the grey clouds into him. Faster and faster he spun, arms winding and enwrapping his chest, his heart. Watching him, Diana felt the energy entering her own being. She screamed, grabbed Majine, and held him close to her, afraid the force would suck her eyes from their sockets and bear her body into a silvery white cloud bank. Songs began to pour forth from her and she was thrust, like the lone man dancing, into a state of transcendent dreams.

Diana wandered barefoot into the kitchen. Miranda sat in her long robe, one leg twisted around the other underneath the table. 'Did you find what you were looking for in the library?'

'I guess. I don't understand really. I brought home some more books to read. I think I have to wait to hear my father speak to me.'

Miranda's head jerked toward her. 'And how will he do that, I wonder?'

Warily Diana spoke of her dreams. Of her visions, of seeing him dancing.

CHAPTER SIX

A BOUT A MONTH AFTER Ria's death, three identical cream-colored envelopes addressed to Anton, Miranda, and Diana arrived. Inside each was a letter written by Maarten Welbroeck on behalf of the law firm of De Keyser and van den Bosch. Miranda took all three to her bedroom. She stuffed the envelope addressed to Anton in the large manila folder in which she kept all matters pertaining to her vanished husband and then opened hers. Later in the afternoon she called Diana into the kitchen, and while they were drinking tea and eating almond cookies still warm from the oven, Miranda explained that her grandmother had left a will and named both of them in it. They read the letter together.

It began with a ritual expression of condolence on the death of Mrs. de Jong and then continued:

As you may be aware, the firm of De Keyser and van den Bosch has taken care of the affairs of the de Jong family for more than two centuries. We have looked after the business transactions, the contracts, transfers of property, and wills for the family from the time that Hendrik de Jong first purchased the house which you now inhabit. It is in that capacity that we have been charged to act as Mrs. de Jong's official solicitors. Mrs. de Jong came to our offices approximately sixteen months ago to update her will and make certain that several bequests were made in the exact form that she wished. In compliance with her instructions, we drew up her final will and testament, which she signed on May 12, 1962. We request your presence at the reading of the will on Wednesday, September 3, 1963. If this date is inconvenient, please inform us at your earliest convenience.

Sincerely,

Maarten Welbroeck.

At the bottom next to the notation *cc:* were the names of Andreas Mieskeeper and Willem Mieskeeper.

On the appointed day, Miranda carefully closed the end of her single braid with a silver barrette. She threw a black cape over the long burgundy skirt and sweater she had chosen to wear and slid her slender feet into a pair of black pumps with sling backs. Diana decided she would wear one of the outfits her grandmother had bought for her. 'But I don't want to go,' she told Majine, as she slid her pale grey jumper over a blouse with delicate stripes. 'I'm afraid I'll cry when they talk about Nanna.'

Mother and daughter walked through the city streets together, although Miranda's long strides soon put her far ahead of Diana. 'Come on, Diana. Our appointment is for eleven, but if you keep walking at this speed we'll be lucky to arrive by noon.'

'I don't want to hear about Nanna from some stranger. It will just make me feel sadder.'

'I know, but walking slowly won't make it go away. Anyway, I expect the meeting will be quite brief and formal. These lawyers have a language of their own and I'd be very surprised if their words made you think about your grandmother in a way that would be upsetting.'

'Why couldn't you just go and tell me what they said?'

'I thought you should be there. Anyway, it's a little late for that now, isn't it?' asked Miranda as they arrived at the tall brick building with a discreet brass number next to the doors.

A man in a dark blue suit sitting behind a highly polished mahogany desk pointed them toward the elevator, where a second man took them to the sixth floor. The doors opened upon a receptionist who took their names and motioned them toward the waiting area where Andreas was seated on a leather couch, distractedly leafing through a magazine.

Maarten Welbroeck appeared just as a clock chimed eleven. Where Diana saw a stern man with deep set grey-blue eyes and pale complexion, Miranda noticed a well-dressed lawyer who had artfully brushed thinning sandy hair over a patch of pink scalp. She thought that his finely tailored pinstripe suit didn't quite conceal the stiffness of his body underneath. He reminded her of a wind-up toy she'd once had – turn a key in its back and it marched forward in an awkward lurching gait. He nodded at Miranda and Diana, giving them a restrained smile that managed to move his large moustaches very slightly from their resting position above his pale lips. He shook everyone's hand and then asked Andreas if his son was expected. 'No,' Andreas answered. 'I can tell him about anything that involves him.'

The group filed into a large and elegantly furnished office. 'First, let me express my condolences at the passing of Mrs. de Jong. We here at De Keyser and van den Bosch always held her in the highest regard. A lovely woman. We saw her several times in the last year and a half. She was quite determined that she put in legal form some feelings and bequests that were important to her. We did everything that she asked, of course. And one of the things that most concerned her was a letter that she made me promise to read before I proceed with the precise points of the will. The letter is a bit out of the ordinary in these circumstances, but being a man of my word, I shall read what she dictated.'

Dear Anton, Diana, and Miranda,
I begin this letter with Anton, my only child. You have essentially disappeared, leaving us in a state of unbearable

suspension. We do not even know if you left of your own will or were coerced, whether you are well, are at liberty or in captivity, whether you are alive or dead.

The family has always adhered to the tradition of primogeniture in passing property to the eldest son. When your father died, he stated in his will that he left the house and all the property on which it stood to you, with the stipulation that I be allowed to continue to live in it with all privileges and rights that I had always enjoyed. Instead, you allowed Miranda to make major decisions, even when they conflicted with what I wanted. When you left without telling anyone where you were going and without leaving much money in the bank, she felt she had no option but to take in travelers and essentially turn our family home into an inn.

As you are well aware, the succession of property has always gone from father to son, but as I write, there is no father in the family – at least not one who can be found – and no son. But there is your daughter, Diana. Since I do not know if you have disappeared into another life or have died without our knowing, I hope that someone will undertake a search if you are still missing when this letter is read aloud. If you have not surfaced within a year of the time of my death, I wish that the house in which you were born and raised should pass to Diana. I specifically leave all the contents – furniture, books, paintings, silver, china, anything large and small, etc., save certain specific bequests – to her.

Diana, I remember how silent and lost you were when you first arrived and how painfully withdrawn you became after your father left. I felt very sorry for you. It took quite a while until we found that the garden formed a bridge between us. In that I was reminded of my own entry into this house and family and how I felt saved by the garden. Once again it came to my rescue in giving us a place where we could be together easily.

Your pleasure in being with me in the garden has been a

great comfort. What we have shared will always be yours, but I want you to feel surrounded by the things that have given life and meaning to this house for many years. That is why I have left to you almost all of its contents.

Miranda, our relationship has never been an easy one. When Anton brought you home as his young bride, I was not pleased. I became unhappier yet when you persuaded him to leave within weeks of your arrival. You were gone for ten years. The war came. Thomas died. Even when the three of you returned, things between us did not improve. Still, you have survived the abandonment of your husband, my son, and you have kept us afloat, although I would have been happier had you chosen another way. You have given me a granddaughter I love very much. To reflect my feelings, I have asked the lawyers to present you with a piece of jewelry that has been in the family for generations. It is large and dramatic, very much in keeping with your style. I only ask that you pass it on to Diana at your death. In addition, I leave to you all the contents of the kitchen that has become your realm over the years. I am certain that your talents will be acknowledged in some important way in the future.

'Surely she left me something more than one piece of jewelry and the pots and pans in the kitchen?' Diana heard Miranda asking in a shaken voice. 'No, I'm sorry, but that's correct,' said the lawyer, coloring slightly. 'She meant you to have everything that you need from the kitchen. She was quite specific in the will itself – bowls and graters, I believe she named, knives and pitchers, punchbowls, ladles and carving boards.' The old woman had shaken him off when he had asked whether her daughter-in-law wouldn't feel slighted. She made it clear she knew what she was doing.

'Not even the silver or linens? The furniture in my bedroom? The tall silver candlesticks I always put on the table?'

'It is all specifically enumerated in the will. We will read the details shortly.'

'And if Anton is found? What happens then?'

'According to the will, he is entitled to the house.'

'And if he doesn't want it?'

'We'd have to hear from him first.'

'Well,' said Miranda, 'since we don't know if he's dead or alive, how do we go about making that happen.'

'I suppose,' said Mr.Welbroeck. 'I suppose you could hire a detective.'

Andreas's head jerked sideways. Send someone half way across the world to find a man who probably had every reason not to want to be found?

'Well, we'd better do it,' said the woman, whose name was barely found in the will.

In the days that followed, Miranda was increasingly invigorated by her anger at Ria and her curiosity at the phrase about gaining recognition for her talents. 'I've been thinking,' Miranda said to Diana as she counted out the napkins needed for the fourteen men who would be at dinner. 'I've been thinking that you might like to move into your grandmother's room. It's bigger than what you have now and more private. When you feel up to it, you could sort through her books and clothes and whatever she kept in her trunks and decide what to do with them all. I'd help you, of course, although I think she'd return from the grave if she saw me touching anything that was hers.'

'Mamma, it wasn't that bad.'

'Wasn't that bad? You saw how she stayed clear of me all these years. She never forgave me for marrying your father and taking him away. What did she expect? When we arrived she took one look at me and lowered those eyelids as if she were gazing on some sort of aborigine who shouldn't be allowed in the house, much less fed at the table with the rest of the family. Anyway, I'll stay where I am. I like being near the kitchen.'

'What about my room? Don't you want to move some of your things into it too?'

'No, I don't think so.'

'Then what? Leave it empty?'

'I've been thinking,' Miranda confessed, 'that it would make an excellent private dining room. A room for special meals and celebrations where people could feel as if they were in a home instead of a restaurant. It would add some extra work, of course, but not a huge amount. And we'll undoubtedly have more money once we've sold some of your grandmother's possessions.'

'Those are mine, Mamma. You know that Nanna left them to me.'

'Have you any idea how little money we have at the moment? Those old silver coins must be worth quite a lot. I'm certain some of the old furniture is quite valuable. What do we really need with the bureaus in the upstairs rooms and the hand-carved bedsteads? Some of the old pictures on the walls? We could easily buy something nice to replace them.'

'I don't know,' Diana said slowly, fearful of challenging Miranda. 'What about Majine? How can I move him into Nanna's room? She wouldn't let him near her.'

'I don't want to seem unnecessarily unpleasant, Diana, but I'm sure you've noticed your grandmother is dead. Under the circumstances she's unlikely to notice his presence.'

'Well, I'd still feel funny. I'd have to do something to make it all right.'

'I'd be interested in what that could be. Midnight conversations at the grave, special signals from the dead?'

'Stop being so mean, Mamma. Just because she didn't like you doesn't mean you should be unpleasant to me. Yes, I will move into her room. Then she'll be all around me. I can still smell her powder, the flowers that filled the vases, the leather bindings of the books.'

Never too soon to start, Miranda said to herself, once she decided that she would definitely open a restaurant in what had been Diana's bedroom. She threw herself into the planning. Most of Diana's furniture would have to go. She had to make room for the highboy from the living room and the hutch whose open shelves would display the handsome antique porcelain plates that had been in the family for more than a century. The room would hold six round tables, space for no more than thirty-six people at any one time. She would paint it a delicate shade of yellow to suggest that the sun was warming its walls, then would hang sconces on the walls to wash them with soft light.

'I suppose I need your permission to move furniture around the house,' Miranda said dryly to Diana. 'Now that you're the legal owner of everything I might want to use.'

'How can you be so mean? You know I didn't ask Nanna to do this. You really think I like it? You want to open a restaurant, go ahead and open a restaurant. Just don't take it out on me.'

Miranda raised her eyebrows, looked at her daughter from under a dark fringe of lashes and was momentarily silenced. 'Here's what I want to do,' she said in a softer tone of voice. 'I'm considering hanging some of the paintings from upstairs in this room. There may be enough tables, but I will probably need to buy some chairs. I'll need the silver candlesticks and damask tablecloths.' She stopped. 'And I'll have to hire someone to help, since I can't do this all by myself.'

'Do you have enough money to do that?' Diana asked.

'You're the heiress, not me,' were the words that flew out of Miranda's mouth. 'You could let me sell a few pieces from upstairs and use the money for the things that I need.'

'What sort of pieces?'

'Just some of the bureaus and old beds. We could replace them with something newer and we just might get enough for them that I could go ahead with my plans. I can't pay painters and handymen with preserves and stews, you know.'

Diana stared helplessly. What did she know about any of this? And she had to admit that no one paid any attention to the furniture on the floors where the men boarded.

'Okay,' she said uncertainly.

Soon there were workers removing the old carpet, pulling new electrical cords, and painting the walls. Men with briefcases came to look at the furniture and figure what they would pay for it. Miranda bought second-hand beds and tables to replace those she sold and pocketed the difference. While all this was happening, Miranda asked Diana to choose what she wanted from her grandmother's room and to decide what could be stored elsewhere in the house or sold.

Each time Diana slid open the drawers in the old oak dresser, which were still filled with soft scarves, silk stockings, kid-skin gloves, and nightgowns, she inhaled the soft powdery smell of her nanna. It assaulted her senses and raced through the passageways to her memory, leaving her disoriented. She found the delicate silver and pearl bracelet her nanna slid over wrist bones as tiny as hummingbirds' eggs. Diana had watched her grandmother put on the bracelet hundreds of times and knew that she took it off only before getting into the bath she took just before bedtime. It was always there, emblematic of her nanna and, when she could bear to, Diana would wear it to keep the old woman with her.

Her fingers continued exploring the contents of the drawers as if they had a will of their own. They came upon baby teeth sealed in an envelope mottled with age, an ancient bulb with dirt still clinging to its frail dried roots, a collection of oversize keys with intricate flanges, and a stockpile of bronze door knobs wrapped in soft cloth. She imagined that the teeth were Anton's and wondered about the dry bulb. She remembered hearing her nanna say how hard they had tried to keep anything out of the Germans' hands during the war. When the order went out that the occupying soldiers would go from door to door making everyone give up their brass doorknobs for the war effort, the old woman had replaced them with inferior knobs and hid the fine old ones where they wouldn't be found. Now here they were, long since forgotten, wrapped in the flannel of Thomas's old pyjamas.

Diana held up the keys she found, admiring their size and workmanship. She and Majine wandered up and down the hallway, trying them in various doors to see if they still fit. She decided to see if one would open the old steamer trunk in Nanna's storeroom. Majine sat down beside her. He patted the lock, then maneuvered a finger in the opening and when it got stuck, he cried out, tugging harder and harder until it was really caught. 'Oh no, Majine, what have you done? Sit still. Shhh, all that noise isn't going to help.' She took hold of the finger and rotating it slowly from side to side, stopping every minute or two to stroke his fur and reassure him, she finally managed to free it from its prison. Once released, he leapt onto her lap, smacking his lips at her.

'Okay, okay,' she said. 'I know you're happy. Me too. That must have felt terrible.'

He jumped up and down and patted his mouth.

'How can you be hungry? I just fed you an hour ago.'

Majine took his small furry hand and cupped it in front of her.

She sighed, knowing she would never get to the trunk until he was taken care of. 'Okay, let's go.'

They heard voices as they walked toward the kitchen.

'Of course it will cost more than the first estimate. And it always takes longer than they tell you. Didn't anyone warn you? There is no way that you will be able to open your restaurant before spring.'

Diana peered around a corner to see a man smiling a crooked half grin while talking to her mother. 'Miranda. Miranda, a beautiful name for a beautiful woman. You need an adviser who has experience in the wicked ways of the world.' Another grin. Giles van Galen was clearly offering himself up for the job.

Just what she didn't need to hear, Diana thought, one more man fascinated by her mother. She backed away, leaving Miranda to wonder who this man was, other than someone who had wandered into her life when he arrived on orders of Mr. Welbroeck to look at the space where she was going to put her restaurant. The first time he came, she waited nervously as he traced his finger over the drawing that indicated where the plugs for new lighting fixtures would go, checked out entrances and egresses, made sure there was adequate protection in case of fire or calamity. He had been pleasantly noncommittal and warned her to expect a second visit. And here he was again. She considered his broad, weathered face with its high forehead and incipient jowls, was reassured by the crinkle of lines around his eyes and the greying sandy hair just beginning to recede. Casting his eyes around the high-ceilinged room with its handsome moldings, he was distracted by the alluring aroma. 'Something smells awfully good. Are you cooking apples with nutmeg?'

'You've got a good nose,' said Miranda, visibly impressed. 'I started out making bread pudding and somehow took a detour into applesauce. Now I wish I had some quince. I'm yearning to make a tart with quince and apples and a drizzle of caramelized sugar.'

'Ummm . . . sounds delicious. You're in luck. I just happen to have a few and I'll bring all of them in exchange for a big dish of whatever you're going to turn them into.'

Miranda made a sound that was pitched somewhere between

pleasure and caution. Giles responded immediately. 'You'll be doing me a favor – I've only got them because a friend has a few experimental quince trees. I wouldn't have the vaguest idea what to do with them. How about if I bring by whatever I have in the morning on my way to work?'

Diana and Majine tiptoed into the kitchen. Miranda caught a glimpse of them and signaled the girl to stay away and be quiet while she was at it.

Giles arrived in the morning with the promised quince. He found Miranda worriedly bent over plans and a sheet of paper on which she'd sketched out the time line for the restaurant's opening. He shook his head. 'It'll be a good two or three months more before you can get this place in order and have all the necessary people sign off on the improvements. That's just reality.' Settling in to the hard work of pulling together the costs of the project, he didn't even realize that he was undoing the buttons at the cuffs of his shirt and rolling up the sleeves of his flannel shirt. 'You still have to convince Welbroeck that you're not changing the house in any way that will have a negative impact on Anton's inheritance.'

Miranda rolled her eyes. 'Anton's been gone for the better part of five years and I'm supposed to worry about a few electrical outlets and a new coat of paint? I don't know what could possibly concern Mr. Welbroeck. Look – Anton's mother didn't exactly leave me with money to keep this place going. I am convinced that the restaurant will bring in money and it will let me use my best talents to do it.'

'Who am I to disagree?' replied Giles, who did briefly wonder whose side he was on. It was Welbroeck, after all, who had sent him to check out the woman's financial commitments and plans, Welbroeck who was paying his fee. Looking at the diagrams, he frowned. 'Is this who's doing the final certification?' he asked, worried by the name he saw stamped in the lower righthand part of the page. 'Hendricks? Look, Miranda – I can call you Miranda? – let me find out why it's taking him so long to get here. And see what I can do.'

'Mmm,' she said, brushing a stray strand of hair back over her ear.

'Don't worry, just make me some of that quince and apple dessert and we're even.'

When he next appeared, Giles brought a spreadsheet to show Miranda how to lay out the numbers the lawyers and bank would require. 'Let's sit in the kitchen,' she said, 'so I can keep an eye on the stove. I'm simmering your quinces with some lemon peel – you don't happen to have access to lemons, do you? – and cinnamon.' She assumed this man was some sort of agent sent by De Keyser and van den Bosch to keep an eye on her plans for fear that they might spiral out of control, but she felt safe in the kitchen, terra firma in her shifting world.

Giles watched as she bent over the steamy pot, inhaling the flavor exuded by the flesh of the fruit along with curls of peel and chunks of its core, then saw her test a slice to see if it had begun to soften. The buttery pastry lining a tart shell stood ready to receive the quince and the mass of apples she was peeling. 'Is it like this all the time?'

'You mean, is there always something cooking?'

'More or less,' he answered.

'More or less,' she echoed him in intonation, although she couldn't duplicate his raised eyebrows, his look of anticipatory pleasure. 'I wouldn't be doing this if I didn't love it. There are not a lot of ways that you're guaranteed to make people happy, but serving them good food has to be high on the list. Anyway, it gives me pleasure and keeps the family afloat.'

'Who's the family?'

'Just the two of us, my daughter and me.'

'Name?'

'Diana.'

'Age?'

'Fifteen.'

'Interests?'

'Don't get me started.'

'What does that mean?'

'Here, hold this handle and help me tip the pot. I have to remove the slices and weigh them so I know how much sugar to add for the syrup. Once I cook them again they will turn the most outrageous deep orange-pink color.'

Giles helped Miranda understand some basic principles of accounting. He was astonished to discover that while she had been running a business, the words 'cash flow' had no meaning for her. 'How do you calculate how much you'll need each month? How much you have to take in to run the house and your lives?' She shrugged and then explained that it seemed to work out, more or less. He couldn't believe that she meant it, and was momentarily speechless when he realized that she did. It took him quite a while to explain the simple system she should use in the future. Taxes, he decided, could wait for another day.

By the time he looked up, he realized he'd been in the kitchen with her for about four hours. Three more than he had budgeted for and absolutely two and a half more than his schedule could afford. He was baffled – he wouldn't have thought that much time could have gone by. He remembered seeing her chop an onion without watching what she was doing. 'Don't worry.' She laughed at his alarm that her fast-moving fingers were in danger. He remembered how she moved effortlessly through the kitchen, grabbing ginger-root and garlic from a basket, a bit of chicken from the refrigerator, and tossing the few simple ingredients in a skillet, cooked them for lunch. 'What do you call this?' he asked afterward, as his fork slid through a tangle of noodles. He couldn't remember if she actually answered, although he still saw her wry shrug and half smile in response.

He didn't look at his watch until she took the quince and apple tart out of the oven. 'My God, Miranda, it's 2:30.'

'Yes,' she replied, drawing the word into one long lightly inflected syllable.

'I was supposed to be somewhere two hours ago.'

'You're going to leave now, when the tart you've been waiting for is finally ready?'

'Hardly makes sense, does it?'

'No. And you'll have to let it cool a bit or you'll scald the inside of your mouth.'

When Giles appeared two days later, Miranda met him in Diana's room, where the plans for the remodeling were spread over various pieces of furniture. She hesitated briefly before asking if he'd mind reading the letter she had just received from Mr. Welbroeck. Taking the two sheets of fine bond paper, Giles was tempted to reassure her that lawyers protected themselves with their dry legal language, but decided to run his eye over the document first. 'This is the part that makes me nervous,' said Miranda, pointing at the offending paragraph:

In view of the fact that you are pressing forward with great haste to put a restaurant in the family home, do you not think it wise to engage someone to find Anton? He is, after all, the legitimate heir to the property and might have an opinion about your incursion upon the house's integrity. Has there been any communication between the two of you, or between your husband and daughter, since his departure? Were any documents left behind that might give clues as to where he went? Could you think of any people with whom he might be or have been in contact? Do you yourself have any idea where he might be?

Giles shrugged. 'He's just doing his job. So the house isn't yours?'

'No, not really,' Miranda replied. 'It belongs to Anton if he comes to claim it in the next few months, something like that. Otherwise it passes to Diana.'

'You can't blame Welbroeck for wanting to get the legal owner to agree to what is happening with the house. It's not an unreasonable request.'

'Don't you think his words are a little harsh?'

Giles nodded a silent affirmative – he'd been struck by the strangely emotional language, but skipped on to what interested him. 'So Anton is your husband?'

'Legally I guess he still is, although he left about six years ago and we haven't seen or heard a word from him since.'

Giles let out a long low whistle of amazement. 'Nothing at all? You don't have any idea whether he's run off or had an accident, whether he's alive or dead?' He stopped, a quizzical look on his face. 'How does Welbroeck's suggestion of sending someone to search for him make you feel?'

Miranda walked to the mantel and removed two dead tulips from a vase, being careful not to disturb the remaining flowers. She dropped them into a wastebasket, then brushed invisible dust from the surface of the couch. 'Nosy, nosy. You certainly aren't shy about asking questions, are you?'

'Oops, guess I overstepped a boundary there. Sorry, but it's pretty natural to wonder. If our roles were reversed, wouldn't you be curious?'

'But they're not.'

'True. But look at it this way. No matter what is going on in his life, he'd undoubtedly want to know that his mother has died.'

Miranda had to admit that she could hardly quarrel with his reasoning. 'What can I do? I don't have the vaguest idea where he is. If he'd cared about his mother while she was alive, he might have written once or twice.' The normally voluble Miranda did not care for the direction in which the conversation was veering. She had no interest in talking to Giles about Anton and wasn't one bit pleased with the thought that the man to whom she was still married might have to be found and brought home.

'If you were allowed only one guess where to find him, what would it be?'

'You're just as bad as Welbroeck. Worse. I'm sorry I ever asked you to look at the letter. Here.' She stretched out her hand, palm up, waiting for its return. She bit her voluptuous lower lip, curling it under her front teeth until part of it seemed to disappear, and then looked up from under her eyelashes. 'Maybe he went back to the islands where we lived when we were first married. I don't know – he left behind a strange message that Diana found when she was searching through a trunk he left behind. Never mind. It's more complicated than I really want to go into.'

'Would you like me to mention it to Welbroeck?' Giles resisted an impulse to walk over and put his hands on her upper arms and lightly shake her, as if to bring her out of the strange resistant stance she'd slipped into.

'I only asked you to take a look at the letter he sent, not take over my life. I'm quite able to do it myself.'

'I'm only trying to help, Miranda. My assumption is that Welbroeck is collecting enough information to send someone to find Anton.'

'Has it occurred to you,' she asked, eyebrows raised, a slight smile on her lips, 'that you may have been reading too many detective novels?'

'Could be,' Giles agreed, mimicking her raised eyebrows and smile, looking briefly like a naughty boy about to be found out. 'But just in case, I think you'd better prepare for the arrival of a detective in your life in the near future. From the little I've seen, I'd say you like to hold your cards pretty close to your chest. That might get tougher now. I only offered to tell Welbroeck to make things a little easier for you. You're one hell of a cook, Miranda, but you might just need a little help with the intricacies of investigations.'

Miranda wondered what made her show Giles the letter in the first place. She hadn't known where else to turn. She couldn't have asked Andreas. He was Ria's great champion and a sort of secondary guardian for Diana, which made him, if not her enemy, certainly not her advocate. But now that Giles seemed to want to help her, why did she bridle and try to get him to back off? Who else knew the lawyer, knew his way around these complicated, unpleasant things?

Her nose twitched. 'Oh no, the apricot sauce!' She raced to the kitchen. She flew through the door, reached out to turn off the stove, and fought through the thick apricot haze to save what she could. As she leaned over the smoking pot, small beads of the concentrated sauce leapt onto her arms and neck. She could hear the sizzle as they hit her skin. Arriving just behind her, Giles registered the look of pain on her face, ran to the freezer, pulled out an ice tray, and dashed to the sink, where he ran cold water to free the ice. 'I'm coming, I'm coming,' he said, to reassure her, and scooping up a handful of ice cubes, pressed them to the blisters beginning to appear. 'Oh yes, oh thank you, so hot, oh yes,' she said, grateful as the cold overrode the heat. She extended her arms toward him and tipped her head back so he could find the burning places on her neck and chest. He was all gentleness as he slid the slowly melting cubes of ice up and down her exposed flesh, until the chill took over and she relaxed. Then he bent toward her and licked first at the spots on her lower arms, then at the soft flesh of the upper arms and finally swished his tongue slowly around the exposed section at the base of her neck. He could taste the thick meaty apricots in the tiny bubbles raised on her skin, could smell the dark musky smoke they carried with them.

'Better?' he asked. 'Ummm,' Miranda mumbled, as his tongue worked its way slowly around each tiny blister and then on to the next and the next. When he arrived at her neck, her body slid toward his. She felt him sliding buttons through their holes until his tongue could resume its voyage over bare skin.

'Oh yes,' she sighed, 'oh yes.' Then she managed to gasp, 'Not here,' and together they found their way to her room, where they fell upon each other. Ravenously, they undressed each other, she tangling with the intricacies of belt and zipper, he slipping silky lingerie off skin he could now caress. She threw her legs around him while he rolled to his side, moving slightly away so he could begin his explorations, finding his way across the declivities and rises of her body, as it arched toward his, breath racing from deep in her interior. She felt his fingers enter the whorls of her ear, the moist recesses of her open mouth, the hollow between the rise of her breasts, the tiny ridges of her umbilicus, the crinkly cover of her soft fleshy mound. She was shaking now, shaking and yearning and he knew it was time, finally time, to plunge into the dark passage for which he had yearned from the moment of meeting his passionate, full-blooded Miranda.

Within days Welbroeck requested that Miranda return to his office for a second visit. He greeted her in the reception area as before, wearing, she was certain, the same pin-striped suit she had first seen him in. She was amused to watch him struggle with the problem of what to call her. He couldn't call her Miranda, but couldn't bring himself to address her as Mrs. de Jong. Mrs. de Jong was Ria, Anton's mother, a dignified, silver-haired woman in a fine old tweed suit who spoke in a low, deliberate voice and behaved in the way a woman of her class should. He looked at Miranda in her flamboyant cape and dangling earrings, was immediately reminded she had been deserted by the questionable Mr. de Jong the third, and chose to slide by without calling her anything. Just a simple nod of the head, a formulaic handshake, and a gesture, once they reached his office, indicating which chair she should take.

He wasn't much for small talk. 'About the house,' he said, clearing his throat. 'I think we'd better try to track down your husband and let him know the sad news. Find out if he plans to come back to claim his inheritance. Get him to sign the necessary papers. There will be taxes to pay. That sort of thing.'

Miranda blinked. Money. She hadn't thought about that. She certainly didn't have any. She felt squeezed into a very uncomfortable corner. She could see she'd have to help them find Anton. 'Mr. Welbroeck, Anton left me with a stack of bills and no money. I had to dream up a way to support Diana and myself, to say nothing of keeping the house going while my mother-in-law was still alive. Don't you think I'd have tried to get him to help us all those years ago if I knew where he was?'

'Yes, of course. It only stands to reason.' He cleared his throat, a dry rasp followed by bobbings of his prominent Adam's apple. 'But now that the situation is rather dramatically altered, I'm afraid we'll have to think on a rather more complex level. I suggest we start by finding someone who will go out to wherever it is to find him.'

Miranda sighed. 'That's really the problem, isn't it? I mean, where is wherever it is?'

'Didn't he give you any clue at all to what his destination was when he left?'

'Mr. Welbroeck, my husband was clearly in trouble. I don't know what the issue was or who was making the trouble. But he left a message that Diana happened to find a while ago that made it clear he's gone somewhere far away. If I had to guess, I imagine that he is somewhere among the 13,000 islands that make up the country of Indonesia, where we lived when we were first married. We started on a couple of very tiny islands and then moved to a larger one. I can tell you their names, although I don't think there's a soul on any of them that could tell you a thing about Anton once we left. Never mind

– it's a place to start. And I'll give you the strange note that Diana found. It gave me the sense that Anton had gone off the deep end.'

'Very helpful. Thank you so much. Would you excuse me for asking' – and here Mr. Welbroeck's normally pale complexion took on the rosy color of spring salmon – 'but had he been behaving differently for a while before he left?'

'Differently? Do you mean strangely? Conspiratorially? Secretively? Or was he just his same angry cooped-up self kept away from the sea for too long?'

'No matter. He will be found. We will engage' – here he hesitated, his voice dropping as if it had been sucked into a pit of quicksand – 'an experienced investigator.' He spoke so quietly that Miranda had to ask him to repeat himself. 'A detective? Is that what you mean?'

'Something like that.' He stopped. 'We'll find someone familiar with the territory and go from there. I'll let you know what happens next.'

Two weeks later she heard from Mr. Welbroeck, this time by phone. 'I think we've found our man,' he said, in a tone more enthusiastic than Miranda could remember hearing him use previously.

'You do?'

'Yes. I hope you'll agree. Pieter van Hoorn spent quite a lot of time in the East Indies some years ago. He's willing to go out there for us now.'

'Just a minute,' Miranda answered. 'This is all going a bit too fast for me. Do you mean that you've found someone living here who has spent a lot of time in the East Indies and is willing to go out and try to find Anton.'

'Why, yes,' Mr. Welbroeck replied in an almost courtly voice. 'That's precisely what I mean.'

'And may I meet this mysterious gentleman?'

'Of course. That's why I telephoned.'

CHAPTER SEVEN

MIRANDA FOUND HERSELF IN Welbroeck's office for the third time in less than three weeks. By now she was familiar with his cursory manner. She slid into his office after his customary brief greeting and found herself confronted with a short, muscular man with an overshot jaw and brilliant blue eyes that stared unabashedly from under thick, wiry, almost white eyebrows. 'Pieter van Hoorn,' he said leaping up from the chair and thrusting his hand into hers for a vigorous shake.

'Yes, yes,' said Mr. Welbroeck slightly breathlessly, as if he were running behind in a race that mattered. 'Let me introduce Miranda de Jong,' he said, using her full name for the first time and guiding her to a chair. 'Very good to have you both here. Yes, yes.' He turned to Pieter van Hoorn. 'We've a bit of a problem and it looks like you're just the man to help us.'

'We'll see,' van Hoorn answered.

'That doesn't sound very positive,' were Miranda's first words. 'Are you some sort of investigator?'

'Never investigated anything other than my own curious interests. But I know the area a bit and Maarten called at a time that I'm looking for a little adventure.'

'A little adventure? Is that how you see this? A bit of a diversion from your ordinary life? A lot of poking around God knows where until you light upon my long-missing husband.'

Here she raised her eyebrows and gave a sardonic nod of her head, looking him straight in the eye until he blinked. 'Have you any idea what we're talking about? The meaning of the trip?'

'That's why I'm here,' van Hoorn replied. 'To find out. No, I don't know much. I only know that I've spent time where you need someone to go and that I made a number of friends there many years ago.'

'Many years ago? What made you go?'

'It was a lark. I was young, between jobs, so I just packed up and went. I traveled around on buses, boats, rickety railroads, every possible means. I was intrigued by the place and all its strange disjunctions. Anyway, it didn't take me very long to learn the language.'

Miranda quizzed him: Where had he lived? Where had he traveled? Did he like the food? How did he feel about the dustiness of interior life? Had he stayed in the small villages or gone to the crowded big cities? She was trying to decide if he was serious or just another man in flight, anxious to go more than halfway around the world to a place where everything was slow and people lived in 'rubber time', where the language existed only in the present tense, and great numbers of feasts and ceremonies threaded their way through the days and months of the year.

Pieter van Hoorn smiled and shrugged simultaneously. He told her about his forays between the islands. She could only imagine how he stood out among the natives with his pink face and white hair. He laughed – 'it was blond then' – and agreed. He was lucky. He hadn't gotten into any serious trouble, hadn't gotten dengue fever, had managed to talk himself out of more than a few dangerous situations. He didn't have any particular plan, just wandered from place to place, island to island, open to adventure.

'I stayed once in a small hotel on an island somewhere between Bali and Timor. It was relatively clean,' he told her, 'but when I woke up, about five in the morning, I found a lizard the size of a small monkey on my pillow. Its skin was silky green, iridescent, pocked with tiny leathery circles. I watched it flick its tongue so fast that no insect within striking distance was safe. I was terrified even though it didn't seem interested in me. I leapt out of bed and got dressed in a big hurry and left it to its own pleasures.'

'Where did you go?'

'I wandered into the main bungalow. In the dim light I could see a young girl with a baby perched on her hip and watched as she put it to her breast. I looked at the family photographs on the old wooden bureaus until someone came and offered me tea. There was no point in walking around the grounds since they consisted mostly of scrubby bushes, wild grasses, and dirt.' Maarten Welbroeck shifted in his chair. 'Yes, yes,' he said, urging Pieter to hurry it up.

'Anyway, it wasn't long before an overweight middle-aged man appeared, asking for me. I couldn't figure out how he knew I was there and he took his own sweet time telling me. He lit a cigarette slowly, blowing the smoke in my direction. He seemed to know a great deal about me – how long I had been traveling, where I came from, where I had sat on the rickety ferry that brought me to the island, what I had had to drink the night before, what I carried in my duffel bag. He never introduced himself, just grinned crookedly at me, exhibiting his gold teeth. Just let me know I'd been watched. Warned me that I should be careful.'

'Careful of what?' Miranda asked.

'Just what I wanted to know. "Mis-ter Pee-ter," he answered me, "I'm going to suggest that you leave here." I could see the girl who had rented me my room drying the same glass over and over. She had warned me about the poisonous snakes that hid in the grasses but had neglected to tell me about the danger-ous rivalry between the owners of the town's only two hotels. When I glimpsed the dagger wedged into the waistband at the back of his sarong, I guessed that her competition held the higher cards.'

'What did you do?'

'I didn't have much choice. I walked back to my room, collected the shirt and shorts that I'd washed and hung on the overhead fan to dry, threw them in my bag, and tossed it over my shoulder. The man was waiting for me. He offered to take me to the bus. I remember telling him not to trouble himself, although I certainly didn't know what I'd do next.

'He took care of that. "Mr. Pee-ter, what I think is that you charter my friend's car tomorrow. He will be your guide. He will show you this side of the island and take you to a nice beach where you can relax. Tonight you will stay at our hotel. Very pretty. Very good food." Want to guess what I did?'

'You went with him?'

'Right. I climbed into his rusty car. He deposited me with his cousin when we got to his hotel. It was beastly hot. The sun beat down upon the place and the heat was inescapable, even at night when I sat in the steamy air of the dining room with its rag-tag collection of rattan tables and chairs. Mosquitoes hovered and buzzed. The hotel owner's wife was hugely pregnant, but that didn't keep her from carrying a tray of glasses full of beer, local whiskey, and sweet orange drinks from table to table. She brought me my dinner, smiling through betel-nut-stained teeth at me.'

Welbroeck cleared his throat emphatically. 'Pieter . . .'

'Yes, all right, just let me finish this one story. The next day I went off for my trip around the island. The cousin was a terror behind the wheel. We'd be driving along at a horrific speed, whizzing by villages with goats grazing at the foot of cottages with tin roofs, ripping by people tending crops in the fields and we'd hit a pothole and *bam* – we were launched, all four wheels leaving the road.

'But I had to hand it to him. He took me to see things I'd never have found on my own. I saw a collection of monumental tombs and watched a group of village ikat weavers using plants like indigo leaf to dye and make the fabric I'd always admired. What really amazed me was when he took me to a burial ceremony in a poor village on a barren hill. The people were believers in the local religion, which required that they prepare their dead handsomely for the long trip to the invisible world beyond our own earthly one, sort of like the Egyptians with their pyramids. We saw them heap up piles of ikat and gold jewelry that would go with the dead into the tomb so they would be free to leave this life and reach the next. After that we saw the community burial ground. Old weathered stone columns and slabs with designs chiseled into them – a monkey on one, some sort of chimerical beast on another. I felt privileged to have seen them. Believe me, there wasn't another outsider there.'

In spite of herself, Miranda was impressed. 'How long ago was that?'

Pieter van Hoorn's caterpillar-thick eyebrows lifted as he calculated. 'Let's see.' He looked at Welbroeck as he calculated. 'I was twenty-four at the time and I'm fifty-six now, so that makes thirty-two years.' The lawyer nodded his head as if he had been doing the problem and had come up with the same answer.

'Thirty-two years? And you think that you'd be able to use what you know to find Anton?'

'Truthfully, I have no idea. I thought I'd rely on my curiosity and connections and any clues that you give me.' Pieter laughed.

Miranda stared. His self-confidence both intrigued and unnerved her. 'I'm curious why you have enough free time that you can volunteer for a trip that might take quite a long time. Don't you have a job?'

'Ah, Mrs. de Jong, you don't hold back, do you?' He did wonder to himself how she had got on in a culture that didn't countenance forthright questions and certainly never answered them with a direct negative. Circumlocution was so much kinder, leaving no one with hurt feelings or a sense of entrapment.

'Do you see these white hairs?' he asked in reply, gesturing at the top of his head, where the collection reminded her of a soft, old-fashioned hairbrush.

'You mean you're no longer working?'

'Right,' he answered, readying himself for the inevitable next question.

'So what was it that you did before your retirement?'

'Shipbuilding. Trade. Gin. The great Dutch triumvirate.'

Even she laughed. 'A perfect combination for tracking down Anton. So it won't be a problem if you're gone for a while?'

'Not at all. May I now turn the tables and ask you a few things?'

Mr. Welbroeck caught Miranda's quizzical glance. 'Perhaps' – he stepped in – 'perhaps Mrs. de Jong and I should have a brief conversation before we continue.'

'Of course. Why don't I wander off a while.'

Once he had gone, Welbroeck turned to Miranda. 'Impressive. Full of curiosity. Clever. Must have good connections. An excellent choice. Don't you think?'

'Who's paying his travel? His bills?'

'The estate, of course. Oh, do you mean, will this money come out of Diana's inheritance? In fact it will only confirm her status, her holdings. You may not like it, but it is a necessity.'

'What if he finds Anton, and Anton decides to come home? Where does that leave me?'

'A fair question, but one I have no way of answering. Until we find him, we know nothing. It's a voyage, an exploration into the unknown.'

'One for which you've chosen Mr. Pieter van Hoorn as our guide?'

'With your permission,' he answered, bowing very slightly in Miranda's direction, a pale smile on his lips.

'How did you settle upon him?' she wanted to know.

'I've known him for many years. I've always been impressed with his abilities. He was being extremely modest when he described what he did. Pieter van Hoorn has been an important leader in major companies, as was old Mr. van Hoorn, his father before him. Pieter plays an extremely good game of tennis and skis well enough to have been an alternate on a Swiss ski team when he was younger. He knows quite a bit about fine printing and has an important collection of the diaries and books of explorers. He's a man who loves risks and appreciates a challenge. If Anton is the needle in the proverbial haystack, Pieter will do everything he can to find him.'

'I don't understand. This man is a financial leader and he's willing to go off halfway around the world in pursuit of a man from whom nothing has been heard for more than five years? There's something you're not telling me. Does he owe you something?' Mr. Welbroeck stared at Miranda. He wasn't used to women who asked so many questions and spoke their minds so plainly.

'Owe me something? If anything we've come along at rather an opportune moment in his life. He's going through rather a bad spell. Something about his wife, I believe.'

'His wife?' Miranda interrupted.

'Yes. Zoe, very attractive. I think they're having a bit of difficulty. And I think he's fascinated by the opportunity of tracking someone down in a part of the world that had a special meaning for him once.'

And so Pieter van Hoorn took on the labor of finding the absent Anton. Miranda gave him a description of the small islands where they had lived in the beginning of their marriage. One was shaped like a turtle, another like an elongated finger, although she was vague about their precise locations. She had more information about their last inland home, the one from which Anton took longer and more dangerous voyages. She remembered the names of some of the people for whom she had cooked and gave a vivid description of the bar where Anton drank and the characters who hung out there. Diana reminded her of the forested preserve where the monkeys lived and reminded her that the name of the keeper of the place was Majine. Miranda told Pieter about the collection of sculptures Max Madoqua had installed at the museum in Rotterdam, but otherwise resisted his prying as best she could.

Pieter questioned Diana with great delicacy. He talked to Andreas about Anton's early life and unearthed information from people who had known Anton at the port. When Miranda handed him the strange letter Anton had left behind, he took one look and thought to himself, 'This doesn't look too difficult. The man's obviously gone native. We just have to figure out where.'

He asked Miranda to allow him to go through Anton's trunks. He had a hunch that they might hold more clues. 'You've never even peeked inside?' he asked in wonderment.

'Look, he left and never sent one word to any of us. What could be in there that would do anything but upset me? So, no, I never did.'

Pieter arranged to come to the house to take a look at the trunks. When he arrived he was astonished. 'My God, this house. I know this house. My parents used to come to parties here. They knew – let's see – they would have been Anton's grandparents. Wonderful, kind people. I was only here once or twice when I was quite young, but I remember this great entry hall. And wasn't there a painting there, over the chest? Yes, I'm sure there was. A beautiful still life. It had a glass of wine that glowed red like the Turkish rug that was somewhere else in the picture. Funny how well I remember it. It was full of food. I'm sure there were oysters and a lobster, a wedge of cheese – and what else? I'm not certain.'

Miranda was amazed. 'You remember all that now, how many years later?'

'It was certainly before the war that I was here. So many awful things happened in those years. Maybe they sold the painting. Or hid it. Or had someone smuggle it to safety somewhere. Wait – I remember the paperwhites.' Pieter closed his eyes, furrowed his forehead, and sniffed. 'Yes, there were dozens of vases of narcissus on the big leather trunk. Well, I see that the trunk's still here at least. It's a very fine piece, you know. It must be at least eighty years old. Not many steamer trunks of that vintage and workmanship are still around.'

Miranda listened as Pieter praised the fireplaces, the oak armoires and cupboards, the extravagant arches and scroll-work of the doorways, the delicacy of the leaded glass windows. His careful observation and deep knowledge made her slightly queasy about letting him see her changes in the room which was to be the new restaurant, but he merely nodded and said that the tempting smells floating through this remarkable house would certainly add to its attractions. She took him to the room with Anton's trunks. 'Since Diana's already been through these, do you think she'd like to come and help me?' he asked. 'A very good idea,' she said. 'I'll ask.'

When the girl appeared with Majine in her arms, she was amazed to see the monkey bare his teeth and hiss in Pieter's direction. 'Majine,' she said in astonishment as Pieter moved backward in a hurry. 'I've never seen him do that before,' she said, apologetically.

'I wonder why he dislikes me so much.'

'I don't know,' Diana fretted, stroking the monkey's fur and whispering to soothe him. She sat Majine on her lap facing her, and wrapped her arms around him as she explained to Pieter how to open the trunk. 'There are shirts on top, but underneath are other things that are probably more interesting to you. Stop – do you see that?' she asked, as Pieter pulled out what she thought of as her father's skirt. 'Do you know what it is?' 'It's a sarong. They are very common there. Men often wear them.' He continued until he found a dark sarong with an unusual pattern. He unfolded it carefully and found something inside. 'Did you see this before?' he asked, holding up a small red silk vest with intricate patterns embroidered in golden threads. She shook her head. 'It's so tiny. I wonder whose it is.' 'My guess it that it's something worn for an important ceremony,' said Pieter.

He worked his way methodically through the contents, and when he had removed most of them he noticed a tear in the lining of the trunk. 'Aha! Here, Diana, your fingers are smaller than mine. Can you get whatever's in there?' She gingerly extracted a small clump of crumbling papers and left it to Pieter to pry them open with extreme care. He tried to decipher the words that had not dissolved in the water. '. . . Oleena was with me . . . Oleena's long fingers . . . Oleena danced . . . Oleena hears the music too.'

Toward the bottom of the trunk he disinterred a simple kris with a serpentine blade. 'You know the note your father left, about dancing into a trance?' Diana nodded. 'This is the sort of knife he was talking about.' She took it from him and studied the carved handle carefully, turning it over to see both sides. She ran her thumb against the blade cautiously. 'It doesn't look sharp,' said Pieter, 'but be careful. It could fool you. And it's a bit rusty after sitting in the trunk all these years.'

He asked Diana's permission to look at her room. Majine was still suspicious, flaring his nostrils and sitting sullenly on his haunches, staring at Pieter. 'I don't mean to pry. I only want to see if there is anything of your grandmother's still there. On the other hand,' he said, by now quite unnerved by the monkey, 'I think I've seen enough. I have plenty to think about if I'm going out to find your father on one of 13,000 islands.'

CHAPTER EIGHT

L IKE ANTON, PIETER TRAVELED by ship. He fell into the
slow rhythms of the sea as into the embrace of a lover. He
let the steady motion cradle and carry him away from the knots
and tangles of his life. He knew that in accepting the challenge
of finding Anton, he was moving into a world whose mysteries
had once both enticed and frightened him.

When the boat finally docked in Jakarta, he left with regret,
walking slowly and tentatively out of its protective isolation.
The air was thick and still. Insects swarmed lazily in the
suffocating heat. As he neared the end of the long tongue of
the gangplank, he saw someone waving a straw hat and smiling
broadly. It took him a minute to recognize his old friend
Varaman pushing through the crowd, gold teeth gleaming
in the sun. The once thin man now had a belly that hung
over his belt, but he still clapped his hands with excitement
and chattered so excitedly that his words bumped into each
other.

'Pieter, Pieter, Pieter. I never thought to see you again. You
look good. So strong.' Varaman stared at his friend's small,
firm muscled body, his decisive jaw. 'White hair,' he giggled.
'Me too. Not so much though.' Pieter smiled wryly, hoping he
didn't show how unnerved he was by the acknowledgment of
how he had aged.

'Now we go to my house. So much has happened since you

left. I called some of your friends from before. They will come to eat with us after tomorrow. It is safe for you now. You can go on the streets, but be careful.'

As they drove into the city, Pieter was amazed by the noise and crowds. Buses emitting dark fumes, newsboys selling their papers at the crowded street intersections, and food vendors hawking fruits and local dishes, each calling out his specialty, trying to be heard over the cacophony of city noises. Since Pieter had gone, the spasms of war had forever changed the country. Vast numbers of people had been killed. The Japanese were gone. There weren't many Dutch people left. Evidence of the army was everywhere. Wherever Pieter looked he saw khaki-colored transport vehicles, soldiers, and huts and barracks flying what was now the red and white flag of an independent nation.

Pieter took some days to acclimate himself. He saw some old friends and slowly made inquiries about the islands, about people who might know about Anton. The sloe-eyed Dutchman had done his best to go unnoticed and unremarked and had succeeded, as far as Pieter could tell. Undiscouraged, he collected the information he thought he needed and after seeing the people he wanted to see, he set off.

Dear Maarten,

When I first read Anton's letter, I was quite certain he'd gone native. But when I went to several of the tiny spice islands, all I found were fragile walls of crumbling buildings fallen beneath a dense growth of ferns and riotous vegetation. On one island I saw a clove tree that was centuries old. It must have been growing when Shakespeare was writing his story of a magical island full of witches and monsters. And, of course, he had his Miranda too, didn't he?

I also visited several remote islands in the seas south of Ceylon, some so small they were really no more than atolls. I thought they might be where Anton and Miranda first lived, especially since it could have been very dangerous for a Dutchman to have been discovered in Indonesia then. I am making it a practice to search out the oldest people wherever I go, but thus far I haven't found anyone who recognizes my descriptions of Anton, Miranda, or their baby daughter.

Diana closed her eyes and imagined swimming to her father, swimming through the seas. Who else will tell her stories of the Indies? The voice rose and fell inside her, ready to rise and darken unexpectedly. Daddy, slow, sleepy-eyed Daddy who wove stories for her in his rich voice. Daddy, the man said, pulling her toward him, say Daddy.

Water was my mother, water was my father, and now my father's gone, like ink written on water, and I cannot find a trace of him.

Dear Maarten,

New islands, same results. So far I haven't found anyone with the names that Miranda gave me who remembers Anton. My descriptions didn't prompt anyone's memories, not even when I hinted that there might be a reward. I'm not giving up, though. Several of the islands are amazingly similar to what Miranda and even Diana described. On one, the sides of a dormant volcano are carpeted with lush forests of dark green ferns, mangoes, and tropical almond trees. Everyone in these particular Indonesian islands gets around in canoes carved of almond wood; I gather that such boats have served as transportation for merchants and traders for hundreds of years. Schools of fish swim in the sea; brilliant green parrots fill the air. Perhaps this is where it all began for Anton. At any rate, I stayed in a crumbling hotel and watched the sun set in an extraordinary violet light.

Daddy, I will swim to you and you will wrap me in your words and tell me tales of red winged birds singing to each other and of the kingfisher plunging into the sea, breaking through silvery waters and returning with a turquoise-scaled fish in its beak. You will watch the fish thrash and struggle until a golden ring falls from its mouth and the kingfisher will dive to retrieve it, dropping the fish, and the ring will become a beautiful woman and the kingfisher will capture her in its beak and fly toward the heat of the sun.

Oh, do not let the rays of the sun sear the bird or singe the woman. You will tell me that they are safe, that the great bird will rule over a kingdom like the island on which we lived, where rosy-fleshed fruit fell into our hands and deep purple berries stained our mouths and fingers when we ate them. They will found a dynasty in that warm-water empire, and I will swim to you and Mamma will return and we will be a family again.

Dear Maarten,

I'd forgotten how immense the spaces are between the many islands that make up this country. When I was here before, I traveled great distances but I was meandering then. Now that I'm on a quest, I'm driven, hardly the thing to be in a country where schedules barely exist and being on time is a highly relative concept.

My present lack of success has led me to give up on the tiny islands for the moment. I am now going on my way to the inland city where Miranda told me she took up cooking and Diana found her way into the grove of trees with its monkey colony. I'm also trying to find out where Anton might have bought some of the sculptures that are now so handsomely housed in Rotterdam. Have a date with a dealer in Yogyakarta next week.

Daddy, water carried you away and now it will carry me back to you. We lived at the water's edge on an island full of fruit trees and we ate what we picked and licked the juices off our fingers. Salt from the sea crusted on our tongues and on our toasted, suntanned bodies, and I watched you lick the salt from my mother's shoulders, from the small canyon at the base of her neck, and from under each arm. Your tongue was long and pink.

Dear Maarten,

A small victory. Although the art dealer in Yogyakarta never showed up – he went home to his island for an annual festival – his young associate took pity on me after two days and showed me a couple of binders with photographs of sculptures not unlike Anton's. He gave me the names and addresses of a few collectors.

Dear Maarten,

The first collector was quite taken aback when I arrived. The associate had evidently neglected to tell them of my existence. From what I can divine, the sculptures seem to have more to them than mere aesthetic attraction. I am quite certain that they are part of some complicated ritual. I got answers to some of my questions, but I have the definite impression that the owners were holding back and didn't want me to dig any deeper.

Water sang lullabies to me as I slept in a hammock slung between two trees. It lapped at my feet until the moon grew full and the tides pulled it onto the shore in great silvery waves. I threw myself into them and loved it when you scooped me up, saved me from the waves. You lifted me with straightened arms over your head and presented me to the sun. Your big paw-like hands held me, dripping, high above your head. 'Saved,' you would say in your deep voice, a voice as true as the silver needle of a compass pointing due north.

Dear Maarten,

I've found the second set of collectors. They were even less forthcoming than the first. I gave up asking about what the sculptures represented and focused on where they were carved. I told them I had been commissioned by a former resident to buy one and wondered if they could steer me to the island that they came from. I am now on my way to yet another island.

Later: Eureka – on a small scale. I have found the island and found a carver. Unfortunately his suspicious nature is making this slow going. I found one or two other sculptures through means I won't describe here and am beginning to understand they have to do with sexual practices that involve some sort of group ritual. A dark way to transcendence and ecstasy. I'm not sure what I expected after I saw Anton's collection, but it all seems shady now that I'm here. On the other hand, the next time you hear from me, I may be the proud owner of a fascinating piece of artwork.

Dear Maarten,

The sculptor asked me if I wanted to meet with a group of collectors this week. I thought I'd better agree. He showed me the beginnings of the piece he is making for me. I don't know how the piece will look when it's finished, but the carving is exceptional.

All the time that I've been here, the sculptor has assumed I want this piece for myself, even when I have insisted that I am merely the agent for a collector. I'm sure he thought that I was pretending because – well, you can imagine any number of reasons. Finally today, I saw the finished product. It is a glorious heron with great dark wings outstretched behind a beautiful woman with a neck as long and delicate as a swan's, immense breasts, and very elegantly carved sexual recesses. I told him how beautiful I think it is and he nodded. But when I described Anton as the real buyer, he looked dumbstruck. I'm certain that he knows Anton or at least knows of him, although he refused to say another word. Anyway, I get the strongest impression that I'm now uninvited to the group gathering and may not even be able to buy the sculpture. I've fallen in love with it and would be deeply disappointed to leave it behind. I have to admit to strong curiosity about how it will be used by the practitioners of the dark arts.

I gathered stones at the sea's edge and made a garden of them, set a mango in the center and watched its rosy flesh grow soft and softer, watched it decompose and rot. Watched the ants come to eat it and bear it away in tiny pieces, long twisted ropes of ants marching into the small circle of stones, breaching the barricade and carrying off the sweet ripe prize.

Dear Maarten,

I took a chance and told the sculptor that I had never personally met Anton, but had been sent to find and tell him that his mother had died. I don't think my explanation allayed his suspicions, so I told him there was a reward for the person who guided me to him. Of course I promised anonymity. He grunted noncommittally, but when I asked if he was acquainted with anyone who knows or knew Anton, he grudgingly gave me a name.

Dear Maarten,

No wonder no one wants to talk about Anton. My informant yesterday painted a rather dire picture of someone at the far edge. It's a long way from Miranda's initial description of a loving husband and father, but I'm now convinced that the more the family moved in those early days – perhaps due more to his being Dutch at a time when his countrymen were definitely unwanted there than to his being in trouble – the stranger he became. He may have been forced to become involved in transporting contraband by his need for money. Things have to be paid for even in paradise. I'm not sure if his heavy drinking preceded the illegal activity or was a consequence. Strangely, I think the sculpture collecting gave him peace for a while, although it surely turned at some point. I don't know if he's deranged, but I'm currently of the opinion that he's making his own perverse, maybe even perverted, use of symbols and taboos that have deep meanings in this culture.

Dear Maarten,

I'm now on an island much bigger than the ones I've been to previously, and it has trance dancers. Presumably they are the same or similar to those that Anton talked about in the letter he left for Miranda and Diana. I've learned that the temples here are a setting for what one man described as 'trance explosions'.

I wonder if the sculptures are what brought Anton here. I've come across a description of men dancing a warlike dance, lifting their knees in slow, advancing steps, like those of a heron. Like the heron in the sculpture I saw no more than a month ago. I am trying to find a way to see a ceremony. I'm preparing myself so I won't be too startled.

Dear Maarten,

I saw my first trance dancing ceremony yesterday. Sampih, the young man the hotel manager found to drive me around, has clearly been bored by my expeditions into the hills and was visibly relieved when I asked to see trance dancing. The look on his face told me that at last I'd found something he would enjoy doing. It was like nothing I had ever seen before. The men attacked the figure of a witch, a bloodthirsty widow with six-inch-long fingernails, hairy knuckles, and tusks (they are on a mask, of course). She *wears the entrails of her victims draped about her neck. The men lunged with daggers, but she overwhelmed them with her magic and forced them to turn their weapons on themselves. Some struggled against being disarmed, leaping and stabbing at their bare breasts and stomachs, and then fell to the ground in what looked like agony. About half of them collapsed into a trance; the rest looked as if they were having convulsive seizures. Later they were liberated by a dragon whose protection keeps the dagger blades from penetrating the men's bodies. Everyone seemed to know their parts and places, and once the men were revived they were carried into the temple for rituals that brought them back to their normal state.*

I can imagine how Anton must have been attracted by such extreme behavior. It fits right in with his collection of sculptures. He probably doesn't realize that the trance dancers are normally gentle people who are only drawn into violent seizures as part of rituals that are as carefully choreographed as dances. Did I neglect to mention that the role of the female witch is played by a man and the male dragon by a female?

Even when you left, you always came back. You always brought me presents when you returned from your voyages. A shell that captured the dark song of far seas, a dried sea horse curled like a parenthesis, nuts with hard shells that I cracked with my teeth, a tiny girl carved out of wood who still sits on my bureau. 'Your sister,' you said to me, 'your companion when I am gone.'

And gone you are.

I will swim to you, through waves and foam, through air and clouds.

I will find you.

Dear Maarten,

It would be hard to exaggerate the beauty of this island. Terraced rice fields with flooded paddies, waters washing down the hillsides, streams and rivers criss-crossing the green valleys, fertile volcanic earth offering up coconut groves, jacaranda and banyan trees with twisted roots reaching up out of the soil. The people here put on elegant shadow puppet dramas that tell all kinds of stories, including how the land was formed and settled. The gods live on top of the volcanoes, ordinary humans live between mountaintop and sea, and devils and terrible beasts live in the sea. Although people travel in boats and fish from boats, they do not swim in the waters for fear of being swallowed by the evil spirits. Funny, isn't it, that Anton, whose love of the sea took him far from his family and home, has come to a place where the sea is much to be feared.

Oh Daddy, far away Daddy, my Majine is sick and no one here can help him. I see you on the steps of a beautiful temple with three roofs, each pointed at the edges and accented with green and golden paint. Dancers perform before the door that leads inside. They motion with graceful hands and sway from side to side, lifting their bare feet from the soft dusty earth and flexing their toes. Men are there, healers who move their hands slowly in front of the faces of the old and sick.

It is for Majine that one of these healers must find a cure. I know you have the power to find out their secrets. Let them wave their hands before you, let the spirit of Majine shine through you. They can open the gate to being. Please, Daddy, I need help.

I see pinpoints of light appear as dancers whirl and stretch and bend their bodies. A small fine-boned woman stretches out her hands and she asks Majine to lie still so she can call the sickness out of him. Oh, she is beautiful. Her tiny upturned face looks toward you and you nod. I watch her hands rise and move like waves on the sea. They flutter upward, then move soft as smoke. I think I see them form the outline of Majine. Yes, there's his tail, a long swift swish of flesh and fur, and there are his eyes, so dull now, not the usual flash of fire and mischief. She wiggles her fingers in the air. She's smiling now, zig zagging her hands and turning around and around. Music like a river turned to sound pours down. I can hear it, it's for Majine, like silvery rain loosed from the sky for him.

Oh yes, you will find the cure. Only hurry. Majine's lying here and doesn't eat anything except cubes of mango from my hand. Let the cure come across the water as you have come across many waters. Heal Majine, let him live here in my arms, let him rise up to health, my sweetest, loveliest Majine.

Dear Maarten,

I'm sorry to have been out of touch for so long. I've been on the move much more than I had expected. Do you think it would please Diana to know that her father has chosen a place where monkeys run free and live in a sacred forest? I wonder if she knows the legends and sagas of the Ramayana – I must remember to bring her a copy. Hindus worship monkeys as the embodiment of Hanuman, the monkey god, who freed Sita, the beautiful wife of King Rama, after she had been abducted. While rescuing her, the monkey discovered the mango, a crime for which he was condemned to be burned at the stake. Fortunately he managed to put out the fire, although his hands, feet, and face were scorched, which is why all Hanuman monkeys have black feet, faces, and palms. I met Diana's monkey, a very unpleasant beast, but I can't remember what color his fur is.

Daddy, I am afraid for you. Do not give in to the cries of the birds that sing to you, yearning to have you for their own.

Do not let the men with dark handled daggers pull you with them into their darkness. Daddy, I will watch you. I will sing for your safety.

Dear Maarten,

I have something I must tell you. On the trip I made thirty-two years ago, I came to this same beautiful island and was entranced by the dances and the shadow puppet plays.

I fell in love with a beautiful dancer, a young woman with skin the color of polished teak. Her hands were long, and when she moved them they told entire stories. But it wasn't just her hands that enchanted me. The rhythms of the gamelan music, the brilliant green of her dress – she was as lithe and green as a grasshopper – the rice paddies brimming with water, oh my God, who could resist?

At first she was afraid of me. Each time she looked at me, she laughed behind the hand that delicately covered her mouth. I came every day to watch her and one day she answered a question that I asked. I began to bring her small presents – a green mango, a tiny green grasshopper formed of long wild grasses. Green things are good luck, she said. The girl's mother was alarmed and stayed as close to her daughter as she could. But I found times to speak to her when no one was around. Moon man, she called me after we came to know each other, and when I asked why, she confessed it was because my skin was so white and I came from so far away. It is from her that I learned so many of the things I tell you about now.

We fell in love. We would sneak away sometimes to be alone in the warm evening air. We talked with more than our hands. And then her father found me. He threatened me with his kris and told me to stay away from her.

Have I told you that a kris is a dagger? Don't get the idea that it is an ordinary knife. People here believe that

*their krisses have a magic power. I wish I could draw
you a picture of some that I have seen. They are quite
extraordinary looking with their serpentine or jagged sharp
blades made from leaf upon leaf of various metals, hilts
carved with intricate designs. I was terrified when I saw
her father's kris. I knew I could not stay and yet I could
not tell her. So I slipped away on a freighter. I left her.
Without even a note. It was a coward's way and I have
regretted it ever since.*

*I do not know what has become of her, but I vowed that
if my search for Anton took me to her island, I would try
to find her.*

Daddy, I am afraid for you. I see you in the shadow of immense
trees with roots that divide and twist in the soil. The white-hot
sun burns a hole in the sky. It is trying to penetrate the darkness
of the great trees, but you are whirling beneath them so fast
that it cannot find you. There are daggers that will pierce you. I
am afraid that you will submit, will fall to the earth and submit
to the demons inside. Then who will save you?

Dear Maarten,

*For the past few weeks I have been meandering around
meeting people, going to nearby cities, watching plays and
dance troupes, and breathing in the aromatic smells of
ginger and cardamom, coconut milk and spicy chilies.
Everywhere I go, I hear shimmering gamelan music.*

*I'm learning as much as I can about trance dances. I
have now been to six. I have seen some men who are
like shamans filled with the spirit of the gods, and I
have seen others who dance with their krisses drawn,
go into violent seizures, and attempt to stab themselves.
When they are overcome with the magic power, they fall
to the ground, trembling and twitching. I wouldn't want
Diana to know, but the up-and-down rhythm of the dances*

is amazingly like slow-motion copulation, complete with shrieking. How fascinated Anton must have been when he first saw the ritual.

Who wouldn't be fascinated? I have seen a trance dancer thrust his face over the smoke from a brazier and inhale deeply, then breathe out with force, expelling the god or demon inhabiting him. Afterward drops of water were sprinkled on his upturned face to bring him back to himself. I had the sense it was very hard for him to come back to this world from the one he'd just left. He looked dazed for a long time afterward.

I have heard in passing about a group of men and women not from this island who come here for the local religious ceremonies. They come to see the leaders entered by the gods and then go into a trance as singers in red and golden headdresses chant and hum. Women dance with puppets wearing fan-shaped headdresses. An orchestra plays. A blind man sings. Leaves are smoked over a brazier as offerings, their essence wafting upward. No wonder Anton was enchanted.

I too am much affected. Perhaps I wouldn't feel so moved were I not yearning for something to fill the hole left by Zoe's absence. Under the circumstances I know I should feel sympathy for the deserted Miranda, but instead I begin to understand why Anton could succumb to the charms of this place. The dancers here are so graceful, their movements so fluid, the stories they tell so rich with meaning. Even the spasms of violence that break out in these trance dances are charged with a significance that carries men across the slow rhythms of their daily lives.

Each night for the next ten nights Diana dreamed. Her dreams were like phosphorescent visions, silvery images on an inky background in which flickering forms gradually took color and shape, became people, animals, and places. It was only later that she saw those ten nights as dreaming herself into her father's core.

Dear Maarten,

The natives here talk about a dark and powerful man who is said to have risen from the sea. He is always with a beautiful woman whom they describe as an enchantress. The couple now live on a nearby island. Evidently some sort of scandal erupted that forced them into exile.

On the first night of dreaming she saw green sea turtles swimming onto moonlit beaches, laying their eggs in abundant sand. Before they could return to the waters, bronze-skinned men swooped down and killed the turtles, plunging finely honed knives into their tender underbellies, then roasted them in fires they lit at the palm-fringed shore.

Dear Maarten,

I am forced to wait to go to the island to see if Anton is really there. A boatload of people nearly drowned yesterday, so I will wait for calmer seas.

On the second night Diana dreamed of merchant ships and galleons, longboats, single-sailed square-rigged boats and out-rigger war canoes sliding silently into the harbor. A Dutch admiral with cold eyes and an unsmiling mouth stood on the deck of his ship and commanded sailors to pillage and destroy, to set fire to the houses, rape the women, and take the men hostage. When the village leader tried to escape, the admiral tied him to a stake and unchained two vicious mastiffs that leapt at him, sinking their teeth into his flesh. Whipping out a knife to cut the man free, the admiral watched him escape toward the sea, still pursued by the two frenzied dogs until, after a frantic struggle, he collapsed and sank slowly to the awaiting darkness at the bottom of the sea.

Dear Maarten,

When I saw a break in the weather, I paid a boatman an immense sum to take me to the island. Not long after we left, storm clouds appeared and enormous waves rose up, threatening to capsize us. The raindrops sounded like balls of sizzling mercury hitting the turbulent waters. They disappeared as swiftly as they came, although the sun remained hidden behind streaks of crimson sky. Now that I am here, I am surprised to find how large the island is. I haven't seen Anton or the woman yet, only small children sitting by the roadside eating melons and mangoes that have fallen from the trees.

On the third night Diana watched swarms of cockatoos and parrots with brilliant red and green feathers fill the air, crowding the blue skies with their plump bodies. White crocodiles floated lazily in the estuaries and jaguars roamed the mossy hills. Without warning dark-haired archers with squat bodies appeared and killed them all with well-aimed arrows. They hacked them apart, leaving the first slices as offerings, before plunging blood-steeped hands into the piles of meat. After they had feasted, the men fell into a deep sleep, while above them floated images of warriors in ceremonial collars made of dazzling bird plumage. Great cats moved in the air as delicately as butterflies and crocodiles swam in the skies feeding lazily on stars.

Dear Maarten,

I have stayed out of the way of the few European males I have seen here, watching and waiting to be certain that the man I have identified as Anton truly is he. Who else could it be? He has Anton's long, oval face, Anton's sleepy eyes with their drooping lids, and Anton's slightly bowed legs. He has the same thick brown hair that falls over his forehead – he could use a good haircut – and the same exaggerated gait of almost strutting from side to side that Miranda described. He looks like a giant next to the natives. Even though I know him only from photographs and descriptions, I am certain that I am right. I can even see a slight resemblance to his father, although his father's features were considerably finer.

Later: It has taken time but I have managed to befriend one of the men with him. It is Anton. He commands the loyalty of a small group of people who moved here with him. My informant, Ayak, told me that they had to leave their previous home after an outbreak of violence. 'What kind of violence?' I asked. He was evasive.

I have asked him to bring a message to Anton, telling him I want to speak with him, and am waiting for a reply.

On the fourth night she watched a volcano erupt in plumes of fire, sending boulders and flaming lava down the slopes, carving paths through the landscape that scarred the lush green cover. She watched women scoop up screaming children under the smoke-filled skies as the lava consumed houses, saw men dance out their fear as they fled toward the sea. One man stood frozen in a ritualistic pose, arms extended and bent at the elbow, fingers splayed and silhouetted as ash sifted over his scarified body.

Dear Maarten,

As I watch him from a distance, Anton looks like a chieftain surrounded by his loyal tribe. He wears a headdress made from dried animal skin that has been stretched as thin as parchment. It has been painted with the sun and moon, with constellations and streams of stars circling around his head. He does not walk, but strides in his peculiar gait, carrying himself like an anointed leader. He always leans upon a ceremonial stick carved with the head of a snake at the top. His followers live in a collection of thatched huts built around a courtyard, while he lives in a larger compound. Songbirds sing in cages hung from the eaves. Strange plants with thorns on both sides of each leaf grow nearby.

Although I have not yet had an answer to my request to speak to him, I have continued to learn about him from Ayak, his only follower who does not shun me. He tells me that the beautiful woman by his side is Oleena, whose name was in the note I found in the trunk. She is small and stands as still and straight as a tree. I am told that she is a spirit-medium practiced in the ancient rites of enticing evil spirits out of hiding.

On the fifth night, screeches filled the dark air. Colonies of monkeys swung from branch to branch. The seas boiled. A circle of diviners hovered over a smoking fire. Men began to dance, their feet beating tattoos in the dust of the now dry earth. They took out sharp daggers and scored their flesh. One man appeared more frenzied than the rest. He sliced parallel lines on his sunburned chest. Droplets of blood hung at the edge of the cuts.

Dear Maarten,

I have finally met Anton. I was taken in the early afternoon to his compound. He eyed me with extreme suspicion and asked why I had come, letting me understand that no good could come of my visit. At the end of each of my answers, he grunted, sounding rather like a feral pig, but otherwise his speaking voice was surprisingly soft, coming out of that large body.

He insisted on Oleena being present, although I do not know if she understood anything we said. She is tiny enough to be the wearer of the ceremonial red silk vest so carefully folded inside Anton's sarong in the trunk he left behind. She listens very attentively to Anton and watches him with unblinking blue eyes. Anton defers to her in his posture, although while I was with them, he sat on a bench and she stood beside him. He never offered me a seat.

I explained that I had come all this way at the behest of his family. He stared at me without any visible response. I'm afraid I was rather blunt when I told him that his mother had died. I could swear that the pupils of his eyes widened until they swallowed the entire iris, but still he didn't speak. Feeling foolish, I plunged on, mentioning the house and asking what he would like to do about it. When he finally spoke, his voice became deep, almost fierce, as he told me that he had left that life behind. He stretched out one arm, pointing his thick index finger at me, and if I had not backed away, he would have stabbed my chest with it. 'That Anton is dead,' he said. I reminded him that that Anton was still married to Miranda in the eyes of the law. 'She knows about my other women,' he said, his mellifluous voice so out of keeping with the message. 'She saw me with them. She saw Oleena. She knows I have left and am no longer married to her.' I suggested that Miranda might not quite see it that way. If he had left for good, he should allow her to divorce him. He fiddled with what I think of as his scepter. Would he sign a paper that agreed to let Miranda divorce him? He looked at Oleena. 'This is my wife,' he said.

On the sixth night the same man whirled under the strong midday sun, throwing back his head and opening wide his mouth as he cut a circle in the fleshy part of his left breast, crying out as he spun faster and faster until the vision overtook him.

Dear Maarten,

I gave Anton both of the agreements you asked me to bring. At first he refused to discuss them because they no longer applied to the life he had chosen. I suggested that I might have to send an officer of the law to bring the matter to a close, although of course it was an empty threat. No one here would have the slightest interest in his family matters. Yet it worked. He looked as alarmed as a man with sleepy eyes and a naturally expressionless face could look, and his shoulders sank into his body. He signed the paper that terminated all his rights, now and in the future, to any property that had been in his family. When I asked him to sign the paper allowing Miranda the right to a divorce, he signed that too. What about Diana? I was amazed to hear myself ask. 'Will you write her a letter so that she may at least have something from you?' 'Yes,' he said, slightly shamed (perhaps this is my imagination). 'You can come for it in two days.'

On the seventh night, the sun glinted strongly off the sand. The mica particles blinded him, inviting him to enter a tunnel reamed out of his own flesh. He threw himself into the sea, opened his mouth to slake his thirst, and was washed in the salty waters that entered the wounds. Stretching out his hands he sang out a lamentation that arose from deep inside him.

Dear Maarten,

I went back to see Anton. Before I could tell him about your letter, he handed me his own addressed to Diana. I read it on the spot. I know it's not up to me to censor her mail but it had hints at practices I can hardly describe: sexual rites, blood sacrifices, a calling out of evil spirits.

If you think that my reluctance to show Anton's letter to Diana comes from some sort of prudishness on my part, I'd like you to judge for yourself. Anton has told me of a variety of rituals in which he and his group of devoted followers participate. In one a priest bites the edge of a brazier of hot coals, letting the red glow cast his cheekbones in relief so that he looks like a death head. That, he assured me, sends the girls and women writhing in a frenzy, pitching themselves onto the ground.

And what do you make of a ritual in which he and the group watched a priest bite off the head of a live chicken and let the blood pour into his mouth as his body thrashed, thighs pumping in spasmodic rhythms. Anton described it as one way of demonstrating that the person is possessed by a demon. Having seen Anton's sculptures, I have a fair idea of the kinds of demons he's talking about, but does Diana really need to make these connections?

He wants Diana to know that he and his followers are seeking transcendence. And I believe that they are, although their way of finding bliss is frightening to me. Anton told me that his body is the sacred channel to transcendence. What he actually said is he 'is giving his being to forces that are ravishing him, taking possession of him.' He reached out, at that moment, to stroke the body of the woman named Oleena. As desperate as Diana may be for any word of Anton, no girl wants to know such things about her father.

I did get your letter about the girl's monkey. I remember her immense attachment to the little beast – did I tell you he tried to attack me when I was with her? Even so, I can imagine her distress must be extreme. I asked Anton if he knew someone who might have a cure. He immediately spoke to Oleena and then told me of a monkey preserve not far from here. I have spoken to the keeper of the colony and he has given me a huge collection of healing herbs that he promises will save the monkey. I will send them immediately.

Although I now have Anton's signed papers in hand, I'm not quite ready to leave yet. My current plan is to stay and find out more about Anton and his life here. I am hopeful that I can convince him to write Diana a different letter.

On the eighth night, she watched him throw himself to the ground and roll in the dirt, saw water thrown over his body so that mud seeped into his wounds and infected them until they oozed.

Dear Maarten,

You are no doubt wondering why I am staying. Of course I feel I must know more about Anton, but I'm also here because I once vowed that I would try to find my dancer if this search ever took me to her island. Unfortunately, the only thing I have been able to learn is that she was sent away by her family not long after I left, all those years ago.

One very old man remembered that she was 'in trouble.' I don't know if that means that she had crossed an irrevocable barrier in her family's eyes by being with me. I am terrified it might mean she was with child. Listen to me, a grown man talking in circles. Could she have been pregnant? Here I have come halfway around the world to berate Anton and make him face up to his responsibilities and now I am afraid I may have behaved even worse than he.

On the ninth night, she saw him lie on the ground. He felt the lash of a whip but nothing could force him to cry out. He remained still while his mind moved slowly away.

Dear Maarten,

I hardly know where to begin. Fortunately I have kept a diary which helps me remember what I have seen.

Even though Anton has not forced me to leave, he has not included me in his group's rituals. I have been allowed to go to the trance dances and the larger community rituals, to share meals with them and be with them in the ordinary moments of the day, but otherwise I have been purposefully excluded. I guessed that their rituals involved sexual practices, but I had no idea what they could be.

I had a clue when I saw a stripe of broken flesh on Oleena's back one day. This beautiful, finely wrought woman, so graceful and delicate, had been marked by a shocking act of violence. I should have realized the second clue when I walked in on two men weaving reeds into what I took be a cage. It was large enough to trap a sizeable struggling fish and was closed tightly with a complicated interweaving of reeds and stones scooped out of the waters of the sea. When I asked what the cage was for, I didn't get an answer.

The next night I watched the men gather in a hut used for ceremonial practices. I heard the percussive beat of a drum, the silvery sounds of the gamelan calling forth the women, of whom there are only five, including Oleena. I could hear Anton instructing them in some sort of wild dance, then later Oleena's voice calling out to evil spirits. 'Come to me,' she said, in a voice that threaded itself around the bodies in that room. 'Come to me from the crevices of all our beings and dance on my fingers, fly out of darkness into the light, to my eyelids, my lashes, the whorls of my ears.' That's when I crept closer and spied a small slit in the thatch of the hut. By squinting I managed to watch as Anton took one end of the long cloth in which Oleena was wrapped. He whirled her around and around and the cloth unspooled from her body. At the end, she stood bare except for a tiny thong of cloth where her legs joined her body. It was then that I saw that lashings had striped her skin. She fell to the floor and instantly two men fell next to her. They pressed in close, one holding her from behind, the other facing her and entwining his legs in hers, and together they immobilized the tiny woman. The three began to undulate as if they were swimming on the bare earthen floor, pumping in unison, Oleena trapped between the men. All the time the remaining group sang a dark atonal melody and the look on Oleena's face remained serene. She had given up her being to the men and was letting them take her where they chose.

Then Anton brought in the cage. I could only make out a bit of what he did, but I saw him clamp it on Oleena's head. She had to stretch her long slender neck to gasp for air. She sang out an incantation and then arched her back, her pelvis thrust forward, while the two men kept swimming, swimming with her on the floor of dark clods. I watched a long shudder ride up her body as noises loud and dark came from inside her.

Her sounds loosed wildness in the other people and they too threw off their clothes and thrashed and indulged in I know not what. Once I saw Anton release Oleena from her cage, I crept away. I could not sleep at all that night.

The same ceremony was repeated for the next four nights. Each time Oleena called forth the evil spirits with the same incantations and each time a different woman fell to the ground surrounded by two new men who wrapped themselves around her limbs and constrained her movements. Oleena leaned against Anton, who slid his arms over her shoulders and down her body as unearthly sounds flowed from deep inside it. Each night he continued to stroke her and she to shudder convulsively, but never again did she fall to the floor or remove the golden-edged cloth that wrapped her beautiful body.

On the sixth night the group performed some sort of ritual at the edge of the sea. The men were clearly afraid of the water and huddled far from it. It took Anton a long time and much cajoling to convince them to follow him to the water's edge. They hesitated, torn between following their leader and intense fear. Slowly he convinced them to wade in up to their calves. An hour must have passed as he got them to let the waters rise to their knees. Then they would *go no further. Not even Anton's seductive voice could talk them deeper into the frightful sea.*

The women cowered and cried. Oleena gathered them into a circle and spoke quietly to each one, stroking shoulders, using her index finger to gently wipe away the tears of terror that fell down their cheeks. She sang a silvery song that wrapped around the stars and enfolded them until finally she lured them to the water's edge. They began to sob anew, so unnerving the men that Anton had to speak to each of them, men and women both, had to enclose the face of each within those large hands, and let his honeyed words pour over their bodies and momentarily dissolve their resistance. They sobbed but did not retreat. They finally allowed him to fill his hands with water and let it sluice down their bodies. I went to sleep that night with a deep sense of foreboding.

On the tenth night she saw a dark room. She saw him pick up a whip and let it slash across the flesh of a woman.

Dear Maarten,

The events of the last days have been so shocking that my hand shakes when I try to write. As I tell you what happened I hope my nerves do not give way.

On the seventh evening, I had already returned to my hidden post to watch the ceremony begin, as all the ones before had begun, with Oleena's silvery voice calling on the evil spirits to swirl about them. Her voice was as low and seductive as if she were speaking to a lover, which in some sense she was, since she invited the spirits into the most intimate recesses of her body.

Next Anton told each of the men to stand before him. From them he chose Surandi, the largest of his followers, to participate in the ceremony about to follow. Although a great honor had been done to him, the man Surandi protested loudly and tried to flee, but Anton's great hands clamped down on him so quickly that he had no hope of escaping.

Now two men brought forth more cages, some large and some small, and laid them on the floor of the hut. Anton stood and spun the man Surandi around so quickly that his sarong was soon a long piece of dark cloth lying on the earth. Next Oleena presented herself and allowed him to spin her too until nothing remained to hide the beauty of her smooth, delicately boned body. Then Anton turned to all the remaining followers and told them to grab the ends of his sarong. Soon he too was without fabric to cover him. And now they laid their hands, one after another, on each other's bodies and invited the rest of the group to do the same. Hands touched faces, mouths, shoulders, breasts, stomachs, touched penises and the inner curve of thighs. The followers sang a song to their bodies and to the spirits swirling around them, and then the hut came alive with writhing bodies until Anton stood up, his member huge and stiff, and commanded them to pick up the cages and follow him to the edge of the sea. They moved away from one another in a kind of slow motion release.

I crept behind, finding cover wherever I could. I watched as the group members fastened the cages about the men and Oleena, carefully setting one cage around each leg, two more around the arms, one around the trunk, and finally the last encircling the head. The man Surandi yelled that he could not swim, that the demons of the deep would rise up and pull him down. Anton growled and swatted him.

The ceremony began. Oleena sang in a haunting voice that called upon the stars in the sky to light a shimmering path in the calm waters of the sea. Then she walked into the water with Anton. The two lay down and floated effortlessly as the water caressed their bodies. Surandi was screaming with terror but the men picked him up and tossed him on one side of Oleena. He reached out blindly as Oleena slithered toward him like a fish, slid her arms around the cage encompassing the cold flesh of his chest, and then she reached back with her legs and wrapped them around Anton.

She was singing softly, she was open to the warm waters in which they floated, and she put her lips next to Surandi's ear to lull him to release. But he was too afraid. He began to thrash just as Anton was giving in to the thrill of the warmth enfolding them, just as the feelings were rising up inside him. Oleena continued to stroke Surandi, her hands wrapped over the bits of flesh that lay open to her. He began to float almost weightlessly, carried to the surface by Oleena's touch and by the swollen reeds of their cages.

Then, without warning, she moved just enough to frighten him and he jerked his head away. She continued stroking him, unaware that his chin had wedged against the cage, jamming his throat so he could not speak. His struggles excited her. Her legs reached forcefully for his body and she drew closer, arching blindly for him, her slippery fingers reaching through the tiny openings in the cages as the sea washed over his mouth and nose.

Anton was bobbing upon the water, wriggling like a snake, and he moved over to where Oleena and Surandi rolled in the water. Those two rolled over once and twice and then in a single motion Oleena pushed her tiny body to slide atop Surandi. Unbalanced, the man crashed against Anton, thrashing blindly. Throwing one leg over Anton's body, he climbed on top of him and grabbed the cage around his face and shook and shook it. He shook it so hard that he thrust it against Anton's throat. And then huge waves were rising up around him and surging over Anton's body, as Anton tried to spin free, but Surandi hung on as if he were riding a demon who was his only wedge between death and the sea. He gripped that cage and pulled it toward him, and he stayed there, he did not let go. Anton looked like a huge serpent caught in the waves, arching his back to thrust upward, seeking the man or Oleena, seeking the warm, receptive flesh he expected to encounter, and when he did not find it, he opened his eyes in confusion. Furious in his frustration, he reached out and grabbed Surandi, who tumbled forward, pressing Anton's head down into the waiting waters. The two men struggled fearfully.

Oleena let out a shriek unlike any I have ever heard. I had left my hiding place to stand with the others who were waiting on the shore, too afraid to enter the water, but by that time it was too late. I could see the fear frozen on Anton's face as it submerged under rippling sheets of water.

Anton's body had pitched downward into the blackness of the water. It bobbed with the waves until his weight pulled him down and he sank slowly in the black sea with its narrow path of moon light.

His followers stood motionless on the shore. They knew the spirits were swirling around them and then unexpectedly they fell upon the sands and upon each other's bodies, swinging their limbs and rolling over and above and into each other, merging in ecstasy. Like fish riding ashore on the lacy crest of a wave, they were sensitive to the rhythm of the tides and knew the time had come for a single instance of spasm and explosive release. The air was filled with moans and cries as the percussive force claimed their bodies and they found their way to the far lands that Anton had always spoken of. They had come to that place. And then they lay there, unwilling to move. Stroking death.

Dear Maarten,

Oleena and I are the only survivors. The natives who remained were disoriented and bereft. They clung tightly to each other but soon they seemed like the limbs of a body *whose heart had stopped beating. Once they saw their leader drowned, they fled as quickly as they could find boats to carry them away.*

And that leaves Oleena. The only way I can think to help her is to take her away from this island and stay with her until she is strong enough to return to life. For now she is neither wife nor widow, parent or child. She is a discard, a toy the world has tossed upon the seas to see if it can float. Her past is gone, her future dark and formless. How will she make a place within herself to rest and repair the damage?

Oleena has told me some of her story. She was born to a disgraced mother who was sent off to relatives in a distant town on the tip of the island of Sumatra to await her birth. When Oleena was born, she was given a second name that translates roughly to Fallen Moon. Oleena Fallen Moon, daughter of an unknown European who ran away and a woman who gave away her future by giving in to him.

It was the girl's fate to be deeply and mysteriously in touch with forces of darkness. By the time she was eight, whole colonies of butterflies collected around her face, a moving mask of fluttering yellow wings with a circle of black at each tip. People came to her with their dreams, and she saw meaning in them, could speak about the future. Once she warned that a nearby town would be buried in lava from a quiescent volcano and those who trusted her vision were spared. Her reputation grew. She became known as the girl who saw into darkness and could cast it away with imprecations and wild movements. The village elders called her to become a priestess in temple ceremonies. People arrived to hear her sing in rich deep notes. She called evil spirits to her, gave them a home inside her so she could know and cast them out. More and more villagers entrusted her with their secrets.

And then one day a man came by sea. He too saw darkness and he too was fascinated by exorcism. But he needed to plunge into darkness, to dip hand and foot and heart and tongue into roiling seas and use the darkness as his way to transcendence. He slid into her spirit and hijacked it for his own, slid into her body and brought it to a pitch she had never known. She meant to cast out darkness but Anton – yes, it was he – invited it in.

She could neither resist nor tame him. She became his familiar, the wife of his spirit. In doing so, she left her mother and her home, and she gradually lost her gift for prophecy as she gave herself up to him.

They slowly collected men and women who were enchanted by the promise of transcendence that Anton held out to them. These followers renounced mothers and fathers, husbands and wives, for they had joined a voyage to ecstasy that bound them ever more closely together as they left the familiar behind. Anton made rules that he insisted they follow. He rewarded them with special private moments with him when they did what he desired, and punished them with banishment when they did not. Those who most displeased him were sent to The Darkness, a special room he had hollowed out of the earth where there was neither light nor fresh air.

He loved them all, he said, loved every man and woman, loved their spirits and their bodies and together they would make their way to glory. When Anton became enraged, the people were afraid, but Oleena could move him. She would take him into their bungalow and her song and her body could bring him back from fury. Then the group slowly returned to the closeness of family and they stood together against the uncomprehending outside world. They had been forced to flee from island to island several times as word of their strange practices got out, until they finally came to rest on the small island where everything I described to you happened.

I understand that you might wonder why I stay with

her. It is simple: she is the daughter Zoe and I might have
had. Oh God, Maarten, I am haunted by the horror of her
life with Anton, by unbidden images of the unspeakable
acts I witnessed. Imagine that I, a rational, successful
businessman, have come to this! I will turn my mind to
other thoughts, but I cannot turn away from her. I only
know that I will stay here until Oleena has found her gift
again or until calm and meaning have returned to her. For
now I am all she has.

But I haven't lost my sense of purpose. A courier leaves
tomorrow with the letters of agreement that Anton signed,
so all legal matters have been concluded. You know his fate
and now Miranda and Diana will know it as well. I deeply
regret not getting him to write a second letter to Diana to
replace the first with its references to black magic and blood
sacrifices. You may not agree with me, but I do not feel
right about its being in her possession, especially now that
Anton is dead. His description of the life he was living was
misleading, to say the least. I've made the decision to hold
that letter back. It will not be in the packet you receive.

Dear Maarten,

I've moved back to the little hotel where I was staying
before I sailed off to the island to find Anton and his
followers. I was afraid that it would be hard to find a
place here for Oleena, that she would be tainted in the
villagers' minds by her connection to Anton, but I've found
a kind family who understand her situation to some extent.
She is living in their house.

I travel around on a bicycle, wandering through nearby
villages. I watch men dig canals for water to fill the terraces
they have created for rice. Vendors come by with crabs and
lobsters hidden in baskets under moistened palm leaves.
Gongs ring. Banners hang upon the houses, fluttering in
the infrequent breezes. It is a quiet life. I have made the

acquaintance of the village elders. They tell me that Oleena will know when she has been accepted by the members of the village because they will come singly, in twos, and threes and each will lay a single scarlet hibiscus upon the porch of the cottage in which she lives. She will know then that she has a home and I will feel that I have done what my heart tells me is right.

I'm as surprised about all of this as you must be. Please send on any news of Zoe as you receive it.

Dear Maarten,

The more I am with Oleena, the more she tells me about her life with Anton. It is an appalling story. The kris that carved the patterns on both their bodies was his. The brazier over whose flames they inhaled the smells of burning leaves that eased them to a further shore was his. The beatings she gave in to were his. The merging of men and women upon the dry earth was a ritual of his devising. It was his hands, his legs, and his tongue that caressed every person, making them his for the claiming.

Did no one realize that they were profaning sacred rituals? That once it had begun, there was no turning back? Surely the natives who had chosen to follow Anton knew that the ceremonies they were imitating were used as protection for the village. They knew that guardians from the village always stood by during the ceremony as those in a trance made their dramatic contact with the spiritual world. And certainly they knew that no one ever let an entranced person get out of hand. To Oleena none of that mattered. Anton was the center of her life, and where he led she followed.

'You never saw the sacrifice of great green turtles trapped in nets and pulled to shore,' she told me. 'You never saw the huge creatures flipped over on their backs, held by two people while another plunged a knife into the softness of an exposed belly. *You never saw Anton try to talk the men and women into wading into the blood and water that washed up in the wake of one of these rituals. We were to be dipped into the seas, washing in what he called 'the fluids of life' so we would be permanently bound together.'*

When I asked if she'd actually walked into the water, she said no. *The members of the group were convinced that beasts and demons would rise up and grab them if they put a foot in the sea and they resisted Anton fiercely. That, ironically, is why Anton taught them to swim like serpents in the dirt of dry land. He loved the water and believed in it with a desperate fervor. He was determined to get his group beyond their fears so he could involve them in the ultimate ritual.*

I will continue in Oleena's words, as closely as I can. *I actually took notes as a way of remembering and also as a way to have a focus so I would not be over-whelmed.*

'In swimming on the dry earth, we were merging with one another, but Anton was determined to have the ritual happen in the sea. There we would enter into the bliss of transcendence.

'It took more than a year before I finally dared to face the sea and I only did it then because I had already given my being to Anton. I had trusted him with everything. He was very gentle. He literally cradled me in his arms as he walked into the water. It barely touched me at first. I felt as if I were a child being bathed. He reminded me in his half-singing, half-chanting voice how water nourishes the rice fields, how it sustains the crabs, how it washes over the roots of the coconut and mango trees. "Water is life," he kept repeating to me, "water is life." And then, "We will mingle our lives in the water and in it be taken to the embrace of paradise." Slowly, slowly he let the water lap at my body. His strength comforted me. I was not afraid because his powerful arms held me tightly. He sang to me. I loved his voice. It wound itself into me. That is how I learned to accept the water.'

As you can imagine, I was unnerved by her story. She accepted the water and then was betrayed by it. I can only tell you how far over my head I feel when I hear her talk like this.

I did the only thing I could think of. I asked how to find her mother. I wanted to bring her here, but Oleena says that her mother died shortly after she left with Anton. And her father? She doesn't know who he is, where he is, or even whether he is dead or alive. She does know an old family story about him. Her grandfather had been badly cheated by a Dutchman and as a consequence he nourished a hatred for all Dutch people. When he found out that his daughter was having a romance with one of 'the enemy', he went after the young man with a kris. He told the girl that she shouldn't ever expect to see him again. You can imagine how enraged he was when he discovered the girl was pregnant. He sent her to relatives far away from their island, which is how Oleena was born on Sumatra. She has always thought that her gifts were compensation from the gods for the sadness she has had to bear.

While she was talking, I looked at Oleena and thought I recognized the shape of my mother's high cheekbones and my own tapering fingers. In my blackest moments I wonder if in trying to track down my dancer, I've found my own daughter instead. No, that's not possible. I am afraid that I have become so enmeshed in the convolutions of Anton's life that I have mixed them in with my own search. Perhaps I'm addled by the tropical heat, the smell of sandalwood, the golden-skinned women, scarlet flowers, and the slowness of time. Personally, I have never felt so inadequate.

Dear Maarten,

Oleena has an admirer. A beautiful little girl who can't be more than nine comes every day and leaves tiny mementos for her: a handful of frangipani blossoms, a small stone, an iridescent bird feather.

The little girl's name is Jaiya. She is one of the young dancers who perform at temple ceremonies. Her big black eyes are serious; her mouth barely moves in the curve of a smile.

She is slowly coaxing Oleena out into the world. Every day now she dances below her window. She motions with the flutter of a finger, the flash of a gold and red fan, the dip of her body as she bends backward toward the earth, hands extended with fingers open and upstretched like the Buddha's palm. She tells me that she wants to dance for Oleena. I asked her why.

'I don't know,' she said. 'I just know that she can help me.'

A week ago the girl was waiting in her usual place when Oleena appeared. They nodded at each other. Jaiya sat next to her but didn't say a word. The same scene was repeated for three days until Jaiya whispered to her, 'I know that you can help me with my dance.'

Oleena looked puzzled. 'I don't know anything about dancing. My mother was a dancer,' she said to Jaiya. 'Here, on this island, long long ago. She stopped dancing when I was born and never danced again as far as I know.'

'Maybe it is time for you to dance, then.'

'I don't know the steps.'

'I will show you,' Jaiya said. We watched her slide slowly from one supple pose to another, dipping and bending and splaying her fingers as she turned them upward. It was the first time I had seen Oleena's face relax, seen light come from within.

Now the girl comes every afternoon. They sit in Oleena's small room underneath a fan that revolves slowly, moving the hot heavy air in indolent circles, and they come outside to dance in the dusty earth. I no longer know who is the teacher and who the pupil. The girl, as nimble as a cricket, shows Oleena how to move. 'Do not be afraid,' she told Oleena, 'to let your body guide you to the dance.'

'It is your beautiful dance that is holding me to this dusty earth, my little bird. Do not expect more of me.'

'I don't expect more. Just watch me. Dancing is a form of magic. People say that you are a seer.'

'Was,' Oleena corrected her.

To see Oleena and Jaiya together is very moving. It's almost as if each had been waiting for the other. Jaiya's mother is very sick. For a while the girl was looking after the four younger children in the family, but she began to sink under the weight of her sadness. Various aunts and cousins have taken on their care, but Jaiya's mother is now so weak that she can no longer leave her bed.

I have heard that some people here are afraid of Oleena, even though she is so gentle with the girl. They say she is a sorceress who knows about black magic. Rumors about Anton's bizarre death and the flight of the group have been circulating, although in a garbled form.

Oleena scoffs at the talk. She says that the only things that possess her now are shame and loss. She is so ashamed of her perversion of the ecstatic moments that she refuses to go into a trance. She will barely dance with Jaiya for fear that her body will lead her to a bridge to the beyond. Besides, she and Jaiya are busily plotting to find a way to grant the girl's deepest wish – that she dance the part of Hanuman, the white monkey. Of course, that's quite impossible. She's too young and anyway, I'm certain that girls are not allowed to dance the monkey. That doesn't seem to be stopping either of them. Jaiya's father has been brought into the plot and I gather he is carving a particularly charming mask of the monkey hero. The girl practices leaps and steps and has even fashioned a tail out of bamboo.

Jaiya's mother lies near death. The girl dances harder every day. She has told Oleena that she must dance the monkey before her mother is carried to the next world. Everyone in the village knows about Jaiya's wish. They are waiting to see what will happen in the performance that will take place within the week.

Meanwhile, I am fascinated by Jaiya and Oleena, by the movement of their bodies that are as supple as the jaguars known to roam the mossy green hills. The girl and the woman dance the story of a world where gods dwell in volcanoes and fanged demons live in the sea, ready to destroy anyone who enters their territory. I remember hearing that 'the melancholy of the East' drove many Dutch soldiers to sickness and suicide. Personally I wonder what effect an enraptured fascination can have.

Oleena accepts my friendship with an almost supernal calm. I have fallen into a kind of quiet peacefulness here. Oleena, however, tells me she scents change. Men are massing in the hills. They blame foreigners for many things that have gone wrong, including a tidal wave last year that rose up without warning, drowning people in their villages and sweeping away their homes. They say that the demons living in the sea will not cease their attacks until the island is cleansed of all the foreigners here. I am beginning to fear for my safety.

Dear Maarten,

The night of the performance the entire village assembled in the open square. Jaiya's sisters and brothers squirmed on the laps of their father and various relatives. Even the family who have allowed Oleena to live with them took care of the littlest one when she got fidgety. As darkness fell, we heard music shimmering like a thousand silver needles. Then from behind the screen appeared shadows of trees in *the forest where Prince Rama had been living peacefully in exile with his brother and his beloved wife, Sita, for thirteen years. Suddenly the ogre-king, a gross and evil giant named Rawana, shatters their tranquillity. He is so captivated by Sita's beauty that he is determined to kidnap her. He is a master of ruses and deceit who changes shape several times until he finally finds a way to persuade Sita to let down her guard. And so he succeeds in swooping down and taking her to his home faraway. Everyone knows the story, even the small children, so there is no suspense and they are not afraid, not really, but even so, the audience groaned when Rawana appeared. They know he will do anything to keep the delicate and beautiful Sita for himself. All these actions take place through the movement of lacy shadow puppets cast upon the white screen.*

I could feel my stomach knotting up as the story moved inexorably toward the time when Rama enlists the help of an army of monkeys. And then, there they were, a phalanx of them, shooting so many arrows that they could not see one another anymore. Enchanting as they were, I could hardly concentrate for wondering whether we would see Jaiya. Although she was determined to be the white monkey and to perform behind the screen, dancers do not do such a thing. Certainly not in this town.

Oleena was sitting quietly beside me, her hands folded in her lap, her head tipped slightly to one side. A ripple of drums. Oleena sat up straighter. Pounce and leap: the white monkey, the great rescuer Hanuman, leapt forward, his presence announced by the shadow of a mask with protruding snout, a long curling tail, the flutter of paws. Oleena let out a sigh of surprise, then clapped her hand over her mouth. The monkey was a whirlwind of energy intent on making the forces of earth bow before the desires of Prince Rama. Leaping, he scaled the highest mountain. When he was unable to pluck from it the herbs that would waken Sita from her deep sleep, he grabbed and twisted the entire mountain from its base. I watched those graceful wrigglings and slidings and boundings and realized that it was Jaiya pantomiming the monkey's great jump across the ocean to Rawana's island. A rumble of applause came when the great white monkey reached the purloined woman. An excited murmur to see her released from her captivity and then a cheer to watch the monkey general, the hero, the wild and playful hero, scoop her up and carry her above the swirling waters that lay at the feet of the great mountain and bring her home at last.

All everyone talked about for the rest of the night was Jaiya's triumphant portrayal of the monkey king. They were thrilled by her performance and astonished at her audacity. Jaiya was still trembling when she slid out from behind the screen. She was instantly surrounded by children and neighbors, until Oleena moved forward and took the girl's face in her hands, speaking so softly that only Jaiya could hear. I do not know what she said, but the effect was electrifying. The girl's face lit up and she leapt, monkey-like, and threw her arms around Oleena. Then her father came and enfolded her in his brawny arms, hugged her and rocked her from side to side. All the brothers and sisters jumped up to reach her face, to kiss her, to have her scoop them up in her arms.

Oleena, who had left the house where she has been staying for the first time in all these weeks, walked home with me. She was more excited than I had ever seen her, thrilled by Jaiya's performance and by the village's acknowledgment and acceptance of the girl.

Two days later, Jaiya's mother slipped into a coma. Began her movement toward the next world, as they say here, with Jaiya sitting by her, holding her hand and speaking to her in a comforting voice.

Oleena has told me again that I must leave, that I am

in great danger of being trapped in the coming upheaval. I have packed my suitcases. I asked her for something that had been Anton's that I could take back to Diana. I worry greatly how the girl will cope with the news of her father's death.

Late yesterday afternoon, I went to say goodbye to the village elders, and as I was leaving, they invited me to join them outside. We walked together and as we proceeded, I watched men come in from the rice fields and women from the dye baths where they were making patterns for batik, saw children draw away from their games and fall into a slow irregular procession. It was then that I realized that each one of them was holding a single scarlet hibiscus. One or two of the littlest children dropped theirs in the dirt and the women stooped to pick them up, while all the others continued to walk slowly until they reached the wooden steps of Oleena's cottage. There they made no noise, called forth no speaker, but merely left the flowers, one on top of another until sprays of blood-red flowers were heaped upon the steps, an enormous bouquet laid at the entrance to the room that had become Oleena's home.

I walked to the door and knocked on it. Oleena emerged to find the entire town still standing there, its tribute laid at her feet. She gasped. Her eyes opened wide and wider, her fingers flew to her mouth and then she made the prettiest little bow, one bare foot behind the other, a slow deep bend of knees toward the earth, hands palm to palm in a narrow steeple. Tears came but she did not brush them away. And then she threw her arms open as if to wrap everyone within them, all of the people and all of their flowers, and she let the tears run down her cheeks. She smiled shyly, bending like a graceful ballerina to collect some of the flowers at her feet.

The villagers mingled and collected her among them. I heard one man say, 'We were suspicious at first, but now that we've seen you with Jaiya, we know that your heart will unfold.' Her acceptance in the community means that I can leave now. I have been witness to her return but I deeply regret that I will not be here to see how she will move in the continually turning gyre of life.

The noise of men coming down from the mountains is beginning to reach my ears. More and more of them are blocking the roads, collecting and telling terrible stories of the cruelty and bloodthirstiness of foreigners. I have told Oleena that I believed her premonitions and have accepted that I must leave quickly. She timidly put her arms around me and made slow patting circles on my back. I truly do not know whether she was consoling me or herself or both of us.

She went inside and brought out two packages. One was for Diana and the other was for me. When I began to open it, she put her hand on top of mine. 'No. Save it until you are safely on the ship. It was my grandfather's,' she told me, 'and it should have been passed to my husband or to my son, but since I have neither, I give it to you.'

Maarten, I have been very thoughtful and attentive to Oleena's wishes, but this time I could not do as she asked. I had to see what she was giving me, so over her noises of protest I began unwinding the wad of emerald green cloth she had handed me. 'Careful,' she warned, as I neared the end of the material.

When I finally came to the gift itself, I was stunned. There in my hand lay the kris with the intricately carved demon's head that had been waved in my direction all those years ago. I immediately remembered the short, compact man whose face was contorted with rage as he wrapped his fist around the hilt, raised the knife above his head, and swung it downward straight at my chest. I could see bottomless hate in his cold black eyes. I didn't think then. I just ran. I ran so fast that I didn't know where I was going or what I would do next.

'Oleena,' I said, 'is this your grandfather's kris?'

She nodded.

'Are there others like it?'

She saw my face. She shrugged her shoulders.

'Oleena,' I asked, like a judge in an important trial, 'it is very important that you answer me to the best of your knowledge. Are you certain there are no other krisses like this one.'

'I don't know. I just know that this one was my grand-father's. Its handle was carved of horn and the sheath is made with wood from the trees of our village. I remember their talking about that.'

'Is this furious demon unusual?'

'Why are you asking me all these questions? Have I done something wrong?'

'Oh no, Oleena, it's not you. It's me. I did something wrong many years ago. Thirty-two years ago. And now it's come back, like some kind of magic, white magic, maybe, if that's what connects families, brings the lost to be found.

'Oh Oleena, your grandfather threatened me with this same kris. Do you know what that means? It means that I am the Dutchman in your family story. I am the one who loved your mother and fled without a word of explanation. If your grandfather had killed me, I think he would have been happy. I was the devil incarnate and I had somehow found my way to his daughter. Your mother. I loved her, Oleena, she was beautiful and enchanting and she had a sweetness to her that found its way deep into me. But your grandfather chased me away.'

'Why did you never come back? Why didn't you write to her?'

'I can't explain myself. I am full of shame. Once I left, I didn't think I could return. I had another life far away. It was so different. I never thought there could be a child.' I looked at her. I could barely speak. 'You. You are that child. You. My daughter.'

'Yes.' *She spoke in a faraway voice.* 'Your daughter.'

I reached out tentatively at first, then wrapped my arms around her and held her close to me. I was filled with confusion. My daughter. My daughter whose innocence had been stolen and twisted by the unspeakable Anton. My daughter who had been part of a life too horrific to contemplate. Thinking about it, remembering what she had done and had done to her sickened me.

The furious cries – aiii aiii aiiiya – *made by the men grew louder as they raced toward the village.* 'How can you go now,' *Oleena wailed,* 'now that I have found you?'

'How can I leave you now that I know?' *I echoed her anguish. The cries of the wild warriors were growing closer by the minute. I looked around fearfully.* 'I promise I'll come back.' *I reached into the top of my bag and pulled out a wide sash woven of vermilion and purple silk. On it many rows of orange flowers were interrupted in the center by a wide navy band and then the pattern picked up again. I took out my pocketknife and swiftly cut the cloth in half across the navy stripe. I gave Oleena one part and kept the other for myself and promised her that we shall be together, father and daughter, just as the two parts of the cloth will be reunited when we are.*

Truthfully, I had bought the sash for Zoe – ever hopeful, I guess you could call me – but it was much better to give to Oleena. I know I will return. I must. You can lose a love once and lose a daughter you never knew you had once, but twice would be unthinkable. I told her that she must write to me and let me know when it is safe. And I flew out of there, the noise of the enraged warriors at my back. I raced to the port where a ship was docked and I left, I left again. But now I know I will keep my promise. Meanwhile when I return to Amsterdam, I will be able to give to Diana what Oleena entrusted to me. And I will tell you more fully the story of this exceptional adventure.

CHAPTER NINE

'A NTON IS DEAD?' MIRANDA repeated. 'How do you know? Are you sure?'

'I had the news from Pieter,' Maarten Welbroeck said, his voice quieter than usual. 'There was some sort of accident.'

Miranda was still. 'What kind of accident?'

'I don't really know. All Pieter said was that he drowned in a freak accident in waters near the shore.'

'I don't understand. Did Pieter say what he was doing?' Miranda could imagine that he had gotten in over his head smuggling contraband or inciting the wrath of a possessive husband. But drowning in waters near the shore? Perhaps he had had a seizure of the heart. Wouldn't that be appropriate, she thought bitterly. Or perhaps some poisonous fish had bitten him, a coral snake, a jellyfish, maybe, its toxic tentacles wrapping him in a fatal embrace.

She was not a woman much given to irony, but she smiled wryly when she realized that he had submitted to the element he loved most. And hadn't it betrayed him as he had betrayed her?

Tears stung her eyes. 'Oh Lord. I'm sad. I loved him once, you know. Sometimes I hated him,' Miranda corrected herself. 'I hated him for leaving, for finding other women. He cast me away without a minute's warning. He made Diana into a desperate girl, leaving her open to the hopes that men throw vainly to women, tantalizing and then discarding them.'

Maarten Welbroeck cleared his throat. First Pieter's tales of unthinkable behavior and now Miranda's outburst. He wished to pass beyond embarrassing emotional disclosures as quickly as possible and was relieved that he could reassure Miranda that at least there were no legal complications from Anton's death. Pieter had taken care of getting all the documents signed in his meetings with the man. 'I suppose that's a relief,' Miranda said. 'But there's Diana. How will I ever tell her? She idolizes her father, you know. She thinks he'd have solved all her problems, and ours, if only he were here. It's going to be a terrible blow.'

'No doubt,' said the lawyer, looking suitably sympathetic.

'You should have seen her when the seeds and herbs for the monkey arrived. She was ecstatic. Her father had come to her rescue just as she knew he would. I'll never forget the smell when she emptied them into her hand. Like a combination of dried animal dung and weird tropical fruit. But they were quite beautiful – black seeds like peppercorns, crinkly leaves, and mustard-colored flowers. She stirred a spoonful into a crushed mango and cradled the creature in the crook of her arm. She spooned the mixture into his mouth, a little at a time, all the while singing his name over and over and then adding a few words about her father. Her personal prayer. She fed him slowly, twice a day, always singing the same thing, until it sounded like a hymn. I was skeptical, but seven days later that poor beast was better and Diana was more convinced than ever that her father had magic powers. So you can imagine I'm extremely worried about how she will take the news.'

'If there's anything I can do,' Maarten offered, twisting the ends of his moustaches nervously.

'Thank you again,' Miranda said, pushing her chair back, standing, and extending her hand for the ritual shake. 'Please let me know when Pieter van Hoorn returns. I want to hear everything he can tell me.'

As she rode home on her bicycle Miranda was so troubled thinking about Diana that she narrowly missed hitting a dachshund trotting behind a mother who had stopped to thrust her head under the segmented black hood of a perambulator. Miranda swerved at the last minute, nearly crashing into the base of a tree. Poor bereft Diana. Miranda worried about how the girl would take the news. She suddenly decided to see if Andreas was at the nursery. Reversing course, she pedaled over a small bridge and rode until she reached the nursery's entrance, where she parked her bicycle against an elm tree and strode through all the planting beds and ornamental hedges to the front door.

It was almost as humid as a greenhouse. Dozens of tulips and narcissus were blooming in pots. Flats of greens lined the counters and crowded the floor. Packets of seeds were arranged on racks. Miranda looked around for Andreas. Not seeing him anywhere, she marched up to the counter, interrupting a clerk who was wrapping a cineraria in silver paper and chatting with a customer. 'Is Andreas here?' she asked. 'I saw him earlier,' said the pale, red-haired woman, tying a bow with a final flourish. 'If you wait until I've finished here, I'll go and see.'

Within minutes Andreas appeared, a rosy-cheeked giant in baggy brown corduroys. 'Miranda,' he said, with unfeigned surprise. He couldn't remember if she'd ever been at the nursery before. 'What brings you here?' He was about to guess that she needed plants when he realized that the expression on her face was not about greens.

'Is there somewhere we could talk that isn't in the middle of things?' she asked.

'Let's go to my office. Oh, wait – it's a mess. Plants every-where.'

Andreas was not exaggerating. Even when he moved the plants from the desk and the chairs, set some on shelves in the bookcase, and called a young man to take some away, there was still barely room for two people to sit comfortably. Miranda didn't seem to notice.

'Andreas,' she said, as if they were friends. 'I've just come from the lawyer's office. He told me the most awful thing.' A long pause. 'Anton is dead.'

'Dead? Are you sure?'

'All I know is that it seems he drowned.'

'Drowned? If ever anyone knew about water, it was Anton. How? Where?'

'I really don't know. Pieter van Hoorn had gone out to the East Indies to find him, and he sent word to the lawyer. I'm upset, I have to tell you, but I'm more worried about Diana. She's built her father up into some sort of god and now he's vanished, just like that, without her ever being able to have a real relationship with him or see him again. I'm afraid it will be a terrible blow.'

Andreas realized that she must be frantic if she'd come to him. 'I'm flattered you've come to talk to me. It's true that Diana and I do get along fairly easily, but I'm not at all sure she'll let me into her inner world. She's a complicated and deeply original girl, Miranda, and I think you're right to worry.' Andreas exhaled loudly and turned his gaze to the floor. He was silent for several long minutes. 'What if I encouraged her to help me here at the nursery? You can see for yourself that I could really use an extra set of hands. I'd keep a good watch over her. It might at least distract her. And maybe she'd be willing to come home and have dinner with Mies and me sometimes.'

'That's very kind of you. I like the idea of keeping her busy. She loved the garden when Ria was alive. You might convince her. It's worth trying. She and I are having a bit of a difficult time at the moment. I've been rather wrapped up in all the preparations for the restaurant and I have to admit I haven't had much time for her.'

Andreas nodded. He bit his lower lip. 'Actually, you may be doing me a favor. I think she could really help out here.'

Miranda bicycled home. She wished she had someone else to talk to. Giles didn't seem quite the right person to ask for advice. Does one discuss the death of a past husband with the potential future one? No, she thought to herself, he wouldn't understand. She didn't really understand herself. She had been so angry with Anton all these years for deserting her, for preferring the open sexuality of his sculptures to her, the woman in his bed. She hated him for lashing her to the mast of the house, making her prow figure and servant, maker of the beds and mender of the sheets. The same sheets that he once tore to bind her with. And yet, now that he was gone, she felt bereft.

Miranda continued her list of grievances. She hated him for bringing her to the cold, grey city of Amsterdam. She hated him for leaving her there and never coming back. We never had it out, she thought to herself. And now he's gone for good and I'll never know what happened, never understand what made him leave without a word.

Miranda offered to take Diana skating that night. The weather had turned cold and the ice on the canals was thick and hard. It was a crisp evening with a hailstorm of stars cutting pinpoints of light into the vault of the sky. 'Let's go, just the two of us,' Miranda said, 'and then stop for hot chocolate and cookies.' Diana was instantly suspicious. For months Miranda had had time for nothing but the restaurant. When she wasn't worrying over details of the construction, she was prowling in shops for furniture or experimenting in the kitchen with new dishes and pastries. She was testing spices she had found and had already made a pantry full of chutneys and preserves.

She and Giles were spending a great deal of time together.

Some days it seemed to Diana as if he was there when she got up and still there when she went to bed. But he was kind and careful to include her. He sometimes invited Majine as well. Even so, Diana could hardly believe that all the decisions had been made and that Miranda was suddenly ready to leave it all behind for an evening of skating.

Giles watched as the two of them walked out to the canal where they strapped on their skates. Diana was much more at home on the ice than Miranda and could literally skate circles around her mother, beginning at a wide outer circumference and circling in tighter and tighter until Miranda looked vexed. 'Am I getting too close?' Diana asked, mischievously skating off until all Miranda could see was a tiny speck of her red coat. Back she came in long easy strides and the two of them, hungry from their exertions, stopped to buy tiny pancakes from an old woman who made them over a coal burner set right on the ice. 'Hot,' exhaled Diana when she took her first bite, blowing white powdered sugar everywhere. 'Um,' agreed Miranda, nodding, her mouth full. Soon they returned for more. Miranda cradled one in her hands to keep them warm and downed a second in a quick bite. Back to skating they went, their blades cutting almost imperceptible patterns on the paraffin-colored ice until they were tired and ready to go home.

'What about the cocoa you promised?'

'We can have it at home.'

Miranda warmed the milk, whisked in the chocolate powder, and poured each of them a full mug. 'Diana,' she began warily, as the girl took her first sip. 'I have something sad that I have to tell you.'

Diana heard the tone in her mother's voice and instantly saw herself falling, falling beyond the seas, deeper than the oceans, falling into a fiery darkness as hot as the molten core of the earth.

'It's my father, isn't it?'

Miranda exhaled audibly. She was visibly relieved that Diana understood. She nodded a silent yes.

Diana flinched but stood her ground. She felt an instant glacial cold. Icicles crystallized along her spine and extremities, petrifying her limbs, freezing every reflex and impulse save for a single swift movement in which she thrust her chin upward toward the arc of darkness above her. She searched the skies to find the constellation her father had surely become – the great speckled fish outlined by thousands of glittering stars – and she listened for the waves of thunder loosed by his leaping from the seas into the night skies. She swiveled and looked from north to south, east to west, staring into the glittering darkness, but she could not find him. An acid bath of orange spilled across her retina and she opened her mouth to loose a long painful howl, a threnody constructed of a single note that rose and fell and rose again.

She envisioned opening her mouth and out flew a thousand fish, golden and silvery fish, fish stippled with red dots and fish with peach-colored scales, fish as long as eels and thin as needles, iridescent turquoise fish, fish with huge glassy eyes and fish with tiny jagged teeth, fish stained the color of sea anemones and fish with enormous open mouths ready to seine a host of tiny fish into their waiting maw, amber-colored fish and fish the indigo of the sea. Above them all hung two knives as sharp as razors, and as each fish jumped into the air the knives came down and chopped them, chopped them fine as forcemeat until only bones were left, pulp and bones, slimy guts and silvery eyes that lay upon the floor at Diana's feet, her father gone, voyages upon the sea finished in a heap of bodies left upon the floor.

Diana fled across the room and down the hall, threw open the door to her room and collapsed onto the bed where, sobbing, she finally fell into a deep sleep that lasted for three days and three nights.

When Diana woke, she still felt drugged with sleep. She dragged around, hardly noticing that the restaurant was beginning to take its final shape or that strange workmen were appearing at all hours to finish their final tasks. Her memories from that time would always remain fragmentary and jagged, as if they had snapped from some now lost central stem of her being. She was peripherally aware of her mother's happiness but remained mystified that the two of them could actually be inhabiting the same house, since Miranda's universe was one where darkness did not reign and deep fatigue did not rule a body intoxicated by grief.

Several days after she awoke, Diana took Majine into the room where her father's trunk still stood. She raised the heavy hasp in which the lock had rested and lifted the top, letting it flop backward against the wall. She reached inside the trunk and began taking out each piece of clothing, methodically sorting shirts from sarongs and shorts. She very carefully unfolded her father's sarong and slid out from its folds the beautiful vest that belonged to the mysterious woman in his life. Next she pulled out the pieces of nautical equipment and laid them in a rough circle on another part of the floor. Wondering what to do with them, she paced back and forth between her two heaps, between the clothes and the anchors, clasps, and chains, the keys with their dramatic flanges and the homemade knives. With her fingernail she flicked flakes of rust off several of the chains and then she coiled them together until they looked like a large copper-colored snake. She set them next to six square headed bolts she arranged to look like a small enclosure. From the pile of clothes she took one of the soft batik shirts and put it on, smoothing it over her small frame, laughing as her knees disappeared beneath its great length. She smelled each of the remaining shirts to find one that kept traces of her father's smell and took it back to her bedroom, where she slid it over her pillow and buttoned it securely in place.

When she finally felt safe to return to the outside world, Diana remembered Andreas's invitation to help in the nursery. She put on two sweaters, a heavy wool jacket, and gloves, wound a scarf around her neck, and left the house, walking slowly, carefully skirting patches of ice that had not melted yet. She was relieved to enter the warmth of Andreas's office and quickly shed her outer layers. 'Well, well,' Andreas said, concerned at how pale she looked, how thin, how lost. 'I suppose you know you are back in the life-saving business.' Diana looked puzzled. 'We have orders from two families here in the city who are both giving immense parties tomorrow night, and they both want all our best plants and insist on having them delivered at the same time. The woman I was counting on has chosen this week to have a baby. A baby,' he huffed. 'Two months early!'

'It sounds like you're accusing her of sabotage. It's not exactly as if she could help it,' Diana teased. 'Andreas, could I have a mug of cocoa before you put me to work?'

'I think that can be arranged,' he said, and sent someone scurrying for it. Diana sat in the chair across from him and swung her feet back and forth nervously, glancing around at the clutter of papers and plants. The radiator clanked and bubbled, sending plumes of steam into the air. 'I was going to have you help Mies plant tulip bulbs in dark loam, but now I think you'd better help pull together all the party flowers.'

'Couldn't someone else do that? I'd rather just be with Mies. I've been asleep for a few days and don't – please don't make me stand up with other women and work while they talk and talk. I can't, I just can't.'

Andreas understood instantly. He found Mies, walked with the two of them over to a separate quiet greenhouse and left them with their hands in the dirt working in a companionable silence. Mies hummed tunelessly and Diana sank into the work, carefully tending the dirt on the onion-like roots of the tulips and cradling each bulb in the protection of her hands. Dark tunes played through her, uninterrupted by the demands of human voices. She was relieved to be away from her mother who was increasingly caught up in the frenzy of the final days before the restaurant's opening.

When Diana and Mies had finished the potting, the girl went to find Andreas. He was sitting in his office with stacks of order forms and letters to be signed.

'Andreas, can I talk to you for a few minutes?'

'You certainly can. Thank you for sparing me one more minute of this awful paperwork.

'When I decided to go into the nursery business, I pictured myself with plants in the hothouses or talking with customers, showing them my most beautiful tulips. Maybe I'd be striding over acreage planted with our trees or designing a garden for a country house. Little did I think that I'd end up stuck behind a desk half the time. Sorry – you really don't need to hear me ramble on about the boring part of this work. How are you and Mies getting along?'

'Oh fine, just fine. We work well together. We like quiet. He's very easy to be with.'

'So what can I do for you?'

'Andreas, I've been thinking about my father. I can barely sleep for all my dreams about him. Over and over I see him in the waters off a turtle-shaped island. I see him turned over with his head held beneath the water . . . I can see that he is going to drown if someone doesn't help him and I start to run to him, but I'm so far away and he's trying to turn over and get his face out of the water and I'm running but I can't get there and I always wake up with my heart pounding.'

Andreas was silent for a long time. 'Diana,' he said in a

low, soft voice, 'do you remember when I surrounded your nanna with flowers and dozens of flickering candles as a way of saying goodbye to her?' Diana nodded. 'Do you think you should do something like that for your father?'

Diana leaned excitedly across the desk. 'I've taken everything out of his trunk and sorted things into piles. I have a heap of clothes and another heap of nautical implements. I was sitting between the two last night and I thought to myself, "Iron and salt – that's what my father was, iron and salt."'

'I don't think I understand.' Andreas crumpled his brow.

'The iron is for all the nautical instruments – most of them are pitted and rusted now, but many of them began as instruments for his sailing journeys, things that guided and steadied the ships and held them together.'

'And the salt?'

'The sea, Andreas. My father was in love with the sea. My mother told me that shortly after I was born my father walked into the sea with me in his arms and dipped me in the warm waters. He poured water from his palm over the stump of my umbilical cord and washed away the blood.

'But now I wake up from dreams in which I see him dissolving atom by atom in the water. I watch his fingers turn pale and wrinkled, see the waters invade the hollows of his cheeks and the cavity in which his heart hangs.

'Andreas, do you remember that strange thing he said in the letter he left among his sculptures? It was about "beyond the beyond" and transcendence and ecstasy. I had to go to the library to look up all those words to try to understand what he was saying. I think that he was saying that he wanted to dissolve, but I'm sure he didn't mean it to happen the way it did. He didn't expect the sea to swallow him.'

Andreas considered Diana with amazement.

'Salt and iron, iron and salt. What could I do with them to honor my father?'

Andreas thought. 'Have you ever seen pictures of Japanese

temple gardens, the gardens with simple patterns raked in the sand and a few rocks placed very carefully for their effect of peace and eternity?'

Diana shook her head. 'What would they have to do with my father? He wasn't a peaceful man. I don't think he ever went to Japan.'

'I was thinking that perhaps instead of sand you could use salt.'

'Oh,' Diana joined in, 'and instead of rocks the rusting nautical implements. And instead of peaceful patterns, Majine could make circles and lines by raking the salt with his long fingernails.'

'You're way ahead of me, Diana, but yes, that's right. These things would represent your father nicely.'

'And every year on New Year's Day or something like that, I would take a cup and pour some water on the salt and watch it dissolve, just as my father is slowly becoming part of the waters off the island.' She looked down, surprised to find tears on her cheeks. She stuck out her tongue to taste one. 'Salt,' she said softly to Andreas. 'Sadness dissolving with salt.'

CHAPTER TEN

'HOW DID YOU DO it?' Miranda asked him. 'I distinctly remember your warning that I'd have to wait another two or three months at least for all the permissions.'

Giles smiled, pleased at her pleasure, her implied praise. 'Shall I really tell you?' Long pause. 'I did what everyone does.'

'What's that?'

'I bribed him.'

'What? You did what?' she asked with icy cool. 'What exactly did you give him?'

Giles laughed. 'Calm down.'

'Calm down,' she said, hands clenched at her sides. 'Good luck.'

'Dear lovely, angry Miranda, here's what I promised. Two meals. In the opening week. And two every year after that. Actually, you bribed him, not me.'

'I did? I never said a word to the man. You know that . . . you, you . . .' Miranda sputtered. Giles remembered that nothing made her pricklier than being blamed. Even when it was justified, she hated being blamed.

'Yes, my darling, you did it. It was the smells of curry and apricot while he was here that pulled him right where we wanted him. The man's a known gourmand – notice that I said gourmand, not gourmet – so my little bribe will require hefty portions and several extra courses.'

'That's a bribe?' Miranda exhaled in obvious relief. 'Then I'm guilty of bribery every day of my life. In that case, my life is a conviction waiting to happen.'

Giles smiled. It didn't take much to move a raging Miranda to more pacific moods. He put his hand in the small of her back and guided her gently toward the upstairs bedroom she had made hers during the construction. When she understood, she looked up dubiously from under raised eyebrows.

'A surprise,' he said, opening the door to the bedroom. On the table by the bed he had set a lunch he had made from food he'd found in the refrigerator. He had piled nutmeg-scented rice in a big bowl, into which he had stirred cubes of cucumber and handfuls of crunchy peanuts. He had ladled cool yogurt and pumpkin soup into shallow bowls and spread crispy rounds of bread with a garlicky topping. Two red-golden mangoes sat separately on a single plate. Miranda shook her head in disbelief. She slid her arms around him and could not believe it when tears came to her eyes. She didn't cry. No, not her. Not Miranda. Well, yes, it seems she did.

Giles took his thumbs and smudged the tears away, the graphite from his pencil leaving little raccoon-like circles beneath her dark green eyes. He fingered the buttons on her blouse, undoing them one by one. He slid his hand over her breasts, then let his tongue go where fingers had first been. Slowly did he remove each item of her clothing as she stood still as a child, feeling blouse, skirt, silken underthings fall to the floor as if of their own will. He watched them become a small clump, her skins shed, interrupting the patterns of red chevrons and orange swirls on the worn Persian rug.

He took charge, lifting her onto the bed, shedding his own clothes, then kissing and tonguing her body into life once again. They lay facing each other, arms and legs tangled in the sheets, and their bodies, the warmth of their breaths, the heat of the movement shaking up and down their bodies, bodies rising and falling. They rode each other over the folds and wrinkles of sheet, past her gripping him between her thighs, past the prickling of flesh down the pathway of his spine, they rode past exhilaration and deep shuddering noises and on and on and in and out until they collapsed, pink flesh against white sheets, his wiry haired chest beneath her arm, her leg left carelessly between his. And they fell asleep, as after a great and filling meal.

They might have stayed there much longer had Giles not heard a cushioned thud, a little guttural cry, then a soft crunch. He sat up in a hurry and saw Majine, who had arrived after somehow divining the presence of food and was now pressing his weight against the door with just enough power to open it. 'Hey, stop, stop.' Giles leapt to the floor, where Majine was wrestling with a mango.

'Oh my God, get out of here, you miserable beast,' Miranda shrieked when she awoke.

'Slow down, Miranda. Look,' Giles said. She watched the monkey smack his lips with his squarish red tongue, watched him hold the mango in both hands and tear into it with his teeth, freeing juices that ran down his chin and into his fur. He slurped as he bit into the flesh and he chewed with delight.

'That's monkey bliss, my darling. You're not going to deny him his bliss after we've had ours, are you? Besides, he's left us all the rest of my carefully arranged meal. Here,' he said, plumping up the pillows. 'Lean back here and you can eat just like Majine.'

'Oh, and do you expect little rivulets of juice to fall between my breasts?' she asked, suddenly very aware of her naked body.

'I do hope so,' he replied. 'I will happily lick them up. Majine, my friend, you are an inspiration. You're welcome here any time. We'll just leave you a mango or two and we can each plunge into the flesh we have chosen.'

'Giles! Are you crazy? You want to invite this creature into our bedroom?'

'That's just what I want. You wait . . . he won't be any bother. Yes, here we are, your loyal servants, Giles and Majine, ever ready to succumb to the food you offer up. To the goddess of the kitchen' – a mock bow in her direction. 'Thank you, Majine. Yes, you are most definitely welcome here any time.'

Giles knew Miranda was not even vaguely fond of the monkey, but he also knew that he had the best chance of getting his way immediately after lovemaking. He looked over at her as she sat cross-legged on the wrinkled sheets, hair loosed from its usual single long braid, eyes half closed, singing a song under her breath. 'Here,' he said, finding a few vagrant bits of mango and putting them in her palm, 'just open your hand and let him take them.' She held back. 'Just lean over the edge of the bed and try,' he urged. 'Have I steered you wrong yet?' She shot him a dubious look, then rolled over on her stomach, extended her hand, and Majine extracted each morsel from her and ate it delicately. Giles was joyful and then, with another glance at her, ravenous again. I've found myself a lady tiger, he thought to himself, stroking her inner thigh, until she cuffed him and slid her two bare feet onto the floor. 'I know what you're thinking and the answer is no. There isn't time now.' She leaned over.

'Okay,' Giles said equably, 'then I wonder whether there's any of that wonderful quince tart left in the kitchen?'

They were besotted with each other, in bed early in the morning and after lunch if they could find a way and again in the evening. They peeled tangerines and let the juices spray across their skin and licked the tiny beads from each other's bodies. Miranda cut a sweet fleshy papaya and slid a slice into Giles's mouth until she took the rest, sucking it slowly from his mouth into hers. He massaged her feet until she shivered. She sat atop him and sang songs in her low throaty voice. They were mesmerized by each other and paid little attention to the monkey who was warmed by their passion. He lay on the ledge that projected into the room just below the ceiling and studied them. When charged by the feelings they loosed, he raced around the ledge. They laughed and left sections of citrus and bits of brilliant fruits on a tissue for him.

In those days Giles could sometimes persuade Miranda to leave the kitchen. He brought her back to her room where he fell upon her, ravenous, 'Miranda, Miranda, Miranda.' Her name came like a chant from his lips. He began kissing her, feeling blindly for mouth and tongue. His hands were hungry for her skin. He fumbled at the hook at the neck of her dress and she laughed softly, raising her arms and reaching behind to slip the prong easily from its moorings. He slid his hands under the soft material and let his hands ride over her breasts, pausing, wanting to have her body, all of it, immediately. She removed the pins from her hair and shook it free, loosed it in a rush of darkness. 'Door,' she mumbled, seeing it ajar. He backed her against it, closing it seconds after the monkey slid in.

Sometimes she appeared with rounds of bread filled with a gingery-garlic spread and slices of lamb with shredded leeks or tiny crunchy shrimp with strips of brilliant peppers. 'Mmm,' he would mumble as the fragrance hit his nostrils, but he always set them aside and reached for her. Later they stayed naked as they ate, tiny crumbs falling into the spongy moss of her dark triangle, and he would reach out, grazing the tender curls, and slowly pluck the little bits of bread and slide them into his mouth. She loved to grab his fingers, suck on their tips as if sucking her own juices from their ridges and whorls. It was one of her deepest satisfactions, tasting herself on him, the sweet juicy places that he loved she too loved, stirred and aroused again by finding herself on him.

One night he knelt over her on the bed, his legs a deep V surrounding her pelvis, and drizzled papaya juice as if they were in a magical rain forest. And then he fell upon her, rubbing the moisture between their bodies until they were caught in a slippery rhythm of gasping and laughing and he, aching with need, first sprinkled droplets of juice into the dark accepting channel between her legs and then released his own into her, his canyon, his tropics, the embracing geography of his desire.

Giles decided it was time to take the next step. He was crazy about Miranda and quite certain that she returned his feelings, although he seldom felt on entirely secure ground with her. By the time that he had finished drinking his coffee that morning, Miranda was already at the stove, stirring cardamom into the sugary syrup in which she was poaching pears for tonight's tart. He slid behind her in a single stealthy glide, lifted her long braid and began kissing the nape of her neck. 'Mmm,' he murmured, breathing in her scent as well as the sweet fragrance of pears that rose from the pot. 'Oh Miranda, you lovely, irresistible woman. I have a confession to make. You have ravished this confirmed bachelor. See,' he said, reaching into his pocket for the white handkerchief that he waved in her direction. 'I can no longer live without you. I sink at your feet.' And he began to drop, allowing his hands to trace the outline of her body as he did.

Miranda turned around and smiled ironically. 'Come now, Giles, you're just angling for a taste of these pears.'

'Marry me, Miranda. I'll look after you and help you with your restaurant in any way that you want. I love you, Miranda. I can't imagine my life without you.'

Miranda had returned to stirring the pears. 'Let's not rush things, Giles.'

'Rush things? I'm practically a resident of the house. I'm certainly the resident councilor of financial prudence and architectural possibility here. I'd hardly say this was impetuous on my part.' Giles took a breath and said, as much to himself as to her, 'You are an unconventional woman, Miranda.'

'You're just discovering that now?

He shrugged helplessly. 'Most women want to get married.'

'I did that,' Miranda replied, 'and I'm still recovering. Anyway, it's not only me you'd be marrying. You'd be marrying Diana, Majine, and a restaurant as well. Are you're sure you want all that in the bargain?'

'Diana and the restaurant, I'm quite certain. The monkey absolutely. Majine is my ally, as you may have noticed. Just tell me you'll think about it seriously.' Giles knew not to press Miranda when she looked ready to back off.

'I'll think about it, Giles.' And she gave him a dazzling smile.

They were in her room when Miranda handed Giles a perfect ripe persimmon and with a quick flick of the paring knife opened it to expose the deep glow of its flesh. The fruit felt as full and ripe as a breast. He watched as she shook her hair into liquid dark waves, then pulled her to him, parting her lips with his tongue. Gasping, she abandoned her clothes, then helped him slide out of his. She sat opposite him then and, without warning, took the fruit into her mouth and sucked at it, before passing it to him. And he to her, then she to him. Back and forth it traveled, its rich flesh feeding them both.

They never took their eyes off each other, just watched as one consumed a share of succulence before passing it to the other. They began to breathe in unison. In out in out, deeper and deeper, breath reaching slowly into their bellies and filling the spaces that opened behind their ribs. Slower and slower they breathed until they didn't know whose breath it was escaping in warm bursts, like clouds that meet and swallow each other.

Flutters started deep inside her body. The slow urgency of Miranda's breath opened her more and more but still she did not move. Giles watched, learning from her, not moving because she did not and when she could no longer remain still, she slid toward him, ready for him to fill the vacancy that she could no longer deny. Slowly did he enter her waiting body. They sat up straight, her legs lying across his but neither of them moved. Her eyes were inches from his. He began to shiver with anticipation. Barely moving her head, she signaled no, not yet. With the stillness her body opened more, and the more her breath filled the empty interior, the more she could feel barriers falling away. They continued to sit this way for many, many minutes until she felt the beat of wings, the pull of the tide, felt her connection to the curve of the earth and then, as Giles shuddered and released breath and body to her receptive being, she felt herself lift off and fall deep within a gorgeous darkness.

Several days later, climbing out of the shower and standing in a cloud of steam, Giles thought to himself that he'd never been happier. He slapped his chest several times to get the circulation flowing, wrapped a towel around his waist, and wiped the steam off the mirror. Preoccupied with thoughts of Miranda, he dipped his soft brush into the shaving soap, swirled it around until it made a foam as thick as beaten egg whites and absentmindedly painted it over the entirety of his face so that he looked like a ghost with dark eyes and eyebrows. He automatically guided the blade of the razor through the lather on the lower half of his face and watched it leave a clean path in its wake. Wiping off the excess foam, he saw that he still looked like a ghost on the upper part of his face and realized what he had done. Giles, he said to himself, Giles, my man, you're in deep trouble if you can't even see or think straight. And, on that subject, he had to be honest with himself. He still hadn't convinced Miranda to marry him, although she was allowing him into her life more and more. They made a good pair, he thought. She knows about food and enchantment and I about construction and money. She is fire and I am earth, she is rapture and I am – let's face it, he said to himself, I am totally besotted.

CAROL FIELD

Giles did count it in his favor that he had convinced Miranda to begin keeping a list of the experiences of opening a restaurant, secretly hoping that his name would turn up so frequently that she would finally realize how important he was in her life. 'Why would I even want to remember all this?' was her initial response. 'Oh, you won't,' he assured her. 'Soon enough you'll sail out of the kitchen into the dining room and charm all the patrons and you will blithely forget what a struggle it's been. Just start making a list of what you remember.'

She saw what he meant. Everything she wrote had to do with workmen, inspectors, and bills. She worried constantly about money. Within a week she was on the verge of giving up. She ran to Giles. 'I can't do this any more. It's only seven days until we open and I'm ragged from the cooking, the construction, the planning, the everything. It's too much for me.'

'I confess that I noticed as much. I suggested to Diana that you might need her help.'

'Diana! She just clings to that monkey as if he were a life raft on a stormy sea.'

'Why don't you ask her, Miranda? Give it a try.'

Miranda thought it over briefly, then decided to gather her nerve by making final lists of all the equipment she still needed. She sat in an armchair, writing with a stubby pencil and wondered, after a bit, if the knocking sound she heard could be Majine. She sat utterly still, listening more closely, and realized there was someone at the front door.

Miranda put down her papers and opened the door to find a young woman in a shapeless grey coat nervously twisting a beret between her hands. 'Excuse me, ma'am,' she whispered, eyes focused on the black lace-up shoes on her wide feet. 'I'm sorry to bother you, but I wonder if it is true, the rumors I've heard, that there would be a restaurant here soon. I need a job, ma'am. I'm a pretty good cook.' Miranda briefly studied the potato-white face with its small grey eyes, saw her large body that looked like two soft pillows joined loosely together

166

at the center, and wondered if she knew anything at all about a kitchen, much less serving at table.

'What's your name?' Miranda asked as she ushered in the girl. 'Anna, ma'am. I've done all the cooking in the family for my brothers and sisters since my mother died a few years ago. But now I need a job.'

'How old are you?' Miranda couldn't guess whether she was twenty or forty.

'Twenty-six, ma'am, and I know my way around a house and a kitchen.'

'Can you wait on tables? Can you write down orders and keep them straight? Pour water and wine into glasses without spilling them? Will you wear a uniform? And cook when I need you to?'

'Oh yes, ma'am.' She smiled timidly. 'I can do all those things.'

'Why is it that you're leaving your family now? Don't they need you anymore?'

'No, ma'am. My father's married a woman just now and she'll be taking over the lot of them.'

'So you're looking for a place to live as well?'

'Oh yes, ma'am. That would be especially helpful.'

'I can hardly hire you without seeing what you can do, can I?' Miranda motioned for Anna to hang her coat over the back of a chair and follow her. 'Come into the kitchen and let's see what you make best.'

'Pastries, ma'am. I made the desserts for my brothers and sisters. I tried to have something different every day when they came home from school.'

'Wonderful. Can you make a pastry crust? I'll get the butter and the sugar and the flour for you.'

'And a lemon, ma'am, if you have one. Or some vanilla. Makes the crust tastier.'

Miranda stopped to appraise Anna. Clearly the girl knew what she was talking about. Large as she was, she moved with uncommon agility and speed. She put the dough together swiftly, asked for waxed paper to wrap it in and then wondered aloud where it might chill.

'Here,' said Miranda, setting it in the refrigerator.

'I suppose you'd be wanting me to make a filling?'

'Do you have a favorite?'

'I always make a plain pastry cream and flavor it with lemon or chocolate, depending on my mood.'

'And what do you feel like right now?'

'I see lemons in the bowl.'

'Good,' said Miranda. 'That's what I was hoping.'

Once Anna put the tart in the oven, Miranda led her into the dining room to see how she served at table. 'Here's a plate, a wine glass, and some silverware. First set the table and then pretend you're serving me a bowl of soup. I'll sit here,' she said, pulling out a chair. 'You can bring me my soup. And pour the wine.' Oh Lord, Miranda thought to herself, I'd take almost anyone at this moment. Maybe I should have put an ad in the newspaper. Now all I can do is cross my fingers. Anyway, the tart looks good.

In her nervousness Anna snatched up the plates almost before Miranda could set her fork down. She was uncertain about which fork belonged on the outside, but otherwise did a competent job. The tart with its creamy, lemon-spiked filling was a very pleasant surprise.

'I think she'll do just fine,' Miranda told Giles that evening. 'She can be in the kitchen and serve in the dining room. I've given her one of the spare rooms. She'll move in tomorrow.'

Knowing Anna was coming made it easier for Miranda to ask Diana for some help. One neutral employee plus one reluctant daughter was a much better equation than one in which Diana was compelled to do whatever her mother commanded.

That night, after cleaning up the kitchen, Miranda made her way down the long hall, where she found Diana lying on her bed reading a book. She seated herself at the foot of the bed at a careful remove from the monkey. 'Candles . . . tablecloths . . . hutch . . . plates . . . newspaper . . . there's just too much . . . I can't do it all. I'm overwhelmed, Diana. I had no idea how much work it was going to be to open the restaurant. I really need your help. We can't do this alone.' Diana put her finger in the book to mark her place and partially closed it. 'We can't do this alone?' she mimicked. 'Who exactly is "we"? I don't remember being consulted. If "we" is you and Giles, well, I'm sure you can. You seem to do other things alone very well.'

'What is that supposed to mean?'

'You're so busy with Giles and the restaurant that I've become invisible. Are you going to marry him? I don't even care.' She shrugged unconvincingly. 'You don't notice me anymore, unless you need something. Like now.

'You don't care at all that my father died, do you? You seem to have forgotten it entirely. I loved him and he loved me. He sent the seeds that saved Majine. I waited for all these years for him to come home and now he never will. And you don't care. You just keep thinking about your stupid restaurant.'

'Sometimes I'm so busy that I do forget,' Miranda admitted with some shame. 'I'm sorry. I know that you're aching without him. I'm not even sure I can fathom how you feel. It's just that in seven days there will be people coming to the restaurant, if we're lucky, and I can't do everything I need to by myself.'

'Why don't you hire someone?'

'Actually, I have, just this afternoon.'

'Then you don't need me,' the girl said, opening the cover of her book, extracting her finger, and beginning to read again.

'Yes, I do,' Miranda raised her voice. 'I need you more than ever.'

Diana thought for a minute and then said in a resigned tone, 'I could help in the kitchen, but I would never go in the dining room to serve. And I could never ever be there when you are.'

Miranda's head snapped back as if she'd been slapped. 'That was unkind, Diana.'

'I'm mouse girl and you're goddess woman. Why would I ever want to be in there with you?'

'Mouse girl? What does that mean?'

'You're tall and beautiful and dramatic. Everyone always turns to look at you. Look,' she said, pointing at her pallid face with its spill of freckles. 'Next to you I might as well be invisible.'

'Diana, when I was your age I didn't look at all like I do now. I felt awkward and out of place and I was desperate to grow up because I thought anything would be better than my life then. No one I knew in those years would recognize me now. Would you like to do something to look different? Pierce your ears maybe? Or buy some new clothes? Look at that skirt. It's been washed so many times it hardly has any color left. And those big pockets – they look like something for a ten-year-old. If you want to look different, let's go shopping for some new clothes.'

Miranda refused to let defeat on one front deflect her from the task at hand. 'So, if you won't be with me in the dining room, what would you do?'

'I'd chop fruits and vegetables, if you give me a list of what needs to be done. I could set out the ingredients for each dish so they were all together.'

'Thank you. I'd really be grateful. After all this restaurant is going to support us.'

'Us. You, me, and Giles?'

'Mmm. And Majine too. Don't forget it's going to keep him in mangoes.'

'Speaking of Majine, I want to have him with me when I'm working.'

'Diana, you know that's impossible.'

'Well, then I guess I can't help you.'

'Stop it. Here I am trying to create a glamorous and warm

atmosphere and you think people want a monkey lurking around?'

'Majine doesn't lurk. I just want him in the kitchen sometimes. We could put his bowl next to the counter where I'll be working and I'll make a little leash for him. But no Majine, no me.'

Miranda had finally given the restaurant a name. 541. The number of the house. Four days before opening Diana cut her finger badly enough to require stitches and the doctor forbade her to return to chopping for two days. She didn't really mind but she felt stupid and clumsy. Majine comforted her.

Miranda was deeply engrossed in pre-opening rehearsal dinners, which meant cooking for and serving the men who had worked on the house as well as friends of Giles' and several suspicious neighbors. The verdict was that her lamb, pumpkin, and yellow-fleshed potato stew was delicious. Miranda was impressed that Anna's delicate crust made a perfect foil for her pears poached in red wine.

Two days before opening a small article appeared in the newspaper about the restaurant. 'It's getting to be real,' Miranda said in her rush from the kitchen to the dining room. 'Oh Lord, there's still so much to be done. Diana, please come and clean out the drawers of the hutch. I bet no one's looked in them for fifty years. I put the paper to line them with on the big table. I don't know why we're bothering with all this. Maybe no one will come.'

Diana debated refusing, but decided to help. 'Why do we have the hutch here?'

'Because the shelves on top hold your grandmother's best Delft plates. Look how handsome they are. They lend just the right character to the room.'

'Ugh.' Diana held her nose at the smell of rot that escaped when she opened the top drawer. Carefully pulling out all the knobs, screws, and bits and pieces of hardware rattling around its interior, she cleaned out the drawer, washed it, and continued with the second and third. When she got to the bottom drawer, she found a heap of old clothing under torn paper scraps that were speckled with age. Carefully removing them, she came upon a cardboard tube wrapped in crumbling straw.

Giles heard her sharp intake of breath and ambled over. 'What did you find?'

'I don't know,' said Diana, holding it up in tentative fingers. The two of them carefully brushed off the dirt that had caked around the ends and worked at sliding off the covering, prying it away and using their fingernails to loosen where it stuck.

'Miranda, come look at this!' Giles shouted a minute later. Miranda heard the unfamiliar urgency in his voice and arrived just in time to watch him unroll an old painting.

The canvas was dark with age and slightly cracked where it had been crimped badly in one corner, but even with its dark surface, she could see a wine glass, a wedge of golden cheese, a platter with some sort of cake, and a deep crimson tapestry disclosing a view of the countryside. 'Oh, it's perfect,' Miranda said, 'absolutely perfect. It belongs right there,' she said, pointing toward the empty space on the wall adjoining the kitchen. 'I've been worrying about that wall.'

'Not quite so fast, Miranda. You can't hang it until it's stretched,' Giles pointed out.

'You must know someone who would do that for me,' she said, assigning him the task and turning back to the blank wall with an emphatic nod of closure.

On opening day, Miranda paced back and forth nervously in the dining room as Diana set the tables. Anna washed all the plates and glasses for the third time, repolished the silverware, and cleaned the glass in the window on which the numerals 541 were painted. Diana took up her post in the kitchen, where she cut up the lamb that Miranda would braise, cubed the potatoes, and washed and dried the lettuces. At midday

Giles brought the newly stretched picture from the framer and hung it.

An electrician arrived at three in the afternoon to fix two of the sconces on the wall that had suddenly refused to work. Miranda spent hours cooking, and by 5:30 was exhausted and wondered how she would ever get through the night. She didn't emerge from the kitchen until six, leaving just enough time to change into a red silk dress with a vibrant purple ikat pattern.

Six people were at the door at 6:30. Four more came at 7:00. Miranda appeared to greet each one. 'How did you hear about us?' she asked the first couple. 'We've walked by for days now, wondering what was happening here. When we saw the article in the paper, we decided we'd take a chance. And if you're good, maybe you'll remember us once you're so crowded that everyone wants a reservation.'

'Welcome then,' said Miranda, smiling at such honesty, hoping to memorize the man's thin craggy face with its eagle-like beak and the thatch of yellow white hair that sat in disarray on the top of his head. 'Let us pour you a little wine,' she said, 'to celebrate our opening.' She motioned to Anna. Miranda then darted to the next small group and introduced herself, offering wine to them as well.

'Curiosity. We're just here out of curiosity,' said the man, who slouched easily into a chair, looking instantly at home.

'Nonsense,' contradicted the woman with him, who Miranda assumed was his wife. 'We heard from one of the people at one of your trial dinners that the food was wonderful. Anyway, we live nearby. We never thought there would be a restaurant here.'

'Yes, it's a bit of a novelty,' Miranda acknowledged.

Miranda retired to the kitchen to sprinkle flakes of red chilies into the sweet pepper soup and to coax a symphony of tastes from the deep golden curry. Giles patrolled the dining room, stopping to talk with the adventurous few who came that first night.

Anna was obviously nervous. She apologized when she spilled a bit of the soup over the edge as she set it down on the table. 'Sorry,' she said, reddening, and then under her breath, 'Sorry, sorry.' She rushed to find a napkin with which to wipe up the puddle on the plate. The woman nodded coolly and returned to her conversation, barely acknowledging Anna's existence. Anna served the curry and rice to the table of six smoothly, but forgot the chutney until they asked. She neglected to pour the wine at two tables and Giles had to step in. 'Don't worry,' he whispered to her as her face turned crimson. 'We're all new at this. Why don't I take care of the wine tonight? It'll give me a real reason for being here.'

Miranda remained in the kitchen, fussing, tasting and retasting, adding a little more turmeric to the curry and urging the rice to cook faster. She dipped a spoon into the vat of curry she had made and tasted it once, twice, three more times. She worried it was flat, the rice too dry. Anna rushed into the kitchen, breathless, ready to take salad to one table, main courses to another. 'How are they liking it?' Miranda asked, but Anna was concentrating so hard on keeping her orders straight that she didn't reply. As it was, one man complained about how long she took to bring the main courses. 'May I offer you some wine? I'm sure your curry will arrive shortly,' Giles said in his most soothing tones, and slid quietly into the kitchen to see what was happening.

'This is harder than I thought,' said Miranda, who was wrapped in a white chef's jacket that reached from just beneath her chin to her knees. 'The rice doesn't want to cook. That's what we're waiting for.' Both Anna and Miranda seemed frazzled. Giles tried to reassure them that the people in the dining room seemed happy with their food.

By the time that the slices of rosy pear in the almond-accented pastry were served, everyone had relaxed. Anna actually managed a smile when one of the women took one look and said to her, 'If this tastes one half as good as it looks,

I'll be back often.' It was Anna's pastry, although of course she couldn't say such a thing.

The restaurant served twelve dinners on the first night. Miranda came into the dining room as soon as all the desserts were served and moved from table to table, collecting compliments and apologizing for any slowness in the service. 'We hope you enjoyed your dinner. You're here at the very beginning. We trust it will be smoother the next time you come.' And to everyone she said, 'Thank you for coming. How adventurous you are. We hope we'll see you again.'

From the smiles on faces as she spoke to them, from the warmth of their handshakes and the congratulations they heard, all of them – Miranda, Giles, Anna, even Diana, who peeked out of the kitchen door several times during the evening – felt that people had, on the whole, enjoyed themselves. As soon as the last person was out the door, Miranda collapsed in the big chair. 'I think they liked it,' she said.

'No question,' said Giles. 'We've got a few rough spots to iron out, but we did it. We survived.' He swooped over the collapsed form of Miranda to plant kisses on her flushed cheeks.

'Yes,' she acknowledged his praise, 'but tomorrow I have to do something about the rice. It took much too long to cook tonight. It's leaving the menu as soon as I can think of what to replace it with.'

Several weeks later, on the bitter-cold night on which a procession of skaters fanned out across the city's icy canals to celebrate the winter solstice, the restaurant was full. Soft light from bronze sconces washed down the yellow walls and candles blazed on each table, illuminating the snowdrops and tulips in their round glass bowls. Garlands of greens lay across the polished walnut sideboard where the wine bottles stood, each in its own elaborate silver holder.

Giles, who had nominated himself maitre d', walked back

and forth through the dining room, looking to see whose wineglasses needed filling and whose empty plates needed to be removed. He recognized Dirk, the man who had already eaten at the restaurant several times, from the exceptionally dark circles around his eyes, and watched as he fiddled distractedly with a pipe. His pale blond wife had a neck as long as a swan's and it rose like a column above an icy white blouse that shimmered with silver accents. She sat as still as an icon, and over time Miranda wondered if the warmth of the food, the almost weekly infusions of ginger and chili oil thawed her enough to continue to bind the two of them together. At another table Giles could not help noticing a man with an over-shot jaw talking volubly to a younger gentleman sporting long moustaches that sprang out from his face like a jack-in-the-box.

Smells floated on currents of air as the plates arrived, the beautiful rosy, orange, and pink food filling the eyes and noses of the expectant diners. Because it was the winter solstice, the longest night of the year, Miranda had created a feast with the colors of the sun, as if to remind it to return and bring its heat back to their lives. Her dinner began with pumpkin and apple soup with a drizzle of curry over the top, a calligraphy of color etching a wild flourish, an invitation to the spoon. Next came lamb braised with pomegranates and served with cubes of yellow-fleshed potatoes fried and then dusted with a tobacco-colored powder made of ground dried red peppers. Anna whisked those plates away and brought a cold crispy salad of mache, lamb's tongue and other wild greens picked hours before from a protected patch of earth tended by a man who had decided to give all his finest greens and vegetables to Miranda in exchange for the pleasure of eating at her restaurant when she permitted. Giles poured deep red Bordeaux and Burgundies, watching as glasses were raised and toasts made. Faces glowed warm and flushed.

There was a general hush and then a collective sigh as Anna transported slices of quince and apple tart with a caramel glaze on top. Giles was surprised when Miranda arrived in the dining room with a bowl tucked in her arm. 'Even if it is a bit cold,' she said with understatement – the temperature had dipped below freezing early in the day – 'I just couldn't resist offering the ice cream I made today.' Not one diner refused as she scooped a custardy cream-colored oval and set it at a slightly rakish angle next to each slice of tart.

'My goodness,' she said, noticing Pieter van Hoorn sitting with Maarten Welbroeck. 'Look who's here.' As she made her way over Pieter leapt to his feet, taking both of her hands into his, and said fervently, 'My compliments, Miranda. An exceptional dinner. So beautiful. So delicious. You are a true magician.'

Miranda glowed under the rush of compliments. 'Can I offer you a little dessert wine?' she asked, smiling, as Pieter pulled out a chair for her to join them. 'I didn't know you were back. When did you return?'

'A little more than a week ago,' he answered, 'and the minute I heard that you'd actually opened the restaurant, I called Maarten. And here we are!'

'There's so much to ask you,' Miranda said, suddenly pensive as she studied his face.

'Of course, and I'm happy to come and tell you all I know, but for tonight, let's just enjoy this feast.' Pieter took the late harvest wine Giles was pouring into his glass, raised it in Miranda's direction, and said, 'To the enchantress Miranda, who has brought light and warmth, elegance and glorious flavors to this frozen city of the north. To your triumph and continued success.'

Miranda bowed her head with uncharacteristic shyness.

'Yes, yes,' Maartin Welbroeck chimed in. 'A drink to the success of this wonderful restaurant.'

Word of mouth brought more and more people to 541. When Miranda saw that some patrons were becoming regulars, she changed the menu frequently to keep them interested. She continued to do all the shopping, to buy the flowers and arrange them, and to cook the food, but she was grateful to have Anna, who had turned out to be such a fine baker. Miranda began to rely on her delicate tart shells and it wasn't long before she had turned the entire dessert course over to the young woman.

'How do you do that?' Diana asked, watching Anna roll her buttery dough into a sheet as fine as silk and then slide it effortlessly into the bottom of a fluted tart pan. 'Here' – she handed Diana a slotted spoon – 'fill it with these poached pears.' Diana took the spoon hesitantly and carefully drained the spices and red wine in which they had poached before she moved the pears to the tart shell. In no time Anna rolled out a second piece of dough and draped it so that it fell in uneven peaks and valleys over the fruit beneath it.

'I've done it for so long I don't even think about it. I think it helps that my hands are cold – see,' she said, extending one so that Diana could feel it – 'they don't melt the butter as I handle the dough. Would you like to learn?'

Diana grimaced. 'I couldn't. If I tried to roll out dough, it would stick to the table or I'd shred it or something.'

'Don't worry so much. Put this flour into a bowl. Now add the sugar. Good. Get the butter out of the fridge and cut it into chunks. Now take these two knives and cut the butter into the flour and sugar until it's the size of small peas. It'll take a while, so don't get discouraged.' Anna turned away to start on the dinner rolls, but kept an eye on Diana as she struggled with the two knives. 'That's looking fine,' she said to the girl after a few minutes.

'It's hard.'

'Of course it is. The first time you do something is always the hardest. You'll get the hang of it and it will seem simple in no time.' Anna bent over the bowl and thrust in a hand, feeling the texture between her thumb and forefinger. 'That's just about right. Now mix in the eggs one at a time and then the vanilla. Well, what do you know? I think you've made tart dough.' Anna turned and smiled broadly at the amazed Diana. 'We can't use it yet. It's got to be chilled for an hour at least, so wrap it up well and put it in the fridge.'

Diana did what Anna told her. 'When can we make the tart?'

'Well, listen to you. We'll get to it in an hour or two. I've a few things to do first.'

CHAPTER ELEVEN

N OT LONG AFTER HIS dinner at 541, Pieter came to see Miranda as he had promised. 'Miranda, Miranda,' he said, taking her hand in both of his, 'what an amazing dinner that was. I can't think when I last ate so well. Certainly not in this city. That lamb.' He sighed.

Miranda smiled and dipped her head. That slight movement was just enough to let the light strike her long silver earrings and splinter into a dazzle of reflections in the windows.

'Do you mind following me to the kitchen? I've got a stew on the stove and I really must get back to it.' He followed her hurried footsteps across the polished wood floors, past the great room with its large upholstered chairs, and kept pace as she pushed open the kitchen door.

He slowed, assaulted by the tempting smells, and looked around, taking in the bowls filled with thick chutneys, the pile of vegetables lying on the cutting board and the deep meaty smells of the stew bubbling slowly in the deep heavy pot. Out of the corner of his eye he watched Miranda in her apron as she stirred with a wooden spoon. He had been forcibly struck by her exotic beauty when she came to the door. The last time he saw her, before he went out to the Indies, she seemed assertively unconventional and opinionated, but now, as she stood in the center of her kingdom, he saw how alluring she was. 'Maarten tells me the restaurant is a great success,' he said, talking to her back as she rinsed a handful of sliced leeks under the faucet. 'I'm not surprised.' Miranda turned around with her spoon in midair and nodded to let him know she'd heard the compliment.

'What can I give you? A glass of wine? Some Italian espresso? I might even be able to track down a piece of lemon tart, if you're lucky.'

His nose twitched in anticipation as she handed him a large slice. Miranda motioned that he should sit at the round table in one corner of the kitchen. She sat across from him, cradling a bowl of egg yolks in the crook of her arm and beginning to beat them slowly.

'You know that I'm here to tell you about my trip.' Pieter barely waited for her answer. 'The trip I made for you.'

'That's not quite how I would have described it,' Miranda responded.

Pieter continued as if she hadn't spoken. 'Six months.' He sighed. 'They felt like two years. I won't pretend it wasn't an unsettling experience. In the beginning I loved going from island to island, chasing down your previous lives, but it became frustrating never to meet a soul who'd talked to you or Anton. I only hit my stride when I got onto the trail through those sculptures.' A tiny frisson shook the man's body. 'I wish I didn't have to tell you some of what I learned. No matter what your life with Anton was like, I'd be surprised if it included some of the things I encountered. My God, what a strange man Anton was.'

Miranda checked an impulse to mock Pieter. Yes, she thought to herself wryly, she had some sense that Anton might have wandered into uncharted waters.

'Did you know that he had collected a group of men and women who made him the center of their lives? He promised them passage to paradise and transcendence – I can't tell you how often I heard that word – and in return they obeyed his every command.'

Miranda leaned further over the table as if being closer would allow her to understand better.

'The group of them moved around quite a lot. It took more than a little ingenuity on my part to find their final island. When I got there, Anton refused to see me. Absolutely refused. If it hadn't been for Oleena, I don't know that I would ever have met him.'

'Oleena,' Miranda interrupted. 'Who's that?'

'I expected you'd ask,' he said. 'She was the woman who was always at his side.'

'His lover?'

'Yes, but she was more. They had an extraordinary relationship.' He watched Miranda closely, wondering how she would react to this news.

'She was the only one willing to take the chance on letting me talk to him. He hated outsiders, but she managed to convince him to let me have an audience. He'd become regal in a demented sort of way. He insisted on sitting on a chair shaped like a throne. He was always waving what I thought of as a scepter, although now I wonder if it didn't resemble some sort of fancy fly swatter. He even wore a crown shaped from the dried skin of a local animal.'

'Good Lord.'

'When I was finally brought into his presence,' he continued, 'I told him about Diana and the monkey, and about you, of course.'

'Didn't he ask about me?' Miranda leapt in. 'He must have been wondering how I was, what I was doing.'

'Perhaps I pressed him so hard about his responsibilities to you and Diana that I deflected those thoughts. I'm sure you know that I insisted on his signing the papers, relinquishing control over any property or goods here. I sent them to Welbroeck. I expect you have them safely in your keeping by now.'

Miranda nodded but said nothing, hoping her silence would

encourage Pieter to remember some interest Anton had expressed about her. 'I took a chance and asked about his ritual, but he waved me away, indicating my audience was over. Of course his refusal only piqued my curiosity. Later I asked Oleena if I could talk to him about it. She looked frightened. "I know," I told her, "it's bad enough that I come from the world he left behind and actually knew his parents. I know that makes me suspect, but tell him that I used to be on the national ski team when I was at university in Switzerland – I had to explain to her what snow and skis were – and that I had the most extraordinary experience once as I was skiing. As I was flying down the mountainside I felt as if my body had merged with it, as if it and the snow and I were all one. I will never forget it. Tell him that, Oleena, and see what he says.'

'It worked.' The expression on Miranda's face made Pieter think she worried that he might have gone over to Anton. 'Oleena said he'd see me in his hut that afternoon. I didn't want to meet him there with his throne, his scepter, his symbols of power all around. And it would be hot and dark, but I didn't dare jeopardize anything, so I went.

'When I got there, I was surprised to find him in nothing but an ikat diaper. My God, he was a mountain of soft flesh, seated on the dirt floor in front of his throne with his ankles crossed over each other. He was hovering over the earth like an immense bird of prey, doing some sort of exercise that involved his swooping low and then swinging in an arc as far as he could reach from left to right and back again. As I watched his gigantic reach and saw how fiercely he grabbed any loose stones or pebbles in the earth at his feet, I was struck that nothing would ever be enough for him. His breathing became like the panting of an animal as he reached low enough that his huge stomach finally almost grazed the earth.

'I told him that I was interested to know how he was preparing for his ritual. Of course I was still totally ignorant of what it was about at that point, but I took the chance.

Still no response. I described my sensation of merging with the mountain as I plunged straight down it, how at the end I wanted to eat the air, the snow, do it again and again, never lose that incredible feeling of possessing and being possessed. It was the first time Anton even noticed me.'

'I can imagine,' was Miranda's acerbic response.

'Next I slid to the ground near him. I reached backward over my head until the palms of my hands were flat on the ground and then kicked my feet up until I was standing on my hands. I could feel the blood rushing to my head, but I held still, raising one hand, slowly, putting it back and then raising the other, again and again until, without any warning, I sprang back to my feet in one fairly fleet motion.'

Looking at his grey hair and the soft dappling of age spots on his hands, Miranda appraised Pieter with new eyes.

'Anton didn't react at all. He began to take deep breaths in and then exhale, panting rapidly like a dog. His eyes were unfocused slits. I watched for a while and then began to count the length of the inhales and to fall into the rhythm of the panted exhales. In out, in out, in out. I have no idea how much time passed. The air began to shimmer around me and I felt as if I were seeing through streaming globules of mercury that blotted out everything. My head was heavy. I was afraid of suffocating in my own breath.

'The silver spheres continued to fill my vision, but when I closed my eyes they didn't leave. It was as if they were expanding ions of energy exerting more and more pressure inside me.

'Through them I could hear Anton's low seductive voice "Watch and you will see me rise, first from the earth and then from the sea. I will give myself to the elements of this world so that they may transform me for the next." I could feel the power of his conviction and for the first time I was afraid.'

'No wonder.' Miranda swallowed hard. She rested her chin

in her palm and looked thoughtfully toward Pieter. If he felt lost as Anton invited him into his bizarre world, she could hardly imagine how she would have responded. And this was the man to whom she had been married for years.

Pieter swiveled in his chair and looked away. When he spoke his words were barely audible. 'Anton reached out and stroked my leg. Somehow I managed to stand up. The air was stifling. It still shimmered, although the silver circles had begun to contract. Anton's preparations were beyond anything I could have imagined. I had guessed only that he had found a bunch of susceptible men and women to follow him. But it was much more complicated than that. Fortunately his breathing was so noisy and steady that I was able to slip away while he remained involved in his rituals.

'He searched me out the next day and with his great paw-like hand motioned for me to follow. "Are you afraid?" He smirked. By then I was too fascinated to turn back.

'This time he took me to a hidden cove near the sea. Again he undressed until he wore only the piece of ikat folded loosely around his private parts. He pushed me to the ground with a rough gesture and seated himself directly in front of me. His huge body obscured the sunlight and the sea. "Watch what I do." He began a series of rapid inhalations and long, slow exhalations. After a while he leaned forward. "Breathe with me." I did as he said. I don't know how much time had passed when he began expelling slow breaths from his mouth into mine. I recoiled but he clamped his hands so firmly on my shoulders I couldn't escape. Then without any warning he leaned forward, encircled my back with his arms and began slapping me, gently at first, then harder and harder as he set up a rhythm like the pounding of drums. His body began to vibrate. I heard his teeth bang against one another and then . . . I hardly know how to say this . . . energy rose up his body – I swear I could see the waves rise in a steady stream, rolling up his soft body and out the top of his head.'

Pieter watched Miranda lean forward on her elbows and bury her head in her hands. The curvature of her fingers reminded him of a fencer's protective mask.

'I wasn't prepared when he gripped my chin in his fingers and turned my head toward the sea. Where minutes before the sand had been unblemished, it was now marked with a perfect outline of his body. He saw the shock on my face. "The first step," he told me. "Tomorrow I will show you the second."'

Miranda was so unnerved that she stood up to make coffee more for the diversion than any need for something to drink. She carefully poured water into the bottom of her small espresso pot, ground the beans and tamped them into place, screwed the top on the pot, and set it over a high flame on the stove. When she heard the familiar bubbling, she picked up the pot, bent over Pieter's cup, and kept pouring until coffee spilled over the lip of the cup into the saucer and onto the table. 'I guess I'm not quite as composed as I thought,' she said to Pieter as she sponged up the excess.

Pieter sipped his coffee slowly and continued as if nothing had happened. 'The next day we sat at the edge of the sea. "This time the shadow leads," was all he said.

'Whoever heard of a shadow leading? Shadows don't go out ahead. He snorted at my objections. "I will cast my shadow onto the sea, and when it is time to rise to paradise it will be waiting for my body."'

Miranda sank into the chair, shaking her head in disbelief. 'I watched him remove the bit of fabric he was wearing,' Pieter continued, 'and then saw him seat himself on the beach at the edge of the sea. This time he did not want me to follow. "I will submerge myself in my interior darkness with long deep breaths," he told me, "and then I will watch my shadow detach itself and rise slowly."'

'Did anything happen?'

'I saw a dark form rise like a swimmer surfacing from deep water. I have no idea how it got there. Did it exit through his mouth? Did it fragment into a million black atoms and rise through his tissues and pores? Was he some kind of trick ventriloquist who could throw his body instead of his voice?' Pieter shivered as he remembered.

'You saw him cast his shadow upon the water?' Miranda began to wonder what Anton had done to Pieter.

'I know it sounds mad, but I swear that I saw darkness rise to the surface, as though thousands and thousands of spores of black mold were leaving Anton's body.'

'And reconstituting themselves in his shape? Come now, Pieter. You can't possibly mean that.'

'I was watching, not judging. I had no idea what to think. Anton saw my bewilderment. "Oh Pieter," he mimicked my voice, "wasn't it you who told me about dancing down the snow-covered mountain into an ecstatic embrace? Your release came through snow. Mine will come with water. Is that so different?"

'And then as if to prove his point, he lay down at the water's edge and waves rolled up and down his entire body. "Come, Pieter," he said in his most silvery voice, "feel the rush of energy here just as you did on the mountain. Release yourself."'

He would never tell anyone, not even Miranda, the next part. That he too had lain on the wet sand and felt its thick granules and small pebbles press into the flesh of his legs and back. That like Anton he had rolled in the warmth of the sand and into the sea, rolled and rolled until he could no longer distinguish whether sea or sand was cradling him. It felt wonderful rubbing the wet sand onto his body and whirling around, as if he were being received into a mystical union with earth, sea, and air.

Pieter was in a state of awe – that's what he called it later – and totally unprepared for Anton's embrace. He had been lured beyond his boundaries. Was violated too strong a word, he wondered, although he told none of this to Miranda.

He lapsed into silence. Without knowing the details Miranda understood. How brave of him to tell her as much as he had. She sat with him quietly until he slowly reemerged, Pieter van Hoorn, cosmopolitan businessman and world traveller.

'Some quince tart?' she offered. He nodded gratefully.

Pieter allowed a couple of days to go by before he returned to give Miranda the full report he had originally intended. 'After what I knew of Anton, I had a strong urge to leave, but I was too curious. The time of the ritual was coming close and I still didn't know what it entailed. It didn't take much to find out that the group gathered every night in a small hut, so I found a safe hiding place where I could watch them without anyone being the wiser. He undressed them, Miranda, men and women both.' Pieter swiveled his eyes to the floor. 'They were naked, their bodies there for them all to see and touch, and then they fell upon the floor of the hut. They . . .' splotches of embarrassment covered his cheeks. 'I couldn't believe my eyes. Anton spinning them loose of their clothing. Anton stroking their bodies. Anton commanding the men to . . . The men were . . . the women lay . . .' She heard the little gasps of excitement, could see that Pieter's professions of horror were shot through with fascination.

'Miranda,' Pieter said, 'he made them . . . oh, I can't even talk about it. He was evil. He had turned into some kind of perverse spiritual commandant. He used anything that would get them deeper into the rituals he was making up – blood sacrifices, extreme trances, cages . . . he called upon the powers of darkness to be their attendants before he and Oleena performed exorcisms. I swear to you that I never thought I'd see such things. You were lucky to escape.'

'Lucky?' Miranda gave a bitter laugh. 'I made him bring us back here. I didn't know what was happening to him but I knew I couldn't go on like that. I could only guess from the bruises on his flesh, the knife he strapped to his leg, the secrecy about his trips. Lucky? The only thing that's lucky is that Diana wasn't infected by his madness, although her connection to him is so desperate that I'm extremely worried how she'll react to what you tell her.'

'I want to talk to you about that. What do I tell her?'

'Pieter,' she said firmly, 'you can't tell Diana too much. I don't know what she has guessed, but even if she *has* seen the sculpture collection, she wouldn't have the slightest idea what a sexual obsession is.'

'But you do,' said Pieter, sounding a good deal less gracious than he had intended.

'Well, I know how he treated me. I knew about his obsession with extravagant forms of passion and punishment, but I was really only guessing. I was young and naïve when all this began.'

'Don't worry. I won't go into lurid details with Diana,' Pieter assured her. 'I could tell her that he had become the leader of a group of men and women who had left their families and friends to follow him. I will tell her that they believed his teachings and believed that he would lead them into a kind of paradise beyond anything they could imagine.'

'And when they didn't do as he asked?' Miranda knew more than Pieter had guessed. 'He punished them, didn't he? Withdrew from them, maybe even threw them into whatever kind of darkness was most painful for them? It's ironic, isn't it, that he's essentially thrown Diana into a terrible kind of darkness too.'

Pieter nodded. 'So what should I tell Diana? I have to tell her about Oleena.'

'Oleena? Why?'

Pieter wrinkled his brow, trying to find a delicate way of explaining. 'The woman who gave up her life to be with him was left behind. She has sent something to Diana.'

'The woman for whom he left me?' Miranda asked.

'I don't know. All I know is that she was devastated. When

he died all his followers were in a state of confusion and panic and they fled as quickly as they could find boats. Oleena collapsed. I tried to help her find her way back.'

'How kind of you.' Miranda arched an eyebrow. 'Where is she now?'

'On the island where she had been before all this happened. I think she will be all right now.' Pieter decided not to elaborate. 'I'm sorry for you that it ended like this. It probably brings back memories you'd just as soon leave where they were.'

'Thank you.' Miranda absentmindedly fiddled with her braid, moving it from one shoulder to the other. 'I'm worried about Diana. Be gentle when you speak to her.'

'I will try my very best not to say anything more than I must, but I have promised myself I'll answer her questions honestly.' He flushed. There was so much that he wasn't going to talk about.

CHAPTER TWELVE

THE NIGHT BEFORE PIETER came to see her, Diana was a volatile mixture of exhilaration, fear, and grief. She tried to calm her agitation by laying her head upon the pillow she had wrapped in her father's shirt. She slowed her breathing to absorb its reassuring smell and lay for long minutes staring at nothing until a series of phosphorescent images gradually arose and appeared to her shimmering in the inky darkness. Diana watched as her father rose from the waves, his body floating in the waters. She heard his soft, hypnotic voice speaking to her. 'Do you remember how we stood on the shore and watched the sun fracture into silvery light that sparkled on the water? Do you remember how we were thrilled by the dazzle blotting out the division between sea and sky, how we fell silent before the power of the light? I am with that light now, Diana. I am with the vast encompassing seas. I have finally come to the place for which I yearned.'

Diana spoke to him in a voice heavy with pain: 'I tried to find you. Night after night I saw you in my dreams. I could feel you sliding slowly toward disaster and I tried to find my way to you. Oh, Daddy, my heart is cracking. No matter how hard I tried, I failed. I could not warn you. I could not come to you. I still look for you everywhere and can never find you. Where are you now? Where have you gone to now?'

The day after his last talk with Miranda, Pieter returned to see Diana. Miranda greeted him at the front door and once again invited him to the kitchen. 'Coffee?' she asked. He accepted with alacrity, ready for a jolt of strong Italian espresso, hoping that she might accompany it this time with a slice of one of the quince tarts for which the restaurant was becoming known.

'I have to thank you, Miranda, for your confidence in me. I had no idea what I'd encounter when I returned to places I had loved so many years ago. I certainly didn't expect the experience with Anton to mark me as it has, but even for all that, I am grateful that I went. I'm a different man now.'

'Really?' Miranda asked, wondering if she should tell him that she could hardly have failed to notice.

'For the first time I really understand how much people can mean to one another. What love and caring are. How important they can be. I've spent most of my life in business and I've been very successful. I won't be modest. I've skied on most of the great mountains of the world, my tennis game is good enough that I can play anywhere without shame, and I've put together a collection of the diaries and manuscripts of great explorers that are desired by several very impressive libraries. I have always tracked down what I wanted and I've refused to take no for an answer, but my trip to the islands opened my eyes to another way. I didn't tell you when I accepted your offer, but my wife, Zoe, had left me a few months before. She had yearned for a close relationship for years, she said, and had finally given up on me. I couldn't believe it. I did everything I could think of to win her back. I sent her armloads of roses one week, tulips the next. I bought her fine leatherbound books with the illuminations she loves. I had a designer make her diamond earrings in a design that has meaning for both of us. I did everything I could to entice her to Venice, the city where we spent our honeymoon.

'She turned it all down. When she told me that she wanted a life of her own, she spoke with finality in her voice I had never heard before. I quickly learned that she had found someone else. I went wild with jealousy. That's when I made my first efforts at detective work. I was determined to find out everything I could about my rival and then beat him at his own game.'

'And did you?' Miranda asked.

'No,' Pieter admitted sadly. 'Nothing I did made her come back. I couldn't believe it. I'd always won, always gotten everything I wanted. I was so certain I could change her mind that I continued to buy her presents while I was in the islands. I thought they might have the magical effect that nothing else had.'

As if she knew they were waiting for her, a sleep-drained Diana trudged down the hall with Majine loping beside her. Pieter got up to greet the girl, then took one look at the monkey and retreated. He was astonished when Majine chattered happily in his direction, even rubbing his furry body against Pieter's pant leg as he settled next to him on the floor.

'Hello,' Diana said shyly, when Pieter thrust out his hand. 'I brought Majine because I wanted you to see that the special seeds and herbs you sent really healed him. Everyone was so worried about him, weren't they, Mamma? And now look. Doesn't he look splendid?'

'Indeed,' said Pieter, who eyed Majine cautiously, worried that the monkey might turn on him at any moment. 'I've brought more seeds and herbs in case you should ever need them again.'

'Are you going to tell me about my father?' she asked, fidgeting with her fingers. 'I'm sort of scared, but I want to hear, I think.' Her face flushed.

'Yes, of course, I am. That's why I'm here. Is this where you'd like to have the talk?'

Diana was relieved that he gave her the choice. 'No, I'd like you to come to my room. I can show you what I've done with some of the things from my father's trunk.' And without any warning, she leapt up and ran ahead, racing down the hallway, her bare feet slapping the wood floors.

Pieter ambled through the large, extravagantly furnished living room and passed through the entrance hall with its huge leather trunk, ebony framed mirror, and mahogany sideboard. He knocked on Diana's door like a proper visitor. The girl invited him in to see her room and the room connected to it, where she had heaped all her father's clothing and nautical equipment. 'My goodness, did all this come out of that one trunk?' Pieter asked. 'What do you plan to do with it?'

'I'm not sure yet.'

'I've brought you one more thing that belonged to your father,' Pieter told her. 'Oleena, the woman with whom he spent his life in the Indies, wrapped it for you. She wrote you a letter that you should probably read before you open the gift.' Pieter reached into his pocket and brought out a box covered in simple bark cloth that had been stained with images of monkeys.

Diana's eyes shone as she looked at their silvery bodies and crested heads. Then she turned her attention to the tiny, spidery handwriting that spelled out her name. With a sidelong glance at Pieter, she slid her index finger under the flap of the envelope and carefully opened it. Inside was a letter Oleena had written that Pieter translated for her.

Diana,

Although we have never met and you perhaps do not even know that I have been your father's companion for many years, I know about you from the stories he told me. I can only imagine how much you have missed him all these years. In some way I can share your sadness, since I never knew my own father. He left before I was born and my mother refused to speak of him. Throughout my whole life I have carried a sorrow that has never left me.

I want you to have the ring that Anton always wore. In all the years we were together, he took it off only once, on the final day of his life, to participate in a ritual that required him to walk into the sea with nothing on his body. I want you to know that you appeared in dreams to your father from time to time. He would wake in the morning telling me that he could hear your voice. He called you his sorceress. Toward the end, he told me that he could not understand why you appeared to him insistently, saying again and again, 'I would save you if I could.' He knew that you loved and cared for him.

When I first saw your father's ring, I assumed that it was chiseled from pale quartz or some unfamiliar stone that got its icy color from being trapped in frost. I do not know why it is carved with such choppy strokes – to me they look like waves gone wild – but the first time your father went into the sea, I was astonished to see the stone turn a brilliant purple color that glowed at the core.

I hope that having the ring will bring you some solace. I assure you that your father felt connected to you even though you were so far from each other.

Oleena

Diana took the ring out of the box. Oleena was right. The stone was carved to look like thick choppy waves. 'I think I see a small figure,' she told Pieter, holding it out to him. 'Do you?' He looked for a long time without answering. 'Look down deep,' she insisted. 'I think it's a man.' He shook his head and said only, 'Maybe your eyes are better than mine.' Diana slid the ring down her finger, but it was so loose that it wobbled and spun around. 'It won't even fit on my thumb,' she said sadly, putting it back in its monkey box.

'Tell me about my father, Mr. van Hoorn. I want to know what he looked like and how he dressed and talked. And who is Oleena?'

'Your father was like a king to his group of followers and

Oleena was like his queen. They loved him and did whatever he asked of them.'

'I would have too,' said Diana. 'I could have been with him and Oleena, the three of us a family moving with the tides.'

'Your father was so tall next to the islanders that he looked like a giant, and after a while he was so tanned by the sun that his skin was almost the same color as theirs. Of course, most of them had straight black hair and your father's was curly, like yours. He sometimes wore a kind of headdress made of animal skin as stiff as parchment and it didn't always want to stay on top of his springy hair, but as with most things, his powerful insistence finally made it behave the way he wanted.'

Pieter searched his memory for details of Anton's 'throne', his long oval face with its mobile features, the way he waved his thick fingers to send people away, his big body gone soft and slack, his deep lidded eyes that looked sleepy but missed nothing. 'You know from his letter that he was driven in his search for transcendence. His followers worshiped him. They had left everything behind to be with him and they were ready to do whatever he said so they could go to paradise with him. They had made their final preparations, but then there was some sort of strange accident in their very first ceremony and your father drowned.'

'But my father knew everything about the sea. How could he drown?'

'I'm sure he didn't think he'd put himself at risk. The way I heard it was that when they were in the water, one of the men became disoriented and grabbed him and held on to him tightly, I'm not sure – I think that's what happened – and somehow your father was plunged into the water and couldn't find his way back to the surface.'

'Didn't they try to save him?'

'They must have, but in the confusion . . .'

'And now he is dead?' Diana asked, knowing the answer. And now all I see are cracks in the dark vaults of the sky, she thought. Maybe you cannot see them yet because they are so tiny, but one day they will open wide as the forces of loss put pressure on the dome that holds the curvature of the earth and sky in place and then the blood of darkness will run into the sea.

'Do you want to know about Oleena?' asked Pieter. 'She's deeply sad too.'

'Is she like me?' Pieter was startled by the question.

'I hadn't ever considered it. You are small, but Oleena is tiny, no more than a meter and a half high at most. She has tiny bones, tiny hands that are so expressive that I think I'd understand her even if she didn't speak a word. Her face is oval, thinner than yours, and her body moves like a dancer's, even though she never danced until after your father died.'

'What color is her hair?'

'Black. It falls straight to her shoulder blades. Her skin is the color of polished bronze.'

'Do you love her?'

'What makes you . . . why . . . ?' And then hurriedly, 'Not the way your father did. I love her like . . . When your father died, she was left alone with no one to look after or protect her.'

'Do you miss her?'

'Oh yes, very much. I haven't told anyone yet, but I plan to go back to her when it's safe.'

'Why isn't it safe?'

'When I left masses of angry natives were marching down from the mountains. They got close enough that I could hear their voices and hear the earth trembling beneath their feet. They had powerful weapons with them and they were threatening to kill any foreigners they found. They blame Europeans for anything that's gone wrong – crop failures, the mysterious death of many birds, explosions of the volcano – and I was afraid that they would kill me, or anyone else they encountered, as a sort of sacrifice, a way to pacify the powers in charge of the world.'

'Oh,' said the girl sadly. 'My father died and I have lost my anchor and my hopes, but you found a girl who could be your daughter.'

'I guess you could see it that way.' Pieter was anxious to end the conversation.

'I tried to save him but I couldn't.'

'No, I imagine not.'

'I've decided to make a salt and iron garden for him,' she said, explaining what she and Andreas had designed. 'If you have anything more you can tell me about him, if you have any more things that belonged to him, I will put them in my monument.'

'I'll look and I'll let you know if I do.'

'And will you come back to visit me and tell me more stories of my father?'

'Of course,' he assured her, although he was hardly anxious to do so. 'I think I should go now. I expect to have a letter from Oleena soon and should she tell me more, I'll pass it on to you.'

'Yes, I'd like that. Come back. Come back and eat the tarts that Anna and I are making.' She took the ring out of the box and held it on her finger so that she could wave at him in the person of her father and herself.

CHAPTER THIRTEEN

B Y THE END OF its first year, the restaurant had found a place in the heart of the city. Miranda was being talked about as if she were Scheherazade in the kitchen. Night after night she created dishes with which to dazzle the diners at her tables, and they responded by returning again and again. The more she cooked, the more she enticed, the more she enticed, the more appetites she excited, and the more appetites she excited, the more people came to eat.

Each evening Miranda appeared in the dining room in one of her long, silken dresses shot through with metallic threads that traced patterns of whirling suns, the moon in all its phases, and sprinklings of stars. A necklace shaped like an elegant spider web circled her throat with brilliant stones sparkling in the irregular openings of its tracery. As she wove her way through the room, she spoke to everyone by name. She greeted those who returned frequently with a special dish. 'Just for you,' she'd assure the delighted recipient. 'Come back,' she would say as each one left. 'Come back again.'

And they did.

A single small article about the restaurant appeared in the newspaper, but it was the excited recommendations of people who had eaten there, the proud bragging of one friend to another about an extraordinary meal, that prompted the crowds that wanted entrance to 541. Miranda received so many letters that she stuck them in a scrapbook, fully intending to straighten them out when she found time.

Giles teased Miranda that she had founded a tiny kingdom and become the official enchantress of its ever-changing population. The only other permanent natives, he pointed out, were Anna, waitress and pastry cook, and her sometimes aide-de-camp, Diana. 'And you,' she inquired, 'where do you fit in my kingdom?'

'A question I ask myself frequently,' Giles replied. 'Am I the keeper of the books that allow the kingdom to function, the man with the enviable position of tasting every dish destined to be eaten by your subjects? Remember,' he prodded her, 'remember how you put me under your spell with that quince and apple tart? I was merely the first to furnish you with proof of your magical talents, and I hope to continue.'

'Do you doubt it?' she asked.

'Aah, Miranda, you give a man hope. I am your suitor and your subject.'

'And more,' she said expansively, 'and more.'

Miranda woke in the middle of the night, fretful and anxious about the growing demands of the restaurant. She turned, she thrashed, she tugged at the sheets until Giles, who slept like a curled prawn, slid sideways and covered her body with his. 'Mmm,' he whispered, as he sucked on an earlobe and let his fingers crawl into the convoluted whorl of the ear into which he hummed. His arm slid over her shoulder, his hand reached down to encircle a breast and feel its full weight in his open palm. He continued to stroke her body until he felt her relax and give over.

Stirred, consoled by his attentions, she rolled over, slid on top of his warm body and stretched out along its full length. They moved together then as if they were swimming in the white sheets, body against body, heat meeting heat, rhythms speeding up, two swimmers now become one as their exhalations released them into the shimmering darkness.

As Miranda's fame spread beyond the cool grey city of Amsterdam, she was astonished to find people coming from towns in the outskirts and larger cities beyond. One night a couple arrived from France and praised the pumpkin soup with hazelnuts, the lamb shanks with sprinklings of grated lemon peel and parsley. At dessert time she swept into the dining room bearing a bottle of champagne to toast the two unsuspecting diners as if they were official representatives of their country of culinary sophistication on a mission to seal an entente cordiale.

Owners of great liners and freighters ate at 541 when they could. A family of five came to celebrate their grandmother's eightieth birthday. A young couple reserved four tables for their wedding dinner. A medical student brought his three closest friends to celebrate the beginning of their careers as doctors.

They had all heard about Miranda. Many of the diners brought with them fragmentary knowledge about the food that she cooked. 'Rutabaga soup,' one said to her. 'Someone told me you serve rutabaga soup.' 'Absolutely not,' she replied. 'I've never cooked a rutabaga in my life. Roots – maybe someone told you that I love root vegetables. Beets drizzled with citrus, potatoes and celery root with grated horseradish for bite. Golden yams sliced like coins and fried until they puff up, crispy to bite into but creamy inside. I've cooked those.'

The more people came, the more Miranda felt she had to keep changing the menu. She was up at all hours, crafting new tastes, new dishes, and still she dashed to Dagstrom's when she ran short of ingredients, to Andreas's nursery for last-minute additional flowers. Giles had told her from the beginning that she'd never get rich, but he had recently started to point out that she could get exhausted. The pace never let up. Indeed, under the lash of her yearning for change, it only intensified.

When he tried to convince her to take a week off, dangling a short trip to Italy before her sleep deprived eyes, he wasn't surprised when she objected, 'What about all the people who have reservations?'

'Pick a time when it isn't so busy. Just tell them 541 will be closed for a short vacation,' he suggested.

'Impossible,' she replied. 'They'll forget us if we go away now.'

Miranda did admit she was glad she allowed Anna to take over the desserts. She had been increasingly impressed with the young woman's delicate hand with doughs, and so while Miranda continued to dream up the fillings and flavorings, it was Anna who made napoleons layered with nectarine jam and vanilla-scented pastry cream, Anna who sprinkled crushed pistachios over the silky surface of a dark chocolate tart, Anna who filled delicate tuile cookies with a wintry custard ice cream flavored with cinnamon and cloves, cardamom, allspice and mace. Miranda watched as Anna taught Diana some of the rudiments of pastry making and saw the girl blossom as she learned to use her slender fingers to shape tiny curls of dough and scallop the edges of pastry crusts.

As the demand for special desserts grew, Diana was provisionally put in charge of cookies. To win over her mother, she practiced for two days and then made butter cookies flavored with tiny droplets of vanilla, cookies spiced with nutmeg and cloves, and silky dark chocolate wafers held together with a thin layer of mint-accented chocolate cream. When Miranda and then Anna nodded their approval, Diana made dozens of cookies in the shape of big buttons. Then she let her imagination take charge. She began making cookies in the shape of the crescent moon and the sun with a blaze of rays. She turned dough into waves on the sea and stars from the sky. Anna praised the beauty of the forms and Diana plunged excitedly into designs in the shape of sea serpents and frangipani blossoms and tiny butterflies with dots of dark pastry cream for the patterns on their wings. 'Yes,' said Anna, hesitantly, 'let's show them to your mother. I'm not sure about that sea serpent.' Nor did she like the frenzy with which her young helper was working. Miranda vetoed the serpents, although she allowed herself to be convinced that they could be ordered for children's plates.

The following week Diana brought Majine into the kitchen early one morning. She slid one end of the leash around his neck and tethered the other to the leg of the stool on which she sat. While no one was paying attention, she began peeling and slicing mangoes, surreptitiously sneaking misshapen slices to the monkey. Next she slit open a vanilla pod, slid it into the pastry cream that was simmering on top of the stove, and let it flavor the cream that became as thick as soft custard. Out came the bean and in went some pureed mango. Majine looked up expectantly. 'Not yet,' she told him, 'it's too hot.'

When it was cool enough to taste, she stuck a spoon into its depths first for herself and then for the monkey who smacked his lips happily and looked expectantly for more. 'That's all for now,' she told him. She laid some tart dough inside a fluted pan and baked it until it was lightly brown. When she pulled it out of the oven, she let it cool just long enough that a bite wouldn't burn a waiting tongue and then carpeted it with a layer of mango slices, which covered the pastry cream. She fanned wedges of mango over the top, and, at the last minute, gave it a delicate glaze of apricot jam. Majine looked at her hopefully, but she just wiggled her fingers in his direction to let him know she'd be back shortly, and walked with the tart into the dining room where her mother and Giles were engaged in deep conversation. She stood there, holding it on a platter, completely invisible as far as she could tell, shifting her weight gingerly from foot to foot while she waited to be noticed.

'I want you to taste something, Mamma. It's a tart Majine. I made it in honor of him. See – it's got mangoes on top.'

Miranda cut a tiny slice for herself and another for Giles, and exhaled with an impressed 'Ahhh'. She refrained from mentioning that most people might think it more than a little peculiar to name a tart for a monkey, and said only, 'It's delicious. We can certainly add this to our list of desserts. You're turning out to be quite a baker, Diana.'

To capitalize on the success of the special dessert orders Giles suggested adding a room purely for baking.

'I had no idea what an entrepreneur I'd gotten myself involved with.' Miranda was torn by admiration for the idea and consternation at being usurped as chef-commander of the realm. It was bad enough that Giles was talking as if 541 were his restaurant, but here he was giving all the work and glory to Anna.

'Darling,' he said, 'it's all a plot to find ways that your restaurant can make money without exhausting you. Look at you, constantly driven to create new and tantalizing dishes for your admiring public. You never stop. Surely it's obvious that it's you who are the source, the creator and cook of the dazzling food.'

Mollified, Miranda agreed.

Once again Giles oversaw a construction project in the house. He stayed on budget by feeding the workers Miranda's food every day, stipulating that meals would stop immediately if the construction fell behind schedule. With that incentive the job was finished on time down to the last coat of paint. Miranda looked at him with new admiration. 'It's beautiful, Giles. It's really beautiful. I never guessed that it could be this nice. Now I almost wish that I hadn't let Anna take over all the desserts,' she said wistfully.

'Great.' Giles sighed exaggeratedly. 'I go to all this trouble and I inspire you to add more work to your already preposterous load?'

'I'm kidding,' she said half-heartedly, still eyeing the pastry room.

While the construction was in progress, Miranda received a letter that she answered with alacrity.

Dear Miranda (if I may),

You may remember me as the man who came up to you at the end of a dinner at your restaurant some time ago and raved on rather too long about the handsome painting you have hanging on the wall. I must have been inspired by my friend Pieter van Hoorn's eloquence that night, since I hadn't planned to say a word. I am embarrassed that I have allowed so much time to pass between then and now. My only excuse is that with the crush of things that crowd onto my desk, I often neglect to pursue those that are my own personal enthusiasms.

Pieter may have mentioned that I am a curator at the museum. When he and I were talking recently, he told me that he remembered first seeing your painting decades ago when he was a very young man at a party given by your parents-in-law. Evidently it had disappeared in the interim and you unearthed it purely by chance when you were cleaning an old piece of furniture you wanted in your restaurant. What a stroke of good fortune! Pieter guessed that your mother-in-law must have hidden the work from the Germans and then forgotten all about it after the war was over.

I wonder if you might let me come to examine the painting more closely. I would be happy to make any arrangement that is convenient for you. You can write to me at the museum and let me know if you would permit a visit, perhaps with an eye to allowing the painting to be seen under closer scrutiny at the museum later.

Yours sincerely,
Jan Witt

When Jan Witt arrived, Miranda recognized him immediately. Tall and thin as a stork, he wore tiny round glasses perched on his nose and a big floppy bow tie. Everything about him was slightly exaggerated. 'I'm delighted you have come to see my painting.' She told him. 'I think it's perfect for the restaurant, but no one else seems to pay it any attention.'

'That is hard to believe. Anyway I am most interested. Perhaps if you'd just show me the way,' he said, shifting a heavy canvas bag from one shoulder to another, 'I can take out these tools and go right to work.'

'Tools?' Miranda asked with a hint of alarm in her voice.

'Nothing invasive, I assure you,' he said, responding to her tone. They arrived in the dining room and he began to unload. 'Measuring tape, camera, a jeweler's loupe, so I can really see details.' He named each one as he drew it out of the sack and laid it on a table. Looking at the picture again, he nodded appreciatively. 'It's a handsome work. No matter what I find, I'd like to suggest that you get it cleaned and stretched properly. See how the varnish has darkened the surface' – he pointed at several particularly murky areas of pigment – 'not to mention the grit that the years have laid on it.'

'I think I'll wait until I hear from you before I do anything.'

'Very wise, although I expect I'll have happy news.'

'You think it might be valuable?'

'I'll let you know as soon as I do,' he promised.

'Can you give me some sort of rough idea?'

Jan Witt looked conflicted. 'It's only a hunch. I wouldn't want to mislead you or get your hopes up.'

'No, no, don't worry. I'm simply curious.'

'Understand I may well be wrong, but the more I look, the more I'm convinced that you may have a Floris Gerritsz van Schooten.'

Miranda looked blank. 'All those names make him sound important.'

'He absolutely is, but if the painting turns out to be by one of his pupils, its value drops quite steeply.'

'Still,' she wondered in his direction, 'what would it be worth then?'

'Let's just say that it's extremely rare to find such a painting in private hands. Now I'd better get to work.'

Miranda wondered if she should mention the visit to Giles. Perhaps not yet. She'd wait to hear if the painting was valuable. Even then she might keep it a secret. Yes, her little reserve in case of hard times. How delicious to think that her fortune might be hanging in plain view and no one would be the wiser.

She wondered if Peter was right about Ria's hiding the work to keep it out of the hands of the Germans. Miranda's theory was that Ria concealed the painting from the creditors who took most of their possessions after Thomas's bank failed. It must have been terrible to lose so much, Miranda thought to herself, especially since she'd begun with so little. And every time she looked at me, it must have reminded her that Anton could have married well and rescued the family's fortunes instead of throwing himself away on an underage Australian with no dowry.

'Miranda,' Giles said one night as they sat in the kitchen nibbling leftovers. 'O goddess of the kitchen, here I am once again applying to make you mine. I would be your consort, protector, the guardian of your tender self. Have I not been provisioner of wines, keeper of the books, and overseer of the construction?'

Miranda looked at him, her guileless Giles, and smiled. 'Yes,' she whispered in a tiny voice that issued from the depths of her. 'Yes, I will. I'll marry you Giles. You've waited so long and now I'm ready. Really ready. Yes, I will. I will marry you, Giles. Yes. I will.'

They set the date far enough in advance that Miranda didn't have to cancel a single reservation. They would marry on a Sunday afternoon and take a two-day honeymoon. 'Just two,' Miranda insisted. 'That's as long as I can be away.'

Diana was hardly surprised when Miranda told her the news. 'I kind of expected it. I mean, Giles already lives here. But that's nice for you, Mamma.' She couldn't see how it would make much difference, although she was gripped by a deep sense of disloyalty to her father.

Anna surprised herself with a spontaneous outpouring. 'Thank God for it. Do you know how much that man loves you? There's nothing he wouldn't do for you. Oh, you look so happy. He's really made us all successful, hasn't he?'

Miranda decreed that the ceremony be small. Diana would be her witness, Maarten would stand up for Giles, and Anna, Andreas, and Mies would be the only guests. 'And Majine,' Diana insisted.

Early on the morning of the wedding, Mies arrived at the back door with his arms full of flowers. Andreas had selected orchids for Miranda, Queen Anne's lace and anemones for Diana, and sprays of scarlet ginger and white tulips for the room where the ceremony would take place. Diana was still in her bathrobe when she opened the door. Mies thrust the flowers in her hands and blurted out, 'You're a skinny bone.'

Diana set the flowers on the table while she thought. 'Do you mean I look thin?'

'Yes,' he said brightly.

'I'm not any different than usual. I'm just wearing this bathrobe because I'm not ready to get dressed yet.' She picked up the white tulips and held them in front of her, obscuring the bathrobe, so he could see her face. 'See?'

Mies shook his head up and down to show her he understood. She put the flowers down with the others and reminded him to come back in a few hours. 'I'm changing my clothes too,' he said, looking down at his dirt caked overalls.

'I'm sure you will look very nice,' she told him.

Miranda had finally given Anna permission to make the wedding lunch, although she asked so many questions and gave her so many reminders that Anna ended up wishing Miranda the Miraculous, as she sometimes thought of her, would just cook it herself. She must have contradicted herself ten times. 'Don't forget to make the stocks while I'm gone. Make just enough pastries for the orders.' Then, 'No, make a few dozen more. People always drop in on Sundays hoping to find something available.' 'Don't take any reservations. I don't care who it is.' Anna nodded 'You have to take reservations. What was I thinking? We can't have tables go empty.'

'Have you toasted the hazelnuts?' and, five minutes later, 'Don't let the coconut milk boil.' While Anna helped Miranda with her hair, all she heard was 'Remember – keep the flame low when you're poaching the red snapper.'

And so it came to pass that Giles and Miranda were married in the living room on a day trembling between the end of winter and the beginning of spring. A milky sky streaked with metallic grey clouds covered the city, while brilliant colored flowers warmed the interior of the house. Miranda had laughed at the very notion of wearing white and appeared instead in a sapphire blue kimono with a single, elegant white ibis, its downy wings extended their full breadth, on the back. Tiny orchids with orange-speckled throats flowed down the river of her long, dark braid. Diana wore a garland of anemones and Majine, sated with mangoes, sat quietly tethered to the leash that Diana had wound with Queen Anne's lace.

Giles could see no one but Miranda, his glamorous bride in her dramatic kimono and flower-filled braid. She stood almost as tall as he in her high-heeled sandals. Andreas couldn't imagine where else he would encounter such an exotic collection of flora and fauna, but found himself moved as Giles swept

Miranda into his arms and kissed her as if he would never let her go.

Before leaving for the Italian countryside, Miranda and Giles fed each other slices of the wedding cake that Anna and Diana had made for the occasion. Quince preserves lay between the layers; sprays of quince blossoms decorated the top. 'Ah, the famous, seductive quince,' said the bridegroom, 'each fruit like the breast of a beautiful woman.' Diana blushed; Mies looked confused. Andreas hoisted his glass of champagne and drank a toast to the happiness of the couple. The small party then followed them out of the living room and down the front steps, where they pelted the departing bride and groom with handfuls of jasmine rice. Majine leapt about, happily picking up kernels of rice and tasting them, crunching them noisily between his teeth. 'Goodbye, goodbye,' the group cried as Giles and Miranda drove off to the railroad station and their two days in the Italian countryside.

While they were gone, Anna taught Diana how to play cards. She cut her hair. 'You look like a shrub from the Australian outback that I saw in a photograph.'

'Mamma's from Australia.'

'Yes, but she looks like she's from somewhere much more exotic.'

'Don't remind me.'

'Let's clean up that bird's nest.'

'Have you ever cut hair before?' Diana asked dubiously.

'Have I . . . Who did you think cut the hair of all my younger brothers and sisters? Don't be so nervous. At least I could give it a little shape.'

'Who cares? Nobody looks at me.'

'Well, I do, and I'd like to be able to see you instead of all that underbrush. Sit still. I'm going to get a towel for your shoulders.'

The clipping and snipping began. 'What are you doing?'

Diana objected. 'Stop. I'm not going to have any hair left at all. No one will recognize me.'

'Don't be silly. Here, let's brush away this fleece and take a look.'

Diana was quiet as she studied her reflection. Her out-of-control curls were gone. What was left lay closer to her head, making it easier to see her face. She looked serious. Thoughtful.

'Majine, who is this?' Anna asked. 'Is this someone you know?' The monkey leapt right into Diana's arms. 'OK? Now are you convinced?'

'He's not exactly the best judge. He'd know me if he were blindfolded. OK.' She spoke tentatively. 'I guess I'll just have to get used to it.'

'Be my guest. Now let's play cards.'

'Honeymoon?' Giles responded in answer to Anna's question when they returned. 'How was the honeymoon? I'd call it more of a sleep cure. Miranda was so tired I swear she'd have slept through the meals if I hadn't woken her up. I kept having to persuade her that everything was fine here, that pastries were flying out the door, and then back to sleep she went.' Miranda scowled, then sheepishly lowered her eyes and smiled sideways at him.

In the next year 541 appeared in guidebooks and magazines in various languages and it was almost inevitably accompanied by numerous stars. Critics declared it the best restaurant in the country. Reservations were almost impossible to get without a wait of several months. People stopped Miranda on the street to tell her how much they liked her restaurant and she noticed fingers pointing and mouths working as she rode by on her bicycle.

On a cold winter morning in late January when Giles and Diana had both already left the house, Miranda made herself a strong cup of coffee. Nibbling absentmindedly on a leftover slice of apple tart, she looked out at the drizzle falling from the grey sky and decided to make something spicy and colorful to dispel the chill of the dreary day. She was contemplating her decisions at the same time that she was looking over the list of reservations for the night. Ooof – she was certain that she recognized the name of a famous French restaurant critic. No time for sitting around. She'd need threads of saffron for a sizzling prawn soup and more chilies to mince with garlic. And what would she serve after the soup? The fishmonger would be by in the early afternoon, but it was clear that she needed to pay a quick visit to Dagstrom's. She put on her raincoat, flipped up its hood, and just before leaving asked Anna to take a pot off the fire if she wasn't back in an hour.

Miranda pedaled slowly over the icy streets, being particularly careful on the slippery brick bridges. Long lines of motorcars were crawling in both directions and policemen stood at intersections guiding traffic. Dark clouds were massing overhead.

When Miranda got to the store, old Mr. Dagstrom waved in her direction. 'You look like you're in a hurry, Miranda.' 'How right you are,' she told him. 'I need your best saffron threads and a couple of big heads of garlic.' 'Nothing more exotic than that?' Challenged, Miranda decided to ask for mint and basil. 'You don't have any persimmons, do you?' 'Persimmons, no. But otherwise you're in luck. The herbs just arrived, each in its own perfect packet, waiting for someone like you to take them home.' 'Do I detect a romantic under that gruff exterior, Mr. Dagstrom?' 'Romantic?' he barked. 'I must be mistaken,' she retreated hastily. 'Will that be all?' She nodded. 'Shall I put it on your tab?' She nodded again. 'Be careful on your way home, Miranda. The streets are icy.' 'Thanks, Mr. Dagstrom. I appreciate your concern.' 'Always happy to look after a pretty woman,' he replied. 'And a good customer too,' she shot back, sliding the hood of her raincoat over her head and setting off again.

As Miranda snaked her way through traffic, she thought about what she would serve the famous critic after the soup. Lamb simmered with slices of quince and a drizzle of the 25-year-old vinegar she kept for special occasions? Duck with apricots plumped in port? She and Anna would need to think of a special dessert. She remembered that she had enough persimmon purée to make a soufflé. Yes, that's what was needed, warm tropical fruit whipped into a cloud of delicate flavor to take the chill off a cold winter night.

Miranda tried to imagine what he would look like. Short and stout, he'd have a florid complexion, a nose with an irregular bump widening at the bridge and a dimple in his chin. He would be wearing a handsomely tailored sport coat with a bright blue shirt calculated to deflect attention from his corpulent midsection. He would arrive punctually but not, she hoped, like many of his countrymen, with a dog. Animals in the dining room – such a barbaric practice! Majine, who was sometimes tethered in the kitchen to keep Diana company, immediately scented another animal and went wild, desperate to claim the territory as his. Long scratch marks low on the kitchen door testified to his previous attempts to attack all intruders.

Miranda's reveries were interrupted by the unpleasant smell of fuel. As she wrinkled her nose and shook her head to banish the odor, she missed seeing the puddle in front of her. Shimmering with an iridescent slick of gasoline, it was deeper than it looked. She struggled to hold the handlebars steady as water seeped into the spokes, slowing her progress and causing her to tilt sideways. The man driving behind her slammed on his brakes, but it was too late. He struck the bicycle, sending Miranda over the handlebars, glancing off one of the elms at the edge of the sidewalk. A passerby watched her fly toward the tree in a low, flat arc, saw her hit it sideways and land in a crumpled heap at the base of the tree. Unnerved by the awkward angle at which she lay, he knelt down next to her. Her face was as white as milk, her breathing labored. She didn't respond to his questions. In the distance a policeman blew his whistle. A horn honked. After a long time an ambulance made its way slowly through the traffic.

When Anna answered the insistent ringing at the front door, she expected to find someone desperate for a dinner reservation. Instead a young man in a policeman's uniform shifted from foot to foot and swallowed nervously as he asked for Giles. 'He's not here now.' Anna noticed how pale his skin was beneath its scattershot of freckles. Cowed by the authority of his uniform, Anna merely shook her head when asked his whereabouts, but volunteered that he would be back soon for lunch.

'Would you come in?' she asked the policeman, and brought him into the living room where he continued to stand, refusing her offer of a chair.

'Would you want a cup of coffee?' He shook his head. 'A glass of water?' 'No, ma'am.' 'A piece of lemon tart?' Anna saw open-mouthed surprise register as he realized that he was at 541, the famous restaurant. 'No, thank you, anyway,' he said, and fiddled with the cap he was holding in his hands.

A little while later the front door banged shut, a great gust of wind blowing in with Giles. The policeman stood. Giles greeted him uncertainly and asked what he could do for the man.

'I am afraid I have bad news.'

'Bad news?'

'There's been an accident. It's your wife, sir. She was on her bicycle.'

'Good God,' Giles interrupted.

'A car hit her.'

'Good Lord, man, why didn't you say so? Where is she?' he

asked, grabbing his coat and pulling the policeman with him. 'You can tell me on the way.'

The nurses at the hospital emergency entrance were sympathetic when Giles arrived, desperate to see Miranda, but they told him that he must wait to speak to a doctor. They handed him a clipboard full of forms to fill out and then left him to pace frantically in the corridor until a tall man with a fringe of grey hair encircling his otherwise bald head strode toward him, stethoscope sticking out of the pocket of his white jacket, X-rays in hand. Giles grabbed his arm as he introduced himself as Miranda's husband and asked to know where Miranda was, how she was. 'I've just had a look at these,' the doctor said, waving the black and white films. 'It looks like there are fine cracks in the spine and the stem of the neck from where she hit the tree. We have to keep her absolutely still. Any movement at all will threaten the fragile connection of spine, neck, and head.

'She's still unconscious, but she'll come to. That much we're sure of. I don't want you to be shocked when you see her, but we've had to fasten an iron rod against her spine all the way to the top of her head. We've connected it to a metal ring that clamps tightly around her forehead and put sandbags on either side of her to keep her from moving.'

The doctor walked him into the room. Giles stared at the pale form in the bed. He whispered her name, but no answer came. The doctor stopped him in midbend when he leaned over to kiss her. 'You mustn't do anything that would make her move in any way. She must stay absolutely still until the spinal column is stable. For now she's in great danger.'

'What do you mean?'

'If she moves, it's likely she will be paralyzed.'

'Good Lord. When will you know she's come through the worst?' Giles asked.

'I wish I could give you an answer, but so much depends

on her, on how her bones knit themselves. You'll have to be patient.' The doctor shook his hand and left.

Several hours later Diana entered the room where Miranda lay as pale as snow drops. She gasped when she saw the iron tree on which her mother was impaled. 'Mamma,' Diana called out. 'Mamma, it's me,' but Miranda did not respond. 'What is that?' she whispered to Giles, pointing at the bar. He put his hands around the girl's shoulders and hugged her. His eyes filled with tears. 'It's to keep her absolutely still. Her spine is cracked. Her neck . . . her neck . . . they don't know yet. They have to keep her from moving. That's what it's for.'

'She looks so fragile and so trapped,' the girl said to Giles, who nodded. They sat in silence, their eyes trained on Miranda.

When Miranda returned to consciousness the next day, she was groggy and disoriented. She recognized Diana and Giles and spoke their names in a whisper, as if she had lost her voice along with her mobility. A young doctor with cowlicks in his unruly red hair tested her reflexes and speech, but he couldn't answer Giles's questions about her recovery. The senior doctor asked them to limit their visits because Miranda would tire easily.

From the very first day Giles refused to allow the doctors to cut Miranda's braid. Each time he came to see her, it lay inert, the only stripe of color in an otherwise colorless world. White sheets. White light. White bed. Even the flowers were white, white with pale centers shading imperceptibly to a pink as delicate as the interior whorls of an ear.

To Diana Miranda seemed as fragile as an egg candled by the light. The fault line lay deep inside where fine fractures were visible only to the eye that sees without seeing, that senses through antennae as fine as filaments of silk.

Diana came every afternoon to the hospital room where Miranda lay immobilized. She was both terrified and enthralled by the internal incandescence of her mother.

Days passed in which Diana watched her slippery-minded mother wander in a borderless state. Often Miranda lay silent, seeing nothing until her interior screen filled up with random images. From time to time she spoke. She spoke of mangoes and ginger, of chocolate mixed with ground almonds and drizzled with honey. Sometimes she seemed to be in the spice islands, 'the islands of desire', she called them in her confusion. Sometimes she saw Giles and thought he was Anton. Once she looked at Diana and murmured, 'You look like a savage. Your father's daughter. A savage.' She twisted the white sheets in her hands fretfully. 'No, Anton no,' she shouted suddenly. 'Stop. You're hurting me.' Her voice sank, her face contracted in pain. 'Don't. Please stop. No . . .' Diana flinched. Her face was as pale as the sheets as she stared at her mother.

Diana was sitting with her one afternoon when Miranda cried out, 'Diana, something is snapping. In the water.' Diana closed her eyes and watched, as if a wafer-thin slat had been raised for her.

'Mamma, do you remember the green turtle in the warm water off the island, how slowly it circled around us one day? You told me she was coming ashore to lay her eggs and that when she returned, her babies would be waiting. Do you remember how she opened her mouth and snapped at our toes?'

'Yes, yes, snapped.'

'What is it, Mamma?'

'My neck. I'm afraid my neck will snap. Help me, Diana. Tell Giles to speak to the doctors. Why aren't they doing something? Why are they just leaving me to lie here for so long?'

'Waiting is the only solution. That's what they all say. The fractures will slowly disappear if you lie absolutely still.'

'My feet haven't touched the floor for weeks now.'

'But they will, Mamma. You have to be patient.' Miranda shot Diana a wary look.

Giles could never get used to how careful he had to be with Miranda. 'My Miranda, who used to fly from one room to the next in a great rush, has been brought to a swift stop. I still can't sweep you into my arms or roll over on top of you. I can't even swoop down and kiss you.'

'No, my love, I'm aware of that,' Miranda said dryly. 'Believe me, when I can't even have a taste of Diana's new cookies for fear one crumb might get caught in my throat, when I can't change position without two nurses, I assure you I know.'

One afternoon as Diana sat with her, Miranda shook her hands loosely in front of her. 'Mamma, what are you doing?'

'I am useless. My hands are asleep when they are not allowed to be at work in the kitchen. I will be forgotten. My life is over.'

'Listen to me. I have seen fire stream around you. I have seen it swirl as you walk in the world, as you plunge into the kitchen. You *are* fire, Mamma, but you must wait as the fire works inside you and restores you.'

'What *are* you talking about?'

'I'm telling you that your fire is banked. It's at work. Think of it burning in a small dark circle deep inside you and then letting its fingers slide up your spine and the column of your neck.'

Mamma, Diana thought to herself, I know your fire. It has singed me many times. I am your opposite, not fire, but air. Air has no color, no form, no substance. It is the space in which I move, barely visible to you, but it sustains me in its stillness. I come here every day so that my cool air can soothe you, wrap you, shelter you.

Another day Miranda held up her hands. 'See,' she said, miming cutting and chopping. 'I can still cut. I can still sliver ginger.'

'Mamma, your spine and your neck are fragile, not your hands. Of course you can still cut. But you have to be careful. Healing is slow.' She leaned over and gently covered her mother's hands with her own, then slowly pressed them downward until they returned to the nest of white sheets in which Miranda now lived.

CHAPTER FOURTEEN

D IANA OFTEN HEARD GILES pacing late at night and noticed the light in his room in the early morning, but she saw little of him except in the mornings when he stopped in the kitchen. She liked how he filched his breakfast from whatever remained from the day before, always choosing her inventively shaped cookies over Anna's more conventional ones and eating them with enthusiasm. 'Sea serpents for breakfast! Yum,' he mumbled, filling his mouth.

Unlike Miranda, Giles had never minded that Diana brought Majine into the kitchen. 'We have to stick together,' he'd say to the monkey. 'After all, we're the only males in this house.' She remembered once when the two of them whirled around and around in the dining room after all the guests had gone home, and another time when Giles picked the monkey up, put him on his shoulders, and danced through the house as if they were part of a conga line in some riotous Carnival celebration.

She was surprised at how much she missed Giles's company. She was comforted when her visits at the hospital coincided with his, although he seemed as much in the dark as she was. He didn't know how well Miranda was healing and didn't know when she could come home. His face looked grey and flabby. His eyes seemed to have shrunk. He was attentive one minute and distracted the next.

The accident forced Anna and Diana to change their lives.

Every morning Anna rose very early, filled her sink with cold water, and then dipped her face in, splashing about in it as if a small group of birds were at play. Once her puffy eyes had opened a bit, she dipped her toothbrush first into the water, then into baking soda, and then ran the brush like a fast train over the two parallel tracks of her teeth. Moving swiftly for a woman of her girth, she soaped her ample body in the shower, rinsed it, stepped swiftly out, and snapped open a towel to dry herself. She slid into one of her shapeless dresses and put on the wooden clogs that reverberated on each tread as she descended the staircase to the kitchen. Once there, she flipped on the light and slipped on a large yellow apron imprinted with the numerals 541.

Diana straggled in a bit later, sleep still crusted in the corners of her eyes. 'Have you lost your brush?' Anna would ask, taking one look at the matted tangle of curls on the girl's head. 'No,' Diana always answered warily, fully aware of what was coming next. 'I know, I know. I haven't brushed my teeth or my hair, but I'm hungry.' 'And you'll do it right after breakfast?' The girl would promise as she did every morning, and then cocoa would be measured out into a large mug, hot milk poured and whisked into it, bread toasted, preserves set on the table, and they'd sit down, the two of them, in companionable silence. Diana hummed. Anna made mental lists of ingredients and quantities.

'Before you go,' Anna would say, watching Diana make her first tentative move toward escape, 'take the usual out of the fridge. Butter,' she'd say 'and eggs. And milk. Heat the water in the pot –'

– 'so you can melt the chocolate,' Diana would chime in. Anna's voice had slipped into the sing-song rhythm of a familiar song. It comforted Diana to hear the same words each day.

She was glad she had finally finished school. No one – not even Anna – seemed to take much notice, but Diana felt relieved that it was over. Now she was restored to her family, and had the time to experiment with new desserts as a way of bringing in more money while the restaurant was closed. It was only when Anna off-handedly asked her what she would do when her mother returned from the hospital that Diana had an inspiration.

'What makes you think anything will change?' the girl asked. 'She'll go back to making the dinners and we'll go on with our baking. We might have to do a little less so we can help her in the kitchen and you'll go back to the dining room, but otherwise it will all be the same again.'

'Do you really expect your life to go on like this, year after year, always the same?' Anna put down the bowl in which she was beating egg whites and turned to look her in the face. 'From now until when? Until you're twenty-five or thirty? An old woman? It never occurred to me that I wouldn't always be taking care of my brothers and sisters but things change. Look at me now.'

'Oh. Well. Yes. Maybe not. I don't know,' Diana replied, 'What else can I do?'

Anna began to tell a story. 'My mother walked by a fortune-teller's house often. A sign in her upstairs window said FORTUNES TOLD, THE FUTURE PREDICTED. It took my mother a while to get up her nerve and actually go in, and when she did, she was surprised at how ordinary the woman was. She was wearing the same kind of dark-patterned housedress my mother wore. The place smelled of cabbage. They sat at a card table in a small dark room at the back of the place, but there wasn't even a crystal ball.

'The lady took my mother's hand in hers and studied it for a long time, tracing the lines with her finger. She was silent for so long my mother got scared and asked what she was seeing. "You're not going to have any more children." Then, "I see two big changes in your life," but she didn't say what they would be.'

'And what happened?'

'An old aunt died and left her enough money to buy us all some new clothes and shoes. We got more to eat. My mother didn't have to work so hard. And then about a year later, my mother got sick and then died. I guess that was the second change.'

'Anna,' Diana said suddenly, 'let's make fortune cookies. Cookies in the shape of hands with some lines on the palms. Then let's write a simple word on each one. *Love. Hope. Luck. Change.*'

'Quite an interesting idea,' Anna smiled.

Diana went right to work experimenting. At first the fingers she made were much too large for the hand. Then the hands weren't big enough for the message. She rapidly gave up making more than a simple life line – always long – and a line for the heart that she varied. Sometimes there were many loves, sometimes only a single one.

The ginger cookies were an instant success. The buttery cookies with a splash of vanilla took a bit of adjustment, but the chocolate were too dark to read.

She fed her experiments to Mies when he came to work in the garden. He was such an enthusiastic volunteer that he rapped on the back door even before he unloaded his equipment. *Surprise*, she wrote on one for him. *Friends*, she wrote on another.

His pleasure inspired her to dream up new messages for the cookies. The next day she came up with *Mystery. A Trip.* She squeezed *Chance Visit* on a wider hand. She made a batch saying *Passion* and slipped them in when Anna wasn't looking. But Anna found the ones saying *Sorrow, Betrayal, Grief,* and *Farewell* and outlawed them.

'Let's make some for Giles to take to the hospital,' Diana suggested. 'What shall we write?' *Health. Get Well. Love* were Anna's suggestions. Diana wrote *We Miss You* in tiny letters on a thin-fingered hand. *Come Home* on another.

Even as they were doing their experiments, Anna and Diana

filled twice as many orders as before. Diana worked in the morning before going to the hospital. Anna baked through the day, and when Diana came home in the early afternoon, she rolled out pastry dough and slid it into already buttered tart pans, made some more test fortune cookies, and then went back to the hospital while Anna finished the orders.

When several weeks had gone by, Anna realized that they might be on their own for quite a long time. Waiting for Giles in the kitchen shortly afterward, Anna made him a cup of coffee. While he stirred in the sugar and slid a couple of cookies into his mouth and a handful more into his pocket, she asked if there was enough money to wait for Miranda's return. 'I've begun to ask myself the same question. If we could live off the reviews, we'd never have to worry, but 541 isn't just food. It's Miranda. Without her, people won't come back. She has managed to set aside a bit of money, but there's not enough to keep us going indefinitely.'

'What if Diana and I started teaching pastry classes in the evenings while the restaurant is closed?' she asked. 'Would that help?'

'It's a very generous idea. Thank you for offering, Anna. Let me discuss it with Miranda. You know how proprietary she is about everything here.'

'That reminds me. I told Diana that we should have been writing down Miranda's recipes from the day we opened. All we have at the moment are some sheets of paper with a jumble of notes and a lot of smudges and stains. The other day I found a perfect fingerprint in cumin. We've been relying entirely on Miranda's magic and you can see where that's gotten us.

'About a week ago Diana reminded me that she has been measuring out ingredients for almost all of the dishes. She knows what's supposed to be chopped or pounded or grated, but the trouble is that we're not at all sure what Miranda does when she puts them together. We're cooking now to test our hunches, and Diana's also been asking Miranda questions during her visits at the hospital.'

'Aha! Does that explain why I've been smelling curry the last few days? I was beginning to think I was hallucinating.'

'We thought we should keep it a bit of a secret while Diana is practicing. She's very nervous about it all. The last time she asked Miranda how to make one of the dishes – I don't remember which one – she told me her mother got extremely annoyed and asked how she was supposed to be able to remember if she couldn't move around the kitchen while she was doing it.'

Giles lifted an eyebrow. 'I can see that we're all going to have to be careful.'

CHAPTER FIFTEEN

G ILES WENT TO THE hospital at least once a day and he almost always had a present for Miranda. He brought her creams for her hands and lotions for her body. He wrapped her shoulders in soft shawls and spread beautiful blankets over her. At least as important, he entertained her with stories about people in the city. When Pieter told him that he had heard from Oleena, Giles immediately told Miranda, and when Pieter began to make plans in earnest to return to the islands, Giles brought that news as well, although no one knew whether it would be months or years before Pieter could travel there safely again.

During his visits Giles told Miranda about Anna and Diana and their adventures in the kitchen, but he didn't mention the recipe recording project. 'You'd be surprised what good friends they have become. They play cards, they take walks, and they even took Majine on an excursion to Dagstrom's. He was quite a hit, diving for the mangoes when he saw them all stacked up. Old women shrieking, the normally placid Mr. Dagstrom rushing from behind the counter and lunging to catch the fruit before it fell to the floor. It was more excitement than the place has seen for years.

'On their latest outing they went shopping for fabric. Don't ask me how, but Anna actually convinced Diana that it was time to replace that faded skirt. Personally, I was convinced she'd grow old in it. But the two of them were intent on finding some material to replace it. I couldn't quite imagine how it would turn out. Anna's not exactly anyone's idea of stylish . . .' Giles smiled his crinkled smile, waiting for her response, wishing he could hear the timbre of her laugh. 'They actually made something quite nice. It has a waistline and there are no big pockets. Diana's kept the old one, but she only wears it when she's baking. She's become quite accomplished. A real baker. You'll see. You'll be proud.'

'Chicken broth with coconut,' Miranda shouted one day. 'Pea sprouts and ginger shoots. Red bananas! Cloves! Rice.'

'Mamma, Mamma, it's all right.' Diana couldn't keep the alarm out of her voice.

She and Giles took turns sitting at her bedside as Miranda began to drift in and out of consciousness. 'Let me out. Help. Something's coming,' she screamed, not once but many times.

'No, darling, nothing's coming,' Giles reassured her. He stroked her arm and sang to her. He tried to distract her with more stories.

'Help, help, save me,' Miranda yelled, and tried to twist away from an invisible intruder. A flurry of nurses came with a doctor and together they added a harness and new sandbags to keep her immobile. A sleepless Giles sat with her through a day and a night as she screamed for help.

When it was her turn to sit with Miranda, Diana studied her mother as she lay sleeping with her mouth open slightly, breath passing almost soundlessly through her lips. Seeing the single long braid lying flat against the white pillow, Diana remembered how she used to find excuses to be near Miranda when she undid her braid. She was fascinated as she watched her mother brush her long, dark hair until it was as smooth as a waterfall and as encompassing as a cave. If only she would let me in, Diana remembered thinking over and over to herself, if only she would let me in, then I would be safe.

After all the years in which she had shied away from looking directly at Miranda for fear of confronting disappointment and judgment, Diana could now safely let her eyes rest on that pale face and motionless form for as long as she wished. As she did, submerged feelings of tenderness began to rise.

Poor Mamma, Diana thought, everything you love taken from you. No delicious ingredients with which to cook, no people to command, not a single diner to applaud your ferocious talents. Your world has shrunk to Giles, who adores you, and me, your strange, plain girl.

Diana watched Miranda drift in and out of sleep. She hoped Miranda was listening when she talked about the fortune cookies she'd invented. Later Diana traced the letters of words on the skin of her dozing mother's arm, wrote them tenderly with the tip of her finger, *Love* and *Sorrow* and *Hope* and *Heal* and *Love* again.

When Miranda awoke from her terrors, she stared blankly at the ceiling. 'Mamma,' Diana said, searching for a way to break through the barrier of silence, 'did I tell you about the caterpillars that are crawling over the trees and eating lacy patterns in the leaves? Mies and I were afraid that there would be nothing left of the garden, but then suddenly they stopped, all at the same time. Now they are wrapped in their thin papery cocoons and we are waiting for hundreds of butterflies to be born. Has that ever happened before?'

The motionless Miranda could not even shake her head. 'I don't think so.'

'It will be dramatic, all the wings slowly filling with life. So dramatic, like you, Mamma, only they are resting in the silvery filaments they spun out of their bodies, and you are wrapped in the beautiful shawls that Giles brings. But soon you too will rise and come home. You'll fill the air with wonderful smells and charge it with the electricity that everyone always talks about. Mamma, I know I'm right.'

Suddenly Miranda responded. 'It's all I think about. I'm desperate to get out of here.'

'I know. I watched a ring of fire moving slowly toward you. I saw its flames circling around you, licking at you, the heat sucking away the air. I was terrified, afraid that it would singe your body. Consume you. Then I watched as it passed through the barrier of your skin and entered your bones, moved into the marrow.

'I watched the fire pass into you and now I know that you will heal. We will bring you home.' Miranda's eyes clouded over as she struggled with Diana's words.

'Even the doctors think you must be all right. I overheard them saying they can X-ray you now.'

And so they did. And when they studied the films, they agreed that something – time, immobility, the mysterious healing powers of the body – had annealed her bones and sealed the fractures. Her spine was once again whole, her neck without a single crack.

Two orderlies in crisp whites came to release her from her iron cage. Even after they had removed it, she could still feel its impress and found it very hard to believe her eyes when they held it up before her.

They helped her as she made her first tentative motions toward returning to the world of the ambulatory. She rolled over in bed and slowly, as they steadied her, sat up. She leaned forward into Giles's embrace and settled there for a while, dizzy from the change in elevation. She stayed until she felt ready to stand up. 'Now?' Giles asked, and she nodded, actually nodded, actually moved her head up and down. She put one foot on the floor, then the other, leaving the crumpled white bed for the first time in months. She rested against Giles's shoulder, took her first shaky steps. She had her first taste of Diana's fortune cookies. 'Delicious,' she said. 'Brilliant.' Diana thought she saw something close to acceptance in Miranda's eyes.

The first time she left the hospital room and walked in the halls of the hospital, Miranda staggered like a baby taking its first exploratory steps into the world. She was drunk with her freedom and would have walked down every corridor and into every patient's room, if only she hadn't felt so weak and tired so easily.

'Now I can come home!' she almost exploded with relief.

'Soon enough.'

'Now, now. I can't stand another minute in this place.'

'I'll see what I can do.' Giles disappeared into the depths of the building, and when he returned several hours later reported his success to Miranda. 'The doctors have granted you permission to go home, provided that a nurse comes every day to exercise your neglected muscles.'

'Don't be silly. Diana will volunteer, I'm sure. How soon can we be out of here?'

When Miranda arrived home, Giles walked her slowly into the large hall and then directly to their room. Despite her pleas, he refused to allow a detour to the kitchen. 'Too soon,' he decreed, steering her artfully in the other direction. She could see that the house was full of apricot tulips that Andreas had sent and she could smell the gingery scents of Diana's latest batch of fortune cookies. She sighed happily when they reached the room that was theirs, the room she had dreamt of in so many lost hours.

She sank down on the bed that Giles had piled high with pillows and looked around with amazement. 'Home,' she said in breathless wonder. 'It's been so long I can hardly remember.' She let Diana release her hair from its long captivity and then brush it again and again, patiently easing away the tangles until it fell like a great dark fan over her shoulders and down half the length of her back. Three times a day Diana's fingers, nimble from baking, kneaded the atrophied muscles of Miranda's arms and legs and rubbed the places still sore from her long immurement in bed.

Giles brought her a walking stick with a top shaped vaguely like a quince. 'Lean on me, darling,' he instructed her.

'I feel like a baby, all flesh and no strength.'

'Not for long. We know you. Did you realize that Anna sometimes refers to you as "Miranda the Miraculous".'

'She does?'

'Yes, but I'm going to call you my phoenix. We were all terrified that you would be a different person if you survived the accident.'

'Out of my mind, you mean, or crumpled and passive?'

'Passive was hard to picture, but we didn't know. Even the doctors didn't know what you were capable of. Diana knew you were in danger and told me that you were putting up a fierce struggle. Once I found her in tears. She confessed that she was afraid you were in serious danger.'

'What did she say?'

'The strangest things. Fire was closing in on you, and she was afraid you'd be consumed.'

'Yes, she told me the same thing. What a strange girl she is. Oh' – Miranda's tone changed abruptly – 'is that why you call me your phoenix?'

'Well . . . maybe . . . so.' Giles spoke slowly. He hadn't really understood until that minute.

'Well, this phoenix wants to rise and return to the kitchen.'

'It'll happen soon enough, but first a few hot baths, some more kneading and massaging those beautiful limbs and some more walks around the house. Let's wait for your energy and strength to return.'

'OK,' Miranda agreed, 'but kiss me first.'

The next morning Giles and Miranda stayed in bed a long time. They were like travelers returned to a land that had enthralled them before they were summarily forced into exile. They were shy with each other at first. Giles's touch was so hesitant that Miranda had to encourage him to let his fingers move as they always had.

'I'm scared,' he admitted. 'I don't want to harm you.'

'Trust me to guide you. Just move closer,' she said, pulling him towards her and taking his fingers, one by one, into her mouth. 'We can pretend that I'm a new island, one you've never visited before. I'll lie totally still and wait for you to explore, let you come to my inlets, my cliffs and passages. Then it will be my turn to investigate,' she said, rolling onto her back, inviting him to explore the contours of her geography.

Later, as they lay next to each other, Giles gave a start. 'I forgot to tell you. Jan Witt told me that he examined your painting very carefully. Says it's by someone – sorry, I forget the name – Floris, maybe, it sounded like a flower, anyway someone quite important – and that it's very valuable.'

'Valuable?' she asked, her voice rising a half octave. 'How valuable? Did he give you a number?'

'Not even a range. I must have looked awfully stupid. I didn't even know he had come to look at it.'

'He thought it needed to be cleaned, so while the restaurant was closed, I let him take it to the museum where there are experts.' Miranda brushed past his surprise. 'Oh, Giles, do you know what this means? Freedom. Enough money that I won't have to work every minute for the next forty years.' And then her voice dropped. 'I forgot. I suppose Diana owns the painting the way she owns everything else in this house. Including the house.'

'Stop it, Miranda. I don't understand what it is about Diana that sets you off. She has never denied you one thing that you asked for. She was at the hospital twice a day. If you could have seen the distress on her face, you wouldn't talk like that. Take one good look. Anyone can see that she yearns for your approval. That's all she wants. And the longer you behave like this, the longer she's going to be stuck in the shadows waiting for recognition.'

He threw back the covers, stood up, and reached for his clothes. 'Pay a little attention to her. Praise what she's doing. Just be kind to her the way you are to almost everyone else. It would mean a thousand times more than all the generosity you pour out to the strangers who pay money to eat your food.'

Diana found a handful of buttons wedged in the back of her nanna's bureau. Some looked like pearls and some were silver with tiny anchors on them. She showed them to Anna who suggested that she could use a new blouse and a dress. 'I'm sure we'll find some material. Let's go now while it's still quiet.'

'I'll get Majine,' Diana volunteered.

'Don't forget his leash.'

Majine loped along ahead of them. Diana kept a wary eye on him as he approached a frisky terrier racing along out of sight of its owner. Suddenly the dog turned, bared its sharp incisors and growled, sending Majine straight to the top of Diana's head in a single leap. 'Majine,' she giggled, 'come down.' But he wouldn't budge, not even when she reached up and tried to detach his agile fingers from their firm grip.

People did double takes as the unlikely trio continued its walk. A small boy pulled on his mother's hand and pointed, giggling. A cyclist waved as he skirted them in a wide arc, but most just stared at the girl with a monkey riding on top of her head, accompanied by a large whey-faced woman of no particular age.

'Diana,' Anna said to her as they waited for a traffic light to change, 'it has just occurred to me that you are every bit as dramatic as your mother. Look at you, striding down the street with a monkey on your head. You may not need to enchant people or cook to thrill them, but I do hope that you can see that you are definitely being noticed.

'And something else. You've taken such care of your mother.

You've baked her cookies with messages that only you could have written, and you've kept massaging her muscles until their tone has begun to return. You've helped run the business that pays the bills and gave Andreas a way to return to the plants that he loved. And let's not forget that you've fed Mies more treats than he ever dreamed of.'

Diana gave a little shrug of pleasure and thrust her head slightly forward like a turtle edging out of its shell. 'Thank you,' she whispered, turning carefully to smile at Anna. 'But you would have done the same. It's normal.'

'Not really,' insisted Anna. 'I could mention it to your mother. She probably doesn't even know everything you've done. But you should tell her. Don't let her keep treating you as a child.' As they stepped into the street, Diana felt Majine's nails dig deeper into her scalp. She turned to Anna and said, 'Let's take a detour by Dagstrom's and hope that he has some mangoes on hand for you know who.'

CHAPTER SIXTEEN

As soon as her arms and legs were strong enough, Miranda went straight to the kitchen. In the throes of nostalgia, she opened cabinets and drawers, peered into canisters and smelled their contents, dipped a finger into chutneys and spiced preserves, sighing happily as she tasted their familiar flavors.

'Now I'm really home,' she said, exhaling so deeply she felt her center of gravity shift subtly. 'Oh Giles, I want to reopen the restaurant as soon as possible,' she announced over a strong cup of coffee that afternoon. 'Two and a half, three weeks, maybe.'

'Don't you think that might be rushing it just a bit? Why don't you spend a little time getting used to being back in the kitchen and then make a plan?'

'I'll start slowly,' she promised him. 'I'll make only the easiest dishes this week, and Diana and Anna will help me. I wasn't sleeping all the time I was in the hospital, you know. I missed my own food. I felt desperately deprived until I started to walk myself through almost every dish I've ever made here. First I collected the ingredients and put them all together. Then I chopped or grated or slivered each one, just as if I were here. I could feel the rhythm of pounding chili peppers and mincing cloves of garlic. I could smell the squashes roasting and the curries thickening as they simmered. Now that I'm finally back in the kitchen, maybe all that I remembered will flow out through my fingers and into the pots and pans.'

'That would certainly speed up the process.' Giles flashed a skeptical smile in her direction.

She told Diana the same thing the next morning. 'I want everything to be just the way it was before. We can do it. I know we can.'

The girl looked thoughtful. 'While you were in the hospital, Anna and I realized we didn't know how to make any of your recipes except the desserts. Anna thinks that you make at least 100 different dishes and she says that they would all be lost unless we watch you carefully and write down everything you do.'

'It's out of the question,' Miranda shot back. 'Do you have any idea how much we've got to do in the next few weeks?'

'If you weren't cooking, 541 wouldn't exist. Do you really want your food to disappear? Because that's just what would happen and it wouldn't take long either.'

'But if we write down the recipes, anyone could use them.'

'Oh, Mamma, if that's what you're worried about, I'll put everything in an ordinary notebook and we can hide it somewhere no one would think to look. But I'm serious. You know you have to cook almost everything again before we open, so let's get started.'

Miranda had been perched on a stool, but now she moved to a chair. 'My back just doesn't want to hold me up for long,' she said with an off-hand gesture. 'Let's try this. I'll stay right here and tell you how I make the curry and you can write it down. I'll just close my eyes and watch myself roasting the coconut and making a thick paste with all my secret special spices to smear on the cubes of meat. They'll simmer for a while and then I'll add, let's see, coconut milk or maybe broth, and then I'll slip in the eggplant toward the end.' Miranda closed her eyes and tried to visualize the next step. 'Do I hear the click of the top fitting on the pot?' she asked herself. 'No.' She shook her head. 'Let's try it this way. You'll put out all the ingredients and I'll tell you what to do. No walking, no standing, no exhausting stirring: a perfect way for me to bring the dishes back.'

Diana smiled at her mother's idea. For all she knew it was as good a way as any for Miranda's memory and musculature to take their first plunge back into kitchen rhythms, although she had always been convinced that Miranda's magic came from the flow of her own special motions as she moved through the process. Without those rhythms that began deep in the body, would she really get it right? And anyway, what good were words when the dance of the kitchen had no music to go with them? Diana would humor her mother – there was time – but in the long run she wouldn't settle for anything less than the entire choreography.

In those beginning days Diana grew into being a cook in her own right. She continued toasting nuts, chopping vegetables, and grating ginger and coconut for Miranda, while making careful notes on everything her mother did, but she also began to cook whole dishes by herself. Miranda finally gave her the secret formula for the mixture of spices that made 541's curries unforgettable and even allowed her to write it down, although she insisted that the paper had to be hidden where no one else could find it.

As she slid into her old life in the kitchen, Miranda found it hard to contain her enthusiasm. Several times each day Diana would grab her arm to keep her from leaping up and dashing around the kitchen in search of tools or ingredients. 'Stay put. I'll bring you whatever you need.'

'How considerate you are.'

'It's easy. You can't imagine how terrified I was that you wouldn't recover. Do you remember how I crawled into bed and couldn't move for days after I learned that . . .' Diana stopped speaking.

'That your father had drowned?'

'Yes,' she whispered. 'I felt as if I'd fallen into a sea of grey ash. I could barely breathe. I was afraid to sleep.'

'Yes, I remember. You *were* gone from us for days. There was nothing we could do.' She paused for a long minute. 'I've been sad too, you know.'

'It isn't a contest, Mamma.'

'No,' Miranda said, without much conviction. 'I don't suppose it is.'

'I have been watching you ever since I began waiting for Daddy to return to me, ever since Nanna died. I've seen how everything and everyone else was more important than I am.'

'What do you mean?' Miranda asked, her face clouding up. What had happened to make Diana say such things to her?

'The restaurant. The restaurant and Giles and the people who came to eat your food and before that all the men who lived here. They were all more important to you. You pay attention to the people who come to admire and applaud you, but I never count. I've already been conquered.' Miranda suddenly had trouble catching her breath. She swayed perilously and wondered if her legs would continue to hold her up.

'While you were in the hospital,' Diana continued, 'I baked and cooked more than I ever had before. Anna made me new clothes that let me look like me. She says that my fortune cookies will be such a big success that they could make up for all the money we lost while the restaurant was closed.'

Miranda was silent as she considered Diana's words. She gave her daughter a thoughtful look and told her 'I thought I'd die in the hospital. One minute riding along on my bicycle and the next waking up immobilized in that horrid bed. I had plenty of time to think. Sometimes I'd open my eyes and you'd be there, looking worried, watching over me. I realized how much I took you for granted, how much I wanted you to divine what I had in mind and then just do it. Even when I was with you, I was distracted, always concerned with my own life, my restaurant and my food. Now you're even recording everything I do here so it won't die.' She reached out her hand and let it fall on Diana's shoulder. She leaned forward and drew her close.

CHAPTER SEVENTEEN

M IRANDA WAS INUNDATED WITH letters as more and more people heard that she had set a date to reopen the restaurant. Some wrote to welcome her back and tell her how much she had been missed, but many skipped the niceties and went straight to the point, asking for reservations as soon as possible.

'Absence and the memory of a good quince tart do seem to make many hearts grow fonder,' Giles teased Miranda. It was hard for him to believe she was seriously afraid of being forgotten during her absence and harder yet to accept her apprehension that at best she would be remembered as a woman who had passed through the city in a brief comet-like flash before returning to obscurity, leaving 541 once again only an address on a tree-lined street. Determined to combat such a possibility, she went straight to work as soon as she walked back into the kitchen. She promised to ease into her first days by making the dishes she knew best, but Giles watched how rapidly she began to experiment with new tastes and combinations of ingredients, determined to intrigue people's taste buds again and cast a lasting culinary spell.

As the time for the opening drew closer, Miranda tried to work at a fiercer and fiercer speed, but she was slowed by the weakness of her back and by the headaches that came without warning. 'I hate this. I used to be able to do everything so easily. I feel like I'm admitting defeat,' she said to Diana ruefully, busying herself with some tamarinds, 'but you know that when the restaurant reopens, I'll need you to do a lot more cooking than you did before.'

'It sounds like you can't find a way around giving me a chance to cook. Maybe I'll surprise you, Mamma. You liked my fortune cookies.'

'I did. They're extraordinary. Witty and delicious.'

'So how bad can I be? These are your dishes. You're the genius – remember what the newspaper article said?'

'Why are you so scared of letting me cook? I'm just here to help you put it together. I'm going to put out the ingredients for pumpkin soup and I'll watch what you do. Anna says you're a magician in the kitchen because you have some secret sleight of hand.'

'Ha! Maybe she's right. So watch me carefully, Diana.' Miranda looked around. 'You'll have to get everything ready for me.'

'Don't I always?' She moved quickly to chop onions, roast pumpkin slices, peel and slice yellow fleshed potatoes.

Miranda melted butter and drizzled oil into a large pan and then added the onions. Her movements were smooth, graceful, almost unconscious, so well did she know her own recipes and rhythms. While Diana removed the rind from pumpkin flesh, Miranda moved the softened onions into a pot. Diana cubed the pumpkin and then watched as Miranda added it to the onions, beating the flesh with a wooden spoon until it was smooth. She drizzled in broth, flavored it with sea salt, strewed a tiny path of hot red pepper flakes over the top and watched them sink slowly into the creamy mixture. Diana wrote down her mother's every motion, and when Miranda dipped a finger inside to taste she did the same.

The only sounds inside the warm kitchen were the clip-clop of Anna's clogs, the sizzle of sautéing vegetables, and the occasional scrape of the whisk against the bottom of the soup pot. Outside rain lashed trees that bent toward the sodden ground.

'Anna found a bag of lemons at the front door early this morning. There was no name, only a note saying they were looking forward to the reopening of 541.'

Miranda picked up one of the lemons and rolled it thoughtfully in the palm of her hand. She contemplated its irregular bumpy rind with pores like tiny pinpricks and the ragged stem end where it had been ripped from a bush. She was puzzled by her rising sense of alarm until she realized that the lemon reminded her of a breast. Beneath the appearance of something as simple as a lemon, she thought to herself, lies a black void in which everything rises and sinks, crashes and cracks apart, exposing the perilous fragility of the world. Miranda looked carefully at the lemon, alarmed now at its brash yellow color, fearful of taking a knife and pulling open the thick flap of its skin. She was horrified to think of slicing into the interior flesh, invading it. Why does it have such a thick peel, she asked herself, if not to protect it, keep it safe from intrusion?

'Diana,' she said in a quiet voice, 'I need to rest. You can simmer the soup another ten minutes and then take it off the heat.'

As Miranda stretched out on her bed, she remembered the silent white hospital room. She had vague memories of Diana sitting there quietly as she slept. Did she recall Diana asking questions about the dishes she made, searching intelligent questions about combining ingredients and creating provocative tastes?

'Why hot chilies and pumpkin together, Mamma? How long should the quinces stew with the lamb? When do you add the mangoes to the custardy ice cream base?' She'd watched, Miranda realized, her sulky daughter, whose closest confidant was a monkey, the girl who preferred her grandmother to her mother, whom she blamed for the disappearance of Anton from their lives – she'd been watching thoughtfully. She cared. She *wanted* to be in the kitchen.

Lucky, Miranda thought to herself as she lay there, lucky, because really the girl wouldn't have a choice. The only way to save the restaurant was to share it, share the cooking and the moments of creative magic. Share the glory. Yes, she knew that would be the hardest.

Better not to think of that yet. Better to think what Diana was doing now. She could hear the girl chopping in swift sharp motions and imagined her leaning over the wood chopping board with the halved white onions, imagined her curling her fingers behind the knife and then moving with sureness through all the hemispheres of onion. While she'd lain sandbagged in her bed Diana had been practicing. Did they already guess that she'd never come back to her previous mastery or did they decide to take precautions just in case? Was that what occasioned all of Diana's questions about recipes, about what went into which pot when? What kind of white wine? Was the ginger minced or grated? She wasn't just giving her mother the opportunity to return to her much-loved kitchen on mental excursions. She really wanted to know.

What was it she had said? Something about what's lost once is lost forever. At first Miranda though she was talking about Anton, but no – it was her cooking, her food. Diana would step into her shoes if she didn't recover. Impossible. No one could take her place and they knew it. Still, were they grooming Diana or was she always to be the aide, the sous chef, still sous but also now chef?

Miranda could smell the sweetness of caramelized onion, hear the sizzle of wine hitting the pan. How she longed to get up, be there to instruct with her wooden spoon and correct with her superior knowledge.

From now on, she sighed to herself with a good deal more resignation than she felt, it's Miranda and Diana at the stove, one wonder worker and one virginal girl slicing and stirring as the heat rises and fragrances fill the air.

Giles was giddy with delight that his old life was returning. One morning he picked up Majine, put him on his shoulders, and the two of them raced through the house, leaping around in a frenzy. 'The goddess of the kitchen is back. Come on, Majine,' Giles urged the monkey, 'let's see what's cooking. We'll ask for a piece of the tart created in your honor.'

Finding Miranda, he skidded to a stop. 'I'm a lucky man,' he said, as he slid his arms around her, worrying her that next he would embrace her and interrupt the crucial timing in the addition of ingredients. 'You survived your accident and Diana has created a whole new kind of cookie that will soon be the talk of the city.' As he nuzzled her, Miranda continued dropping green coriander leaves into her ginger broth. 'Is this your way of telling me you're famished, or are opening night tremors making you giddy?'

'Neither, my love, but if tasting a small bowl of that ginger broth would help you decide its fate, I'd be delighted to be of service.'

On a morning about two weeks before the restaurant would reopen, Miranda was sampling chutneys that Diana had made from her instructions. She passed Giles a spoon and said to him, 'While I lay in bed at the hospital, I thought about what it would be like to reopen the restaurant. I don't ever want to feel as much pressure as I felt the first time.' She watched Giles open his mouth to speak. 'I know – you're going to say that I've done it once and it would never be that hard again. But I'm scared. I know that expectations are so high this time. Let's do it as quietly as we can. Let's invite the people we'd like to be with us on the first night. No critics, no journalists, no chefs. It would be like a big dinner party.'

'Who would you have?'

'Pieter, of course, and Maarten and Andreas. Dirk and his wife, our steadiest customers. And the neighbors, what are their names? The ones who wrote that nice note you read me in the hospital?'

'Nicholaus, I think. They'll certainly be happy that you're back. She was so relieved to be out of the kitchen and he seemed even more grateful. They must be waiting every day to see the lights go on again.'

'Do you remember Mrs. DeLeeuw?' Miranda asked Giles. 'The woman who celebrated her eightieth birthday with her family about a year ago? There were six of them in all – two sons and their wives and a man about her age, probably her brother, since she was a widow. You could feel the warmth and see how easily they all got along. We made a special cake and put eight candles on it, but when we brought it to her, one of the sons insisted on a ninth. "To grow on," he said. I remember thinking I wouldn't mind looking like her when I got old. She had so much character in her face. Good strong bones. A beautiful smile. And masses of gorgeous silver hair.

'I've just opened a letter from her asking for a reservation for three. Her granddaughter has just gotten engaged and she says she can't think of a better way to celebrate than to introduce the two of them to the full power of my food. Don't you think they'd be pleased to be included?' Miranda asked Giles.

'Of course they would. And years from now they'll be among the hundreds of people remembering the amazing meals they had here. They'll talk about you and probably compare notes on exactly what they ate. And that's how you'll live on in the minds of many people long after you've forgotten them.'

'Culinary immortality? Is that what you'd call it?'

'Something like that.'

'Why are we talking about me as if I were already dead? Did I ever tell you that Ria wrote in her will that my talents in the kitchen would make me famous? I always thought it was her way of taking the sting out of leaving me nothing but a bunch of pots and pans, but maybe she was right. Or maybe she pushed me to it.'

On the Saturday before the opening, they were all in the kitchen. 'Does anyone want a taste?' asked Anna as she slid her ginger-spiked chocolate tart off the oven shelf. 'Spectacular,' said Miranda, 'but I've made up my mind that the opening night dessert will be Diana's mango tart.'

Diana was astonished. 'You like it that much? Will you call it Tart Majine?' Miranda was tempted to respond sarcastically, but said only, 'Why not? If anyone asks, though, I'm leaving it up to you to explain what a Majine is.

'Mrs. DeLeeuw is coming to the opening night dinner, but now she is requesting a dessert specifically for the grand-daughter and her fiancé. Something special that would make their evening even more perfect, to quote her.'

'My fortune cookies,' Diana said immediately. 'They would be perfect. I'll think of special messages.'

'Does that mean they won't have the Tart Majine?' asked Giles.

'Of course not. We'll make some cookies just for them and fan them out around it.'

On Sunday Pieter wrote a letter to his friend Varaman. When he finished, he walked to 541 and rang the doorbell. He exhaled with relief when Miranda opened the door. 'I knew you'd be here.' She wiped her sugary hands discreetly on the inside of her apron pockets and invited him into the kitchen.

'It smells so good in here.'

'Let's see. It could be the ginger cookies or mango-flavored pastry cream or even the ginger-spiked chocolate tart.'

'Maybe I should come back when you're not so busy,' he offered in a disappointed voice.

'When would that be? No, no, come in and taste. There's more than we can eat. We're in high production today.'

Miranda filled a plate with desserts and insisted that he sit at the table and then looked at him expectantly.

'I had to tell someone and I just couldn't wait until Saturday. I've had a letter from Oleena. Things are very bad there. Crazed men slaughtering everyone in sight. Annihilating entire villages. She is living in terror. So far the people are protecting her, but things can change without warning. She feels vulnerable and alone. I'm in agony. I'd go in a minute to protect her, but it's much too dangerous.

'I just wrote to my friend Varaman asking him to look after her. He's a good man and I think he'll do what I ask. It's torture to be so far away, unbearable to have to sit here and just wait. What can I do? What can I do? I had to come and tell you. I couldn't keep it to myself any longer.'

Miranda nodded thoughtfully. Diana looked distressed.

On Tuesday Jan Witt brought the newly cleaned and framed painting back from the museum. Miranda looked sheepishly at Giles as the two men hung it in the dining room.

'Don't worry,' she told Giles later. 'I talked to Diana about it. We agreed that if I want to sell it, half the money will be hers and half mine.'

'Very generous on her part. Does she know how valuable it might be?'

'Don't be so suspicious. Yes, I told her. It's an amazing amount. I guess there just aren't paintings like this one still in private houses. But she said the strangest thing. When I asked why she would need money, she took a long time before she finally answered. "I just might want to leave this house someday. I might want to be with Oleena. She could tell me about my father. And about beyond the beyond." I was horrified. I thought she'd come through it, we'd come through it. But I was wrong. She's still bound by him, still a captive of his fierce magnetism.'

Five days before the restaurant was due to open, Miranda was lying lazily in bed, resisting the need to get up. Giles was wandering around the room, buttoning his shirt, sliding loose coins into his pocket, and brushing his hair with his fingers. He sat on the edge of the bed while he put on his shoes.

'Five more days,' Miranda said, 'Five more days until we put the sign in the window.'

'Sign?'

'The one saying TODAY.' Miranda saw the quizzical look on Giles's face.

'That's all? Just TODAY? After everyone has waited for months for the big reopening?'

'What more does it need to say? "Miranda, with the exceptional help of her daughter, Diana, is back in the kitchen cooking extravagant dinners"?'

'Oh, I see. Diana again. She's not asking you to make a big fuss over her, you know. She seems quite content. I haven't noticed her calling the newspaper or rushing off to tell Mr. Dagstrom of her sudden elevation in status in the kitchen.

'I know it's hard on you, darling, not being in total control, but Diana's helping you. She's been working hard herself, trying to make each dish from what she's written down in that thick notebook with MIRANDA'S MIRACULOUS DISHES written on the cover. Think of it this way: she's immortalizing you. Future generations will know your incredible food because she's worked so hard to put the recipes in order.'

'Oh, Giles, I know, I know. All the time I lay trapped by those horrible sandbags, I kept wondering when I would get back to my restaurant. Not our restaurant. Mine. I know it's ours, darling, but I never thought of Diana as really being part of it. Not an important part. And now because of my back and my hopeless headaches, it's ours, all right, ours up the middle with maybe even a bit more of the weight on Diana now.'

'You might look at it that she's saving it. That you have a

talent and she has a talent, put them together and you have a restaurant that will permit you to work less and have a vacation now and then.' He leaned over to kiss her but missed as she swung her legs over the side of the bed and threw on a robe. She felt around with her feet for her slippers and then, holding on to his arm, she stood up slowly, and together they walked down the hall. 'I couldn't smell that coffee another minute,' she announced, as she poured herself a cup and eyed an apple tart cooling near the open oven door.

Diana was chopping vegetables and didn't look up. Miranda heard the steady rhythm of the knife on the cutting board. She watched as the girl slid the roughly chopped vegetables into a wide-mouthed wooden bowl, then picked up the mezzaluna and rocked its half-moon shaped blade back and forth, cutting through celery and carrots, through onions and garlic and parsley. Her rhythm was slower and more deliberate than with the knife, and save for the sharpness of the blade, she might have been using a child's tool, rolling it from hand to hand like a tiny seesaw in the kitchen.

Miranda remembered rocking Diana in the hammock she and Anton had slung between trees when they lived on the island. She remembered Diana climbing on Anton's shoulders and wiggling down his back as he pretended to be a sea serpent, rocking her back and forth and creeping down the dusty road until they arrived at the water and slithered in.

Diana continued her chopping, moving now to golden squashes and green beans. Next she would strip rosemary branches of their needles and chop them. Something in her movements made her think of her father, but why he should arise in her thoughts now she did not know.

Diana moved toward the stove, her eyes vaguely focused as she considered the vegetables she'd diced. 'What will you do now?' Miranda asked, as she slid a spoonful of five-spice custard ice cream into her coffee.

'Soup, soup from the faraway Indies,' she said in a dreamy

voice, ginger and hot peppers and chunks of chicken in broth, what they referred to as Miranda's miraculous healing broth, although that's not what it would be called on the menu.

Diana already knew how it would feel to make the soup. The long simmer of chicken parts and vegetables for the stock, the slow skimming of froth as it rose to the surface, the poaching of the chicken in its broth, what she thought of as bathing it in a sea of its own juices. Then a sudden change as she traded the giant spoon for a knife and flew into high speed chopping of ginger and chilies. Diana could feel herself slide into each rhythm and without knowing why, she felt herself coming home. Home to her body and its own idiosyncratic rhythms, home to its history, to life long ago with her mother and her father. Standing at the stove, she felt consoled and revived as she cooked and chopped and ladled and stirred.

On Thursday morning Anna spread the crisply ironed table-cloths on the tables. She and Diana set all thirty-six places with the newly polished silver and sparkling crystal glasses. Giles had surprised Miranda with a new set of plates. Dragons undulated around the cobalt edges, dancing over and under red ribbons that were woven around golden fruits. 'Come and see how beautiful the tables look,' Anna called.

'Now I can begin to believe it's really all going to happen again,' Miranda said with wonder in her voice. She still had moments of shakiness, when her body remembered how close she had come to paralysis, to being immured within herself with no possible escape. 'I feel as if years have passed since we were last here. And now there are only two more days,' she said.

On Friday, the day before the opening, a forager rang the doorbell and presented Miranda with several wild ducks. 'Wonderful,' Miranda said, mentally appraising how many they would serve. 'The chickens have just flown out of the curry. Duck curry – splendid – and I think there will be enough left for crispy duck salad as well. You'll have to come back and have a meal with us.'

'Thank you,' he said, lifting his chin and looking straight into her blue eyes. 'Thank *you*,' she said.

Diana baked fortune cookies for the young couple and showed them to Miranda. The words she chose were *Deep* and *Passion* and *Happiness* and *Strength*. 'Strength?' Miranda pondered the choice.

'Perfect,' said Anna, confirming the girl's decision.

CHAPTER EIGHTEEN

L ATE IN THE MORNING of opening day Anna and Diana were in the kitchen baking the tart shells for the evening's dessert. Majine was sitting on his silvery haunches, slowly peeling the thick skin of a mango away from its juicy flesh with an off-hand expertise. As he devoured it, Diana scooped up the peel and flat pit and added them to a bowl that already contained onion skins and pumpkin seeds, potato peels, parsley stems and old lettuce leaves. She tossed in the remains of orange and lemon peels Anna had used in baking and then hoisted the monkey on her shoulders and wandered outside, where she deposited him on the branch of the nearest tree. She watched him grab the coarse bark with his fine fingers and swing easily hand over hand to where Mies was kneeling, planting new bulbs. The monkey dropped onto the ground next to him and proceeded to imitate his motions with the trowel. Mies laughed and patted him like an old friend.

Diana walked slowly, almost dreamily, toward the far end of the property. Years ago Andreas had chosen a spot that was well screened from view where he could leave discarded leaves and garden clippings to become compost. Whenever he or Mies worked in the garden, they added to the pile but they also took from it, spreading the organic cover to nourish the plants and replenish the soil. Diana tossed her collection of kitchen trimmings on top and watched as they sank into the steaming mass. She could smell ripeness in the fruit peelings and got a strong whiff of rot as the scraps joined the pile that was fermenting in the sun.

Majine looked around for Diana. When he didn't see her, he shrieked. 'Here I am,' she called out, signaling with a nod of her head that he should follow her. She walked slowly to the memorial she had made for her father. Anchors, chains, hasps, clamps, and various nautical implements rose like islands from the circle of crystalline sea salt. Majine leapt into the center, racing around and around, leaving new marks from his curved nails, a calligraphy of remembrance in the sparkling white sea.

Diana stooped to pick up a handful of the crystals and put a few on her tongue. She waited as they dissolved. Some tasted briny, some round and creamy, but they all had the ancient wild taste of the sea. 'I will never forget you,' she whispered.

Diana looked at the garden and thought sadly that her family was as deciduous as the trees along the city streets, members falling away one at a time, her grandmother in her bed, her father in the sea. As the maker of memorials and preserver of memories, she kept them with her, let them live on in the silvery-black expanses of her interior life.

She spent the rest of the day in the kitchen with her mother, grating ginger, chopping herbs, roasting squashes, adding vegetables to the big pot of lamb which would be flavored with the quince Miranda had preserved before her accident. 'The curry, oh no, I almost forgot the curry.' Diana unearthed the recipe from its hiding place, and once she had mixed the spices she furtively dipped in her finger to be sure she had it right. 'Try it,' she urged Miranda, who shook a little mound in the center of her palm and licked it with the tip of her tongue. 'Yes,' she said as a smile of pleasure took over after a moment of serious consideration, 'that tastes as if I'd made it myself.'

Miranda came and went during the day's preparations. After a morning of intense cooking and a lunch composed of whatever was taking up space in the refrigerator, she disappeared for a rest and returned later to taste and put finishing touches on every dish. On her way she stopped in the dining room to rearrange a few flowers in the big vase on the sideboard and to be sure that the highly polished surface of every knife, fork, and spoon sparkled in the soft golden light. Satisfied, she pushed open the door to the kitchen and walked first to the oven to peek at Anna's tarts, then to the stove, where she lifted the top off the bubbling pot of lamb and let steam envelope her face in its fragrant aroma. 'Wonderful, absolutely wonderful,' she said to Diana as she took a taste. She put down her spoon and encircled her daughter with a hug.

Miranda was alarmed when she noticed how much time had passed. 'It's almost six. I've got to get dressed.'

Diana lingered uncertainly, then decided to change her clothes quickly so she could return to the garden before it all started. She put on the dress Anna had made for her. Its alternating waves of color – sky violet, sea blue, foam green – made her feel as if she were swimming in the sea when the light shone down through its layers. She tiptoed down the hall so no one would catch her before she slipped out the back door with Majine. The monkey leapt into the branches of a tree while she stood silently.

After a time Diana realized that Miranda must have already changed into her sapphire-blue dress with its swirling silvery suns and moons, must have already made her way into the kitchen, where she would be moving from pot to pot, lifting lids and dipping in spoons, tasting quince and lamb, loosing their smells as she tasted again and again to make sure the flavors were perfectly balanced. By now Giles would certainly be in the dining room, where he would already have lined up the bottles of red wine in their silver holders, opened with an expert pull of the corkscrew to allow their deep flavors time to breathe.

Family. Giles was part of their family now. Was Anna? She lived with them and ate with them and shared their lives. What happened to families, she wondered, as people wove in and out of them? Would Oleena be part of her family if her father were still alive? Could she travel one day to the far away Indies to be with her? Would Oleena teach her to dance to the beautiful silvery music Pieter had described?

Diana looked up into the sky. I know you are there in the night sky, thrashing darkness as you must have thrashed as you sank in the waters you loved. You'd been thrown from sea to sky and I could see you, leaping, as lithe as the fish we used to catch. But now you have leapt out of my dreams, slapping your tail across the arc of the heavens, and I can track you.

Oh, you cracked my heart. My heart's a fish now flapping crazily in the darkness, seeking solace, looking for the past, the promise, the paradise. Oh yes, I know you are there, but I don't want a fish in the sky, I want you.

It was getting late. Diana could hear the faint voices of the first guests. She knew that she should have been in the kitchen long before now, but she wasn't ready to go in yet.

She stood quietly, feeling the darkness settle inside her. She wondered how much the ghosts that whirled slowly in the inky darkness inside of her circumscribed her life, wondered whether they would loosen their grip and allow changes in her life. Tonight, Anna had suggested, might be a departure, the beginning of a new life for her when she went into the dining room and took her place beside her mother, the celebrated cook and enchantress.

Diana watched as the stars began to shimmer, saw her being travel out to them, circle around the constellation of the great fish that was her father, and then begin the voyage back. She waved her fingers in his direction, a benediction and a blessing, and bent down to scoop up Majine. Stroking his fur, she turned back for one last look at the garden and took a long slow deep breath. It was time now. They were waiting. She knew they were waiting.

MIRANDA'S MIRACULOUS
DISHES

PUMPKIN SOUP

Soup

4 tablespoons (60 grams) unsalted butter
1 tablespoon (15 grams) olive oil
2 pounds (900 grams) pumpkin or butternut squash,
peeled, seeded, and cut into ½-inch-thick slices
1 white onion, minced
10 to 15 cloves garlic, enough to make 3 tablespoons,
minced
3⅓ cups (780 ml) chicken broth, preferably homemade
Coarse sea salt

Croutons

4 thick slices rustic country bread, crusts removed
2 teaspoons (10 grams) unsalted butter
⅛–¼ teaspoon dried red chili pepper flakes

Warm 3 tablespoons of the butter and the oil in a 3- or
4-quart pot and sauté the butternut squash slices over low
heat until lightly golden, about 15 minutes. You may need
to do this in two separate batches.

In a separate sauté pan, melt the remaining tablespoon
of butter over low heat and sauté the onion until soft and
translucent, about 15 minutes. Add the garlic after about
10 minutes and cook until it is soft, being careful that it
doesn't brown or burn.

Combine the onions and garlic with the butternut
squash in the pot and mash to a thick paste with a
wooden spoon. Pour in 3 cups of chicken broth and
simmer for 20 minutes. Taste for seasoning and grind the

coarse sea salt into the mixture at the end. Transfer to a blender and purée or press through a fine sieve. Stir in extra chicken broth, if necessary. It is best to chill this in the refrigerator and skim off any fat.

To make the croutons, cut the bread into small cubes. Melt the butter in a medium sauté pan over medium heat, stir in the pepper flakes, add the cubes of bread, and sauté until they are golden brown on all sides.

Warm the soup and serve with a sprinkling of croutons over the top.

Serves 6

SIZZLING PRAWN SOUP

Fish stock

2 ¼ pounds (1 kilo) head, tails, and trimmings of mild white
fish, such as haddock or snapper, cleaned and chopped
3 tablespoons (45 ml) mild olive oil
3 large onions, finely diced
3 celery ribs, finely diced
2 carrots, finely diced
3 garlic cloves, crushed
4 strips lemon zest
6 parsley sprigs
10 black peppercorns
2 small bay leaves
Pinch dried thyme
1 walnut-sized piece of ginger, peeled
1 cup (240 ml) dry white wine
6 cups (1½ liters) water
1 pound (450 grams) prawns, shelled and deveined
(reserve the shells)
Small pinch of saffron threads, soaked for 15 minutes in
1 tablespoon warm water
Salt

Rinse the fish well. Remove any gills or skin.

Warm the oil in a large saucepan or stockpot over
medium heat and sauté the onions, celery, carrots, garlic,
lemon zest, parsley, peppercorns, bay leaves, and thyme
over medium heat, until the vegetables are tender, about
10 minutes. Add the fish and ginger and sauté for 3 or
4 minutes. Pour in the white wine, bring to a boil, reduce

the heat and simmer for 5 minutes. Pour in the water and simmer for 35 to 45 minutes, skimming off any scum, until the stock is rich and somewhat thickened. Strain through a cheesecloth-lined strainer and cool to room temperature. Refrigerate. Skim off any fat before using.

Rinse the prawn shells well and tie in cheesecloth. Cut the prawns in half. Bring the broth to a boil in a large saucepan, add the shells, and simmer until pink, 4 or 5 minutes. Add the saffron with its soaking liquid and the prawns and cook until they turn pink, about 3 minutes. Remove the cheesecloth packet and discard. Season with salt to taste.

∿

Seasonings

4 large garlic cloves
1 dried red pepper pod or ½ teaspoon (2.5 grams) dried red pepper flakes
3 tablespoons (45 grams) mild olive oil
6 scallions, thinly sliced
¼ tightly packed cup (20 grams) fresh cilantro, minced

∿

Mince the garlic and hot peppers together. (See note about hot peppers on page 264.) Warm the oil over a very low flame, add the garlic, peppers and scallions and sauté slowly until the mixture sizzles.

Use a slotted spoon to add the seasonings to the prawn-filled broth, ladle the soup into individual bowls and garnish the top with cilantro.

Serves 6

∿

CHICKEN WITH GINGER, GARLIC,
⟨ AND CHILLIES ⟩

Chicken stock

6 pounds (2.75 kilograms) chicken whole or in parts –
necks, backs, wings, thighs
12 cups (3 liters) cold water
3 medium onions, coarsely chopped
2 celery ribs, coarsely chopped
3 medium carrots, peeled and coarsely chopped
Green tops of 3 leeks, cleaned and coarsely chopped
3 garlic cloves, crushed
1 bay leaf
4 parsley sprigs
8 black peppercorns
3 thyme sprigs
3½- to 4-pound (1.5 to 1.8 kilograms) whole chicken

Seasonings

3 tablespoons (45 ml) peanut or light olive oil
4 pieces of ginger, each about the size of a quarter, peeled,
thinly sliced, and finely chopped
4 scallions, minced
3 garlic cloves, crushed with the side of a knife
and finely chopped
½ to ¾ teaspoon chopped dried red chilies or dried red
chili pepper flakes
1 teaspoon sea salt

⟨⟩

Wash the chicken and chicken parts well. Place in a large
stockpot, cover with the cold water, and bring to a boil.

263

Reduce the heat and simmer uncovered, skimming off the froth that rises to the surface, about 1 hour. Remove the whole chicken and set aside for another use. Leave the chicken parts, add the vegetables and herbs, and continue simmering uncovered for 2 hours. Pour the broth through a strainer into a large bowl. Cool as quickly as possible, then refrigerate. Before using, skim fat from the top.

Pour the broth in a large heavy pot or stockpot and boil until you have about 8 cups. Add the new chicken, bring to a simmer, and cook uncovered 45 minutes to 1 hour, turning two or three times to be sure the chicken poaches evenly. It is done when the meat flakes easily with a fork. Remove from the pot and let cool to room temperature. Using your hands, tear off pieces of chicken and set aside. Cover well.

Warm the olive oil in a small sauté pan, add the ginger and scallions, and sauté until the scallions are soft. Chop the garlic. Use rubber gloves when you chop the dried red chili peppers. (Remember that the seeds are the hottest part. Do not touch your eyes, lips, or any sensitive parts of your skin.) When finished, wash your hands and the chopping board thoroughly with soap and warm water.

Warm the chicken broth over medium heat, add the chicken meat, and cook until the broth is almost boiling. Stir in the seasoning mixture, taste for salt, and serve immediately.

Serves 4

ROAST DUCK WITH APRICOTS
∽ PLUMPED IN PORT ∽

1 4-to-5-pound (2 kilograms) whole duck
1 garlic clove, minced
1 teaspoon (3 grams) cinnamon
½ teaspoon ground ginger
½ tablespoon grated fresh ginger
1 tablespoon (15 ml) lemon juice
Salt and pepper

Sauce

12 dried apricots (best quality)
1 cup (230 ml) good quality port
¾ cup (180 ml) chicken stock
¼ teaspoon cinnamon
⅛ teaspoon ground cloves
Grated zest of 1 lemon
3 tablespoons (45 ml) orange juice
2 tablespoons (30 ml) lemon juice
Salt and pepper

∽

Preheat the oven to 500 degrees F. (260 C.).
Wash the duck inside and out and dry well. Discard
the neck, giblets, and liver or save for another dish. Make
a paste of the garlic, cinnamon, ginger, salt, pepper, and
lemon juice and rub inside the cavity and out. Prick the
duck skin all over with a fork. Place the duck on a rack
in a roasting pan and roast for 1 hour to 1 hour and
10 minutes, until tender.
While the duck is roasting, put the apricots and port

into a small saucepan and bring to a simmer. Remove the pan from the heat and let the apricots plump, for about 10 minutes.

Boil down the remaining port to ⅓ cup and the chicken stock to ¼ cup. Combine in a small saucepan and add the cinnamon, cloves, orange and lemon juices, and the grated lemon zest. Simmer for 3 to 5 minutes. Season to taste with salt and pepper. Add the apricots at the end.

When the duck is roasted, cut it into quarters. Heat the sauce so that it is warmed through and serve immediately.

Serves 4

LAMB AND QUINCE WITH A SPLASH OF
~ AGED VINIGAR ~

3–4 tablespoons (45 to 60 grams) olive oil
2 tablespoons (30 grams) unsalted butter
2 pounds (900 grams) lamb stewing meat in
1½-inch cubes
2 onions, minced
¼ teaspoon red pepper flakes
½ teaspoon ground ginger
1 teaspoon (3 grams) ground coriander
1 teaspoon (3 grams) grated lemon zest
1 tightly packed cup (45 grams) fresh parsley,
finely chopped
1 cup (240 ml) beef broth
1 to 1½ teaspoons (5 to 7.5 ml) well-aged red wine
vinegar (optional)
Salt and pepper

For the quince

1½ pounds (675 grams) quinces
3 tablespoons (45 grams) unsalted butter
2 tablespoons (30 grams) sugar
1 lemon

~

Warm 2 tablespoons of the olive oil and 1 tablespoon of the butter in a large sauté pan over high heat. Add as many lamb cubes as will fit easily without crowding and sauté until lightly browned on all sides. Transfer to a plate. Repeat with the rest of the lamb.

Heat the remaining oil and butter in the same pan over

medium-low heat, add one onion, and sauté until soft and translucent, about 10 minutes. Stir in the pepper flakes, ginger, coriander, lemon zest, and parsley, and cook briefly. Return the lamb to the pan, cover with the beef broth, and simmer, covered, until the meat is tender, about 1 hour. Add the second minced onion and continue cooking until it has almost melted into the sauce, about 30 minutes. Add the splash of aged vinegar and taste for salt and pepper.

Meanwhile, peel, quarter, and core the quinces. Discard the seeds. Put the fruit in water with the juice of a lemon so it won't discolor. Slice the fruit into wedges and pat dry. Warm the butter in a large sauté pan, add only enough quince to cover the bottom of the pan, sprinkle the tops with sugar, and sauté until the quince is lightly golden on both sides, about 15 minutes. You may need to do this in two steps.

Thirty minutes before you plan to serve, add the quince to the lamb and simmer just until the fruit is tender. Serve with marble-sized Yellow Finn or Yukon Gold potatoes.

Serves 4

~

MASHED POTATOES AND CELERY ROOT
~ WITH HORSERADISH ~

1½ pounds (675 grams) celery root
1½ pounds (675 grams) Yukon Gold or Yellow Finn
potatoes
Water
Milk
¼ cup (30 grams) grated horseradish root
1 teaspoon (5 grams) sugar
1 teaspoon (5 ml) lemon juice
3 tablespoons (45 ml) heavy cream, chilled
Salt

Peel and cut the celery root and potatoes into quarters.
Place them in a heavy-bottomed saucepan that will hold
them comfortably in one layer. Cover with equal amounts
of water and milk. Bring to a boil, reduce the heat, cover,
and simmer until a knife easily penetrates the vegetables,
about 25 minutes.

While the vegetables are cooking, grate the horseradish
root into a small bowl. Stir in the sugar and lemon juice.
Whisk the cream to thicken it slightly and then stir it in.

Drain the potatoes and celery root, reserving the
cooking liquid. Press through a food mill into a large
bowl. Beat in enough of the cooking liquid to achieve
the soft texture of mashed potatoes. Add the horseradish
mixture, season with salt to taste, and serve hot.

Serves 6

BEETS DRIZZLED WITH CITRUS

1 pound (450 grams) red beets
Grated zest of 1 orange
1/3–1/2 cup (80 to 120 ml) orange juice
Freshly ground sea salt crystals
Freshly ground black pepper
3 tablespoons (45 grams) walnuts

Place the beets in a large pot, cover with abundant water, and bring to a boil. Cook over high heat until they are tender, 35 to 50 minutes.

While the beets are cooking, toast the walnuts in a 350 F. (180 C.) oven for 12 minutes. Set aside to cool. Chop coarsely.

Peel the beets as soon as they are cool enough to handle. Slice into 1/2-inch rounds and set on a serving platter. Drizzle the orange juice over the top and season with freshly ground salt and pepper. Garnish with the coarsely chopped walnuts.

Serves 4

FIGS STEWED IN RED WINE WITH
~ CINNAMON AND CLOVES ~

*16 to 18 firm Black Mission figs, tough stem ends cut
off 2 cups (500 ml) full-bodied red wine, such as a
Cabernet Sauvignon
¼ cup (50 grams) sugar
3 whole cloves
3 long strips lemon zest
1 teaspoon (3 grams) ground cinnamon*

Have the figs at room temperature. Pour the wine into
a 2-quart nonreactive saucepan and add the rest of the
ingredients. Gently boil until reduced to 1 cup, 10 to
15 minutes. Slide the figs into the syrup and cook over
medium heat until tender, turning once to poach them
evenly, 5 to 10 minutes. Turn off the heat and let the figs
sit in the liquid for another 5 to 10 minutes.
Using a slotted spoon, transfer the figs to a serving
bowl. Strain the poaching liquid; discard the cloves and
lemon zest. Pour the syrup over the figs and serve while
still warm.

Serves 4

QUINCE TART

Pastry dough

1 cup (140 grams) all-purpose flour
Pinch salt
3 tablespoons (45 grams) sugar
Grated zest of ½ lemon, unwaxed
1 large egg, room temperature
½ teaspoon vanilla extract
6 tablespoons (90 grams) unsalted butter at room
temperature

Place the flour, salt, and sugar in the large mixing bowl of an electric mixer. Grate the lemon zest over the top. Mix the ingredients briefly on the lowest speed. Combine the egg and vanilla in a small bowl.

Cut the butter into small pieces and scatter over the top of the dry ingredients. Mix on the lowest speed for about 2 minutes, until the mixture has the texture of cornmeal. With the motor running, pour in the egg mixture and mix only until the ingredients come together.

Place the dough on a clean, dry work surface. Divide it into small pieces and with the heel of your hand press each piece of the dough against the work surface, pushing it away. Combine the pieces into a single ball of dough and push it away a couple more times until it is smooth.

Refrigerate for at least an hour, until the dough is cold and slightly firm.

Quince

2 cups (460 ml) water
1 cup (200 grams) sugar
3 or 4 quinces, 2 to 2½ pounds (900 to 1125 grams)
1 lemon, in 1½ inch slices
½ teaspoon ground cardamom
¼ teaspoon ground coriander

~

Bring the water and sugar to a simmer. Quarter, core, and peel the quinces. (Be very careful when cutting the raw fruit because it is extremely hard and resistant.) Discard the seeds and cut the quinces into ½ inch thick slices. Add the fruit, lemon slices, and spices to the sugar syrup, cover, and cook at a bare simmer, for 2 to 2 ¼ hours, or until the fruit has turned rosy pink. Discard the lemon slices. Chill the quince in their syrup.

~

Tart preparation

2 tablespoons (30 grams) unsalted butter
⅓ cup (65 grams) sugar
Poached quinces, above

~

Preheat the oven to 400 F. or 200 C. Melt the butter in a 9-inch cast-iron black skillet over medium high heat and immediately add the sugar. Stirring constantly, cook until the mixture is pale golden brown in color. To check you can take it on and off the heat, always stirring. When it has reached the desired color, immediately remove from the heat, still stirring and being very careful that the caramel doesn't take on a darker color. Spread the caramel evenly in a thin layer over the bottom of the pan and set aside to cool.

Arrange the first row of quince slices over the caramel with the round edges against the sides of the pan. Continue arranging the slices in concentric circles until you have covered the caramel. Mound any leftover slices in the center so the tart will be a little bit higher there.

To roll out the pastry, flour your work surface lightly. Set the dough on top of a large piece of waxed paper or plastic wrap, sprinkle the exposed surface of the dough with flour, and roll into an 11- or 12-inch circle no more than ⅛ inch thick. Brush off any excess flour and set the pastry, exposed side down, on top of the fruit. Slowly pull the waxed paper or plastic wrap away, trim the edges with a knife, and let the pastry stand until it has softened.

Just before baking, press the pastry between the fruit and the edges of the pan. Bake for 35 to 40 minutes, until the pastry is golden and shrinks away from the edge of the pan. Remove from the oven and leave for a minute or two. To serve, set a serving plate upside down over the pan. Lift both together, holding the plate tightly against the top of the pan, and flip over quickly so the hot juices don't spatter. You can resettle any pieces of fruit that may have stuck to the pan. Serve warm, possibly with the Winter Custard Ice Cream.

Serves 6 to 8

CHOCOLATE CAKE SPIKED
~ WITH GINGER ~

½ cup (60 grams) hazelnuts, toasted
2 tablespoons (30 grams) sugar
3 tablespoons (20 grams) cocoa powder
1 tablespoon (15 grams) finely minced or grated fresh
ginger with its juice
5 ounces (150 grams) bittersweet chocolate
1 ounce (30 grams) unsweetened chocolate
2 tablespoons (30 ml) strong espresso coffee, cooled
1 teaspoons (5 ml) vanilla extract
2 teaspoons (10 ml) ginger liqueur or Fra Angelico
hazelnut liqueur
8 tablespoons (1 cube, 112 grams) unsalted butter
½ cup plus 2 tablespoons (120 grams) sugar
3 tablespoons (45 grams) hazelnut or filbert butter
4 large eggs, separated
Pinch salt

For the pan

2 tablespoons (30 grams) unsalted butter
3 tablespoons (30 grams) flour

~

Preheat the oven to 375 F. (190 C.).
Grind the hazelnuts, sugar, and cocoa in a blender
to a fine powder. Add the finely grated or minced
fresh ginger.
Place the two chocolates in the top of a double boiler
over boiling water until they have melted. Remove the
top pot immediately and continue stirring briefly. Pour in

the coffee, vanilla extract, and liqueur and then mix well. Cool to room temperature.

Cream the butter and sugar until pale yellow and fluffy, for about 10 minutes in an electric mixer. Beat in the hazelnut or filbert butter and then the egg yolks, one at a time. Stir in the cocoa and chocolate mixtures.

Beat the egg whites with the salt until they stand up in peaks. Stir one-quarter of the egg whites into the chocolate mixture and then fold in the remaining egg whites delicately.

Use 2 tablespoons butter to completely cover a 9-inch-round baking pan with a removable bottom and high sides. Sift the flour over the surface and sides until they are all well coated.

Spoon the batter into the pan and smooth the top with a rubber spatula. Set the pan in the middle of the oven and bake for 30 minutes. Reduce the heat to 325 F. (160 C.) and bake for another 15 to 20 minutes, until the top is cracked and a tester comes out almost but not completely clean. Cool for 20 to 30 minutes in the pan set on a rack.

Very carefully invert the cake onto a large plate and let it cool completely. Place a cake platter on top of the cake and, holding the two plates together, flip the cake onto the platter so that it is right side up. Serve the rich, moist, deeply chocolate cake in thin slices, perhaps accompanied by Winter Custard Ice Cream with Five Spices.

Serves 8

WINTER CUSTARD ICE CREAM WITH
➤ FIVE SPICES ➤

Custard

4 large egg yolks
½ cup (100 grams) granulated sugar
½ cup (125 ml) milk
1 5-inch vanilla bean, slit up the center
3 cardamom pods, crushed
6 espresso coffee beans, crushed
1 cinnamon stick

Ice cream

Custard base
1 cup (230 ml) heavy cream
1¼ cups (300 ml) milk
¼ cup (50 grams) sugar
Pinch of salt
⅜ teaspoon ground cinnamon
⅛ teaspoon mace
⅛ teaspoon ground cloves
⅛ teaspoon ground allspice
⅛ teaspoon ground cardamom

To make the custard base beat the egg yolks and sugar together until light and frothy. Heat the milk with the vanilla bean in a saucepan until lukewarm. Gradually whisk in the yolk mixture and stir well. Pour into the top of a double boiler set over boiling water and stir continually until the mixture thickens and coats the back of a spoon. Do *not* allow it to come to a boil. Immediately remove the top pot from the bottom of the double boiler and stir the contents for another minute. Wrap the cardamom pods, espresso coffee beans, and cinnamon stick in cheesecloth and add to the custard base. Set aside to cool for one hour.

Stir the cream, milk, sugar, pinch of salt, and the five spices into the custard base. Cover and refrigerate for at least 8 hours. Discard the cheesecloth packet.

Freeze the mixture in an ice cream maker according to the manufacturer's directions.

Makes 1 quart

A NOTE ON THE AUTHOR

Carol Field is the author of *In Nonna's Kitchen:
Recipes and Traditions from Italy's Grandmothers*,
The Italian Baker, and *Celebrating Italy*. *Mangoes
and Quince* is her first novel.
She lives in San Francisco.

A NOTE ON THE TYPE

The text of this book is set in Linotype Sabon,
named after the type founder, Jacques Sabon. It was
designed by Jan Tschichold and jointly developed
by Linotype, Monotype and Stempel, in response
to a need for a typeface to be available in identical
form for mechanical hot metal composition and hand
composition using foundry type.

Tschichold based his design for Sabon roman on a
fount engraved by Garamond, and Sabon italic on a
fount by Granjon. It was first used in 1966 and has
proved an enduring modern classic.